# IRON-FORGE CROSSROADS

## METANOIA

GWYDION ROYCE

ORACLE OF LOST PATHS BOOKS

Cover Design by Damonza.com

1st edition 2024

Oracle of Lost Paths Books

author@gwydionroyce.com

979-8-9902074-0-0 (paperback)

979-8-9902074-1-7 (eBook)

Thanks, Ma.

# CHAPTER ONE

*If I'd known how this day was going to end, I would've left the house with more than just a knife...*

The leaves crunched underfoot as Jake and I made our way up the trail, heading toward the sunset overlook that would give the best view of Lake Superior.

My feet knew the way on their own so I could enjoy the sights unhindered. After I'd moved here twelve years ago, I secluded myself to the vast expanse of forest reserve, wandering, putting down my own roots, and trying to learn how to breathe again.

Now a little more than a year old, Jake was curious about everything, sniffing every trail he could find, diving into the underbrush with abandon and chasing whatever moved. I quickly learned that a Bernese mountain dog equaled stubborn, smart, and built like an ox.

Jake bayed and went sprinting by me, plunging into the trees.

"Great." I'd bet money he'd just found something sticky and smelly to roll in. I grimaced, resolving myself to the struggle that would be bath time.

I continued up the path, lost in my thoughts and just enjoying the late afternoon quiet. I'd seen a few other people on the trail, but it had been a solo journey most of the way.

Crashing leaves and snapping twigs startled me enough to make me jump and I whirled to see Jake plowing through the woods toward me. He raced up the path, yipping and baying after an unknown quarry.

I started after him but stopped when something brushed the edge of my consciousness. Peering into the trees I searched, sliding my eyes in and out of focus a few times before my Sight kicked in. Small runnels of ether were snaking around the trees, pooling around one before another tendril sought out the next.

The trees were talking to each other. Not that that was unusual, but the speed with which they were communicating was. Something was out there, and they were spreading the word. I moved farther in, toward the ether, and placed my hand on one of the trees in the chain.

The bark was warm, much warmer than it should have been.

"What's happening?"

A hand pushed out of the tree bark and wrapped its fingers around mine. A face appeared next, round and undefined, childlike. The nymph opened its eyes and smiled kindly, teeth the color of the inner wood. The dry bark of the spirit's skin crinkled at the eyes, making a few bits flake off, and I stared calmly into the large black pools as they blinked slowly.

Once the nymph was strong enough to speak it pushed its head out farther and the friendly look became serious. "Something came through from the Strangefells. Nobody seems able to tell what it is. It must be cloaking itself somehow."

"How dangerous?"

"Dangerous enough to forewarn about." The nymph's sly grin twisted the bark.

I smiled despite my annoyance. "But not so dangerous that you can't still be a vague smart-ass about it." I gently extricated my fingers from the spirit's grasp. "How fast is it moving?"

"It doesn't seem to be in any rush. It's been milling about on the other side of the forest for a little while now. Not sure if it's here for anything other than some sightseeing."

"Come for the views, stay for the vast expanse of unoccupied land with few witnesses." I shrugged. "Just as good a sales pitch as any."

"Just be wary," said the nymph firmly.

I nodded and it faded back into the tree.

Daylight was running out fast, so I jogged back to the trail and headed up quickly. There was nothing for it anyway. I wouldn't make it back to the car before dark even if I left now. Might as well enjoy the sunset.

Jake caught up with me after having made a wide circle following my scent. I crested the last of the hill and was greeted by a spectacular watercolor, accentuated by the clouds and rains earlier that day.

I sighed, letting myself get swept up in the sights. The vibrant pinks and oranges bled into rose and indigo as I stepped onto the old overlook deck, weathered boards creaking under my feet, and took a deep breath of the fresh lake air. It was cold, even for the middle of fall, but I paid it no mind.

I stood in silence, Jake sitting still at my feet staring across the water, until the last of the light disappeared below the horizon and gave way to nightfall.

Now that the show was over, I turned back to the dark woods with trepidation. Mage night vision was just as good as any nocturnal animal's, but it still wasn't the best circumstance to run across a large unknown predator. I straightened Jake's harness and checked that my knife was still securely in my ankle sheath.

All good. Let's roll.

Truth be told, I may have a bit of an overinflated sense of confidence even compared to other mages. We're a battle-hungry sort, but it wasn't an uncommon occurrence for me to be accused of having more bravado than common sense by others of my kind.

At some point on that giant universal tree of creation, mages had splintered off from normal ol' humans and became magickal beings in our own right. I had a sneaking suspicion that it was thanks to the myriad fae getting busy with prehistoric humans, but no self-respecting fae would ever fess up to that.

However it happened, mages, sorcerers, witches, and druids all earned their places amongst the other beings of the Strangefells, our peoples flourishing in the magickally charged atmosphere of that alternate dimension as we continued to evolve.

We all have our strengths and weaknesses, but mages seem to have perpetual "middle-child syndrome." I know *I* used to do really stupid things for attention. Why else would I be roving the dark woods with an unknown creature lurking around?

Or maybe that's just me making excuses...

The darkness pressed in around us. Every stick cracking, every rustle of leaves had me straining all my senses to make sure that whatever that thing was it didn't get the drop on us.

Jake was sticking close, walking slowly with me, and constantly scenting the air.

A faint whisper caught my attention. I looked into the forest where a fog was forming in the pockets of less dense greenery from the drastic change in temperature after sundown.

Something was off. I stopped in my tracks and sent out some feelers to check if there was normal wildlife keeping an eye on us or if I needed to find a way to get Jake to safety in a hurry.

A lesser elemental was stalking the borders of its territory, hissing angrily about an intruder as the trees tracked and reported the unwanted visitor's movements once again. Damn.

Jake barked and stared at me with his big brown eyes and there was something more than just a dog's empathic knowing looking back at me. It was like he knew exactly what had me worried.

I spoke sternly. "Whatever happens, stay away from the action, got it? If I tell you to get away, just go. Don't worry about me."

Jake barked in response, head darting side to side.

I set off up the trail, hoping that I could distract or even defeat whatever was out there with nothing but a four-inch blade and cursing myself for packing light.

The air was filled with the damp smell of the leaves and the lingering scent of rain. Far off in the distance I heard thunder rolling as another storm approached.

The fog was denser now, heavier pockets lying low and swirling in the occasional breeze that came in cold and bitter. Other than an owl call and a small rustling from a mouse or other critter, there was just dead air. The eerie stillness was punctuated by the tremor in my bones and the fear gripping my chest.

I bent down and slid the knife out of the sheath like it would disintegrate in my hands if I wasn't gentle enough. What little light there was from cloud breaks overhead was unforgiving as it reflected in the blade.

There were sounds now, larger ones, something big moving through the woods with ease and stealth, but still confident enough in its rank on the food chain that it wasn't trying to be silent.

Jake stuck close to my side, his hackles raised. A low growl rumbled deep in his throat, but he didn't bark.

The creature coming toward us was bipedal, that much I could tell from this distance. Tall, judging by the way the sounds were bouncing. A growl laced the air and carried toward me on the wind that chose that moment to pick up. It wasn't menacing as much as it was curious.

I never thought I'd be wishing that it was just a bear.

The creature moved closer, not making any pretense of being quiet anymore. A whiff of something musky and wet announced its arrival before a bulky figure finally moved into view. I clutched my knife tightly and took stock of the visitor. Jake wasn't reacting as I would have expected him to, standing silent and watchful but not overtly aggressive.

Long, powerful legs leading into the torso of a man, muscled like a body builder. Terrifyingly broad shoulders... and a head that was equal amounts wolf and domesticated dog. All covered in thick dark hair. I bit back my irritation.

It wasn't his fault the trees got me worked up for nothing.

I waved at the dogman. "How's it going?"

He shrugged and looked overhead.

"Got a place to wait out the storm?" It did feel like the incoming rain was going to be on the severe side.

The dogman nodded his shaggy head, his ears twitching a few times. Then he flexed his claws and, with a slight nod, went sprinting off in a blur of speed.

Once he was gone, I turned to the trees at large, knowing the message would get back to my nymph friend. "Seriously? You got me all worked up about dogman? How bored are you guys?"

There was only stillness in response, so I angrily sheathed my knife and huffed off down the trail.

I was paying far less attention than I should have been in my frustration and didn't notice that Jake was hanging back.

He started barking madly just before an impact like a wrecking ball knocked me off the path and into the trees on the other side. The air was pummeled from my lungs as a couple of trees brought me to a halt and a loud crack rang out into the night. I hoped it was the trees and not my back, but it was hard to tell through the numbness.

I hit the ground and light blasted across my vision when my head smacked against a rock. A flurry of movement and more frantic barking filled the night as Jake skirted whatever it was that had found us, trying to get to me.

I gritted my teeth and shouted, the words slurred. "Jake, stay back!"

Through the pain I looked in the general direction of where the attack had come from. A demon had stepped out into the open, squat bodied with clubbed feet, gnarled joints that jutted at weird angles, and an overbite that was smiling around tusked teeth. The clouds scudded over the moon and turned his skin into a mottled, rotten shade of gray. A real looker, this one.

It stepped onto the packed earth and advanced on me, one clubbed foot in front of the other, steam rising from the ground as he moved. Nothing about it screamed assassin. Every movement it made was labored, and I didn't even see any weapons.

But I couldn't imagine a demon just happened to be passing through for any reason other than a bounty. I'd worry about how anyone knew I was even alive later, if there was a later.

"Get up," it hissed.

I nodded and held up my index finger for the demon to wait a minute. At least it seemed to want a fair fight.

Ignoring the screaming pain in my back I reached down to grab the knife from my ankle and struggled to my feet. I adjusted my grip on the blade. Knife fighting was just like riding a bike; just sharper, and with a much higher chance of bloodshed.

I gathered as much confidence and nonchalance into my words as I could. "If you're looking for directions, you could've just asked."

The demon kept advancing, a smile growing on its face, lips twisting awkwardly around the tusks. When it spoke, its voice was almost indistinguishable from the deadfall it was walking across. "You can't hide your fear behind jokes."

Fine, my poker face needed work. "I'm giving you fair warning." I flipped the knife in my hand in a quick round of circles, the pain in my body already subsiding. "I'm rather good at this."

It closed the distance in a flash and grabbed me by the throat, knocking the knife out of my hand. "You're too long out of the game, mage." The demon lifted me off my feet and I choked. "The definition of 'good' has changed."

I grabbed the demon's wrist and squeezed until I heard bones start to pop. It screeched and flung me to the ground, lifting a massive foot to stomp on my abdomen.

I caught the foot and twisted inward to set the demon off balance. It crashed to the ground beside me, and I pounced on top of it, raining down blows on the demon's face and chest. It took a wild swing, and I rolled to the side, spotting my knife and scrabbling toward it.

The demon grabbed my leg and hauled me away from my weapon, but I kicked out with the other and nailed it in the crotch.

A grunt and it let me go. This time I retrieved my knife and jumped to my feet just as it lunged at me, losing all decorum and slashing at me with claws bared. I ducked backward and slashed with the knife, severing its hand. The demon screamed an unholy howl and backed away.

I felt my pupils dilate and my pulse even out as the predator in me took over. I advanced on him.

"Who sent you?" I asked, light and singsong.

Its eyes got wide at the change in my demeanor, and it began to look around for an easy escape.

"Oh, are you scared now? It's not befitting a demon at all." I smiled with a few too many teeth. "What will your friends think?"

"They just wanted me to scare you," the demon said by way of explanation, nursing its stump with its other hand.

My head cocked to the side sharply. I advanced, taking one step for each three of its shuffling retreats. "Who did?" I spat. Its back hit a tree and it flinched, folding in on itself to protect the vital organs. I grabbed its throat, picked it up and slammed it into the ground.

"Who sent you?" I screamed in its face, resting my knife on its throat. Jake redoubled his barking and I saw him inching closer. Without taking my eyes off the demon I motioned with the hand signal that told Jake to stay still.

When it remained silent, I pulled back my fist and punched it in the face. The demon sneered around a mouthful of blood and said with a sickening smile, "I only know the broker. The money was too good to pass up." It growled. "They want you to know that you're not as hidden as you think you are."

I growled back and pressed my knife farther into its flesh where it hissed and left a black line of blisters. "I won't ask you again."

It bit back a yelp and glared at me. "Aldous Kildaire." The demon smirked. "I'm guessing you're aware of who he brokers for."

"The Briste."

The demon nodded and I grimaced. "Well shit."

"It's only a matter of time before someone else shows up. I got the feeling whoever sent me here was very... keen... on you."

I could feel my lip twitch in a sneer. "Tell them they have an open invitation." What was I doing? This life was behind me, I'd made sure of it. I didn't want to get involved in this.

But it was habit that was talking now, habit that dictated that I not back down from an outright challenge.

A thick branch snapped in the distance and that moment of distraction was all the demon needed. It pushed me aside and ran back into the trees, the crack of its disappearance echoing through the woods as it returned to the Strangefells.

Jake barrelled over to me and stopped an inch away, whining. I scratched his ears.

"It's alright, baby boy." I held his face in my hands and rubbed his cheeks with my thumbs.

A loud boom of thunder echoed across the sky and I looked skyward. "Better get back to the car, quick."

We'd parked on the side of an access road since they closed the parking lot off after sunset and made good time the rest of the way down the trail. We made it back to my car just as the rain began to fall, quickly becoming a deluge.

Jake stuck his head between the seats and looked at me, concerned. "I'm sorry to have dragged you into this, Jake. I never meant for them to find me."

In response he wiggled up from the backseat until he could sit in the front passenger seat, sprawling uncomfortably around the gear shift and resting his head in my lap. I stroked the blaze on his forehead, and he quickly fell asleep, tongue sticking a small ways between his teeth. I didn't have the heart to move him, and he didn't budge when the engine roared to life so, once the rain lightened up a bit, we headed home.

The small cottage set back in the trees at the end of a rural road used to feel like a sanctuary, but now... every shadow felt like a threat. I sat in my car for what felt like hours, Jake snoring away. My home wasn't safe anymore, my attempt at disappearing and starting over completely blown to bits.

When the majority of your life was spent in the dark shadows of a mercenary society, your past will always catch up with you.

My name is Evyn Urquhart. Welcome to the madness.

And don't say I didn't warn you.

# CHAPTER TWO

The shrill bleat of my cell broke into my sleep. I groaned as my eyes opened to a bright light stabbing through my window. What kind of monster calls before noon?

"Dammit," I mumbled, angry at having been woken up. Here's the math: late night demon fight + early afternoon call / new target on my back = pissed-off Evyn.

"What," I grumbled into the phone, groggy and not caring who was on the other end.

"Good morning, lass." The melodic voice on the other end had a cheery Scottish accent, fading from a couple hundred years in the States.

I sighed. "It is *not* a good morning. What do you want, Derfael?"

"I have a job for you." I could practically see the sly smile on his face.

"You know what time it is. You know that I was sleeping." I propped myself up on my elbows and continued my listing. "You know I hate it when you talk like that because I know that you're up to something. There's really only one reason you *wouldn't* be calling me, and that's if it was just another job." I sat up with a sigh and pushed some hair out of my face. My fingers caught in the tangled dark chestnut strands, and I fought for a second to get them free. "What is it?"

"The leader of the Briste has come back to the States."

"And?"

Silence on the other end. Not the response he expected.

"And I've already heard rumor that you were paid a visit last night. Courtesy of the Briste's top contractor."

"Word gets around fast." Anger flared as the demon's smug face flashed in my mind. "But I don't want to get into this. I hung up my guns, it's over. I finally built a life here, made friends."

"They're aware that you are alive. Are you just going to run for the rest of your life, until someone finally catches up to you again? You can't fake your death a second time. They won't settle for anything less than a body to prove it."

"If I have to run, so be it."

"Do you really think you can do that?" Derfael's tone turned knowing. "That you can bring yourself to do that, I mean. You've never run away from a fight."

Before I could stop them, the words I'd never said tumbled out, barely audible. "It's not the fight I'm running from."

A heavy silence where Derfael sought for the right words, settling at last on the nickname he'd used ever since I was a child. "Talulla."

I brushed it off. "I just have to do a better job concealing my location next time." Where could I go that was more remote than the tip-top of Michigan's Upper Peninsula? "Maybe I should start looking at Australia. Everything there wants to kill trespassers so I wouldn't be the only one out for blood."

I looked down at Jake who was pawing at my arm, head buried in the blanket. My heart melted and I smiled. "I'm sorry, am I interrupting your sleep?"

"Who are you talking to?" I could hear the narrowing of Derfael's eyes.

"My dog." I waited for the scorn or mockery I was sure was on the way. Instead, I just heard a small huff, and he ignored it.

"Griselda Moreno is the new heir apparent to the syndicate."

"Grizz-mo?" She hated that nickname, broke my nose once for using it. "How does an Unseelie fae become a vampire queenpin?"

An old "friend" from my days coming up as a merc, Grizz and I had a falling out years ago. Something about her wanting to cut my still-beating heart from my chest and me vowing to light her on fire and watch her Unseelie ass burn.

"Somehow she convinced an established Briste vampire to turn her. She survived the transition and then she killed Jeremiah in hand-to-hand combat."

"The old-fashioned way, then?" I shook my head and whistled. "The kind of power needed to take down a Master... I didn't think she had it in her. But what a lateral life move." I grimaced. "She just traded being an evil bitch for being an eviler bitch."

"Be that as it may. You know what lengths she will go to if there's a vendetta unresolved."

I flopped back on my pillow and pinched the bridge of my nose. "So basically you're saying I might as well come back because she'll be like a dog with a bone now that she knows I'm alive."

"Basically."

Jake was looking at me from sleepy, half-closed eyes, catching on that an interesting conversation was happening. Or he heard me say "bone" and thought he was getting a snack. I scratched his chin and his tail started to thump happily. "Dammit. Where do I have to be?"

Derfael laughed, and I heard a sound in the background like he had slapped his hand on the table. "That's the Evyn I know! You told me once that you were only truly happy at the moment you wrenched life from an enemy. That instinct is not something you grow out of."

I rolled over and buried my face in the pillow. "I'm already saying yes, so why are you trying to ruin it?"

He ignored me. "Come home, where you belong."

"Home." My stomach clenched as I thought of everyone from my old life, thought of seeking them out after so many years. I just up and left, without so much as a goodbye.

Percy was still holding a grudge from when I spilled wine on her carpet in 1973; forgiveness was not something any of them were familiar with. I expressed none of this to Derfael. "Fine. I'll be there by tomorrow night."

"Good. I will see you then."

We hung up without goodbyes. It was just habit. In this business, goodbyes were always assumed.

"Okay, Jake, here's the deal."

The decision to get a dog was a big one for me. I was used to destroying lives, not caring for one, but I finally felt that I was settled into this place for good and wanted a companion. Now here I was, packing up my "settled" life and upending everything again.

I didn't have to think about what to take with me, that much was for certain. Guns, ammo, and tempered steel were tops on the list. But of course there were other things that would need to be shoved in the limited space of my '69 Chevy Camero SS hardtop.

I'd just recently updated the interior to sleek black leather and had it painted with that color-morph purple. You know, back when I didn't need to worry about being inconspicuous.

"The passenger seat is yours, alright? Don't make me regret it."

Jake ducked his head and looked back up at me, smiling.

"Good man." I scratched behind his ears. "You've never been to a city before, so you need to learn the ropes. I have faith that you can pick it up pretty quick, but just stick by me at all times, got it?"

He nodded and again I said, "Good man."

I turned to my steamer trunk and sighed. I had kept this thing locked since the day I moved in and had put everything inside that I wanted to keep out of my life.

I stood in front of it and debated what it would mean to open it; if this would be a point of no return. Mercenary life sucks you in so fast because you earn your fair share of enemies that you always have to fight off or you'll sentence yourself to death. I'd been doing this since 1838, so that list was pretty long. Mages age at a seventh the rate of humans but the real trick was surviving long enough to enjoy the extended life span.

I swallowed, feeling the lump slowly work its way down like it was trying to choke some sense into me. I ignored the sense of foreboding, bit my thumb with my incisor and drew a small line of blood perpendicular to the left latch. I softly spoke the words that would break the spell that had held the lid fast and kept the monster I feared the most contained.

There was a series of clicks as the multiple hidden locks unlatched. A hiss like an airlock coming undone caused Jake to cock his head and then the trunk popped open a fraction.

I lifted the lid and pulled out the series of accordion drawers that made up the top half of the trunk and surveyed the layout. Knives, guns, a whip, a crossbow, and several shelves of ammunition all sat in pristine condition, not a speck of rust or dust anywhere.

These were the tools the Council raised and trained me on, honing me into their perfect enforcer, one of the claws on the iron fist they ruled the Strangefells with. They were our leadership, composed of the heads of the individual guilds that represented each race or type of Stranger—Strangers being the common term for those that hail from the Strangefells.

For example, the shifters had their guild, vampiric beings had theirs and fae of both courts were represented individually. Druids, witches, and sorcerers were grouped together but the mages had our own guild since we were naturally inclined towards causing trouble the others were not.

We were a bloodthirsty bunch and required a heavier hand with governance at times, but only when the Council wasn't using mage proclivities to their advantage.

They'd chosen me from an early age, seeing "promise" in me. Seeing a perfectly malleable monster, destined to be a psychopath.

I exhaled heavily and extended my hand, gently touching the grip of my one and only sword. Sensory images flooded my sight and for a moment I could feel the bloodlust all over again, as strong as if it had never stopped.

I tore my hand away and the images vanished. I slammed the lid shut and sat back on my heels. "Everything looks fine anyway, don't need to bother with it too much."

I wasn't sure who I was trying to convince.

The storms had moved out, making way for clear blue skies. As I went about collecting all the random weapons I had hidden, I took in the house, my house, for what might be the last time.

It was a small, cozy A-frame, only meant to function as a summer home when it was first built. It had been long abandoned by the time I bought it, but it was a great project to keep me busy and keep my mind off everything that I left behind. I restored everything myself, from the spindles on the loft railing to the gingerbread ornamentation on the roof and the masonry on the low garden walls.

I was born a few miles northeast of the Summer Isles, in the Highlands of Scotland. In 1818. If you think it's remote now, try living there before the invention of electricity or the automobile. Needless to say, I was raised to be self-sufficient.

I ran my hand over the coffee table I'd hewn from a fallen log, remembering each dig of the awl as it took shape, before sliding my hand underneath it and removing the pistol secured there.

I'd leave a generous tip for the movers in case I missed any, but at least I was certain I'd gotten all the ones on spring triggers.

Once that was done, I packed all the essentials the two of us would need until we got settled and then I climbed up to the loft and settled on the balcony overlooking the forest. You could just make out the water from this view now that the trees were shedding some leaves. When the wind blew the right way, you could hear the ferocity of Lake Superior crashing against the shoreline.

"It's not fair, Jake."

He lifted his head and trained his soulful eyes on me.

"We had a great thing going here. A little boring at times, but there's nothing wrong with that. I made a good new life here." Dismay overtook me and emotions were still compounded for me in ways I wasn't able to understand. The chest tightness, the stomach dropping, the hurt that had no physical cause.

Battle wounds, cuts, broken bones, bullet holes, scars. Those I could understand. Those I'd felt many times before. But now I knew a lot more about emotional pain, trauma, grief, even fear. Was I broken now? What kind of merc has *feelings*? It wasn't only bad for business, but there was no telling what kind of weaknesses I would discover at the worst possible times when the stakes were life and death.

Living a quiet existence of solitude and reflection had made me well suited to being a scholar or a monk, not a better mercenary. If Griselda Moreno was back in town, it wasn't just because she heard about me being alive and well and wanted to change that dynamic.

Something else was going on, and I was just the cherry on top. Now the real question I needed to figure out was why she wanted to draw me out into the open. But there was only one way I was going to get those answers.

"Enjoy the peace and quiet while we can, bud." I sighed. "I have a feeling it'll be in short supply for the foreseeable future."

After a nine-hour drive, we finally crossed the invisible borders of the city, stretching through the boundaries like a thick layer of plastic wrap. There was a lot of power in this place, and I had forgotten just how intense it was. Jake yipped and put his front paws on the dashboard, staring out the window.

"Never seen anything like it, have you?" I asked him with a strained smile. He barked in response. Copper Harbor was tiny and almost as far north as you could get before hitting Canada. Grand Rapids was a world of difference, a city in southwest Michigan finding its stride after the Industrial era furniture boom was over and making up for lost time.

Though in regards to Canada, there's a lot to be said for nearby international borders —even if there's a giant, ferocious lake in-between— when there's a high potential for having human law-enforcement on your ass.

As we wove through the tangled knot of streets, I began to remember the old days, how it was when I stalked this city like an urban legend. My name was infamous. If someone heard that I was after them they either booked it out of town or sought protection, but neither option ever worked out for them.

There were even a couple marks that came to me themselves in order to receive a quick death instead of the manner in which I usually doled out the punishment.

I was an ice-hearted killer that never lost a fight and never let anyone get away. Well, I suppose I did lose a few fights, all but one of them pitted solo against a Briste vampire. To this day I don't know how I managed to get away.

I bit my lip and pushed those thoughts aside, the memories coming back with a little too much fondness, and glanced at the dashboard clock. I'd be arriving at Wolfe's Mercantile just in time for tea.

Druid high priest as he was, Derfael put me through my paces growing up. I wasn't the easiest foster kid to raise I suppose. But no matter how much we butted heads there was never a day where we didn't sit down together for tea. He insisted on it, even when my teenage angst started to take over and I became a raging hormonal mess that had powerful budding magick at my fingertips.

How's that for a nightmare?

I maneuvered through traffic, making my way deeper and deeper into the city. We passed posh restaurants and high-priced shops that catered to the Gaslight district crowd, and then those started to fade into boarded-up windows and empty shop fronts. The unhoused crowded the alleys, trying to stay warm in the late autumn air.

Pretty soon I was surrounded by lonely, neglected buildings that had gone out of business a long time ago; an old theater, barber shop, shoe store, pharmacy. Many of them still had faded 30's to 50's era lettering peeling off the windows and no doubt some ghosts from the same time period rattling around the empty shelves and rusted tin ceilings.

Wolfe's Mercantile was in a part of the city that was just starting to see new life again. The Heartside district still had the gorgeous architecture that hinted at art nouveau and the lasting memory of a vibrant community that still thrummed along the sidewalks.

I found a parking space that wasn't all potholes and had no intention of feeding the meter. No one in the traffic authority ventured to this side of town, and even if they did, I had a few tricks up my sleeve.

After writing a few sigils on the dashboard that would make anyone's attention slide right past my car, I got out and called Jake to my side. He looked around with interest and sneezed a couple of times as he breathed the first of the unfiltered city air.

"You'll get used to it."

We casually walked up the sidewalk to Wolfe's and I peered in the windows of the new businesses that had cropped up. What looked like an artist's co-op with bright and colorful window displays, a hair and nail salon, and a Salvadoran shop selling pupusas. The mouthwatering smell wafted onto the street.

"I know where we're getting dinner," I told Jake. He looked up happily and his tongue lolled out of his mouth. The thing I was looking forward to the most now that I was back in the city was finding some decent grub. The spicier the better.

We finally stopped in front of the storefront we'd come here for. My smile faded and I pulled my jacket tighter as I looked at the gold writing on the window, spelled in old Gothic letters. *Wolfe's Mercantile.* And under that, *Fine Purveyors of the Mystical since 1902.*

I approached the door and as soon as I touched the handle the shades on the windows flipped shut and the sign switched to closed. "Very funny, Derfael," I said under my breath. I opened the door and Jake marched right in with head held high, not even waiting for me to lead the way.

"That is quite a dog you have, Talulla." Derfael's broad face appeared around the curtain to the back room. "It's been too long, lass. You're just in time for tea."

I gave a begrudging grin. "I suppose I could say the same." He disappeared behind the curtain, and I could hear cups clinking into saucers. He peered back around when I didn't show any signs of joining him.

"Do not be afraid to step past the doormat." He lowered his head and appraised me slyly over the top of his wire-framed glasses.

I frowned, both at him and myself for my childish fear and stepped purposefully off the mat and onto the aging flagstone floor. Shallow grooves had been worn over time on the most traveled paths through the store, and Derfael had no intention of repairing it.

I looked around me and remembered the two centuries I had spent here. Before the occult became more acceptable to display in public the shop had hosted a spiritualist church and table-tipping shows to distract from the reality of who the customers were and what services it provided.

There was always a human-friendly veneer over the ancient magicks that resided here. I couldn't help but laugh that the current mask it wore involved a large display of crystals, incense, and tarot cards, pendulums, and cheap scrying mirrors.

"This place hasn't changed a bit."

"Is that a good thing or a bad thing?" asked Derfael, a half smile on his face.

"I haven't decided yet." I had trained and studied within these walls, Derfael never letting me slack off for a day with the reminder that I could be fighting for my life tomorrow and I could only blame myself for my death if I didn't keep working. Perhaps a little overly dramatic, but it was effective as shit.

"There is something different about you, Talulla." Derfael moved closer. "I did not notice it before."

"You've talked to me a few times since I left. What could I have gotten past you?"

"No more is there a thirst for blood behind your eyes. You don't look ready to kill anything and everything that crosses your path." He looked at Jake. "And you have taken it upon yourself to care for a living thing." Derfael shook his head. "I never would have thought it possible."

"People change, Derfael." What was happening right now? Was he honestly disappointed?

"But not you. You have not changed since you became a fully indoctrinated mage and started your life as a mercenary." He sighed. "Perhaps I have made the wrong choice in bringing you here."

"What, just because I'm not a stone-cold soldier for the Council anymore? According to you there's a job that needs doing, and I packed up my life and drove nine hours to do it."

"But are you prepared to do it?" Derfael's brow creased. "Can you?"

I shook my head, trying to clear the buzzing anger threatening to show itself. "You knew my trepidations coming into this." I clenched my fists to my sides and Jake snuck around behind me, unsure of what was happening.

Derfael turned away and walked toward the back room. "I did not know the severity of your change of heart. I don't think you're able to fulfill the duties that this task will require." He disappeared behind the curtain.

I followed him, confused. "What are you saying?" I tore the curtain aside. "Are you dismissing me?"

"Evyn." Derfael was seated at the table, and he looked up at me with tired eyes. "I'm sorry. I didn't realize how far off the path you'd strayed."

"What path? You wanted me to stay the way I was?" I sat across from him and leaned over the table. "I was so far gone there were moments where I almost killed you! Just for funsies!"

"Humanity is a sign of the weak willed and soft minded. You are better than that." He looked at me and then through me before correcting himself. "You *were* better than that."

"I'm still perfectly capable. You should have a little more *respect* for me than that."

"First you run and then you say that I should respect you? Respect is earned. And I don't think you have what it takes anymore." Derfael rose from his chair and made for the door that led to the apartment upstairs.

The anger flared and broke free. "Don't walk away from me!" I shouted, smashing my fist on the table hard enough to crack it down the middle and break it in two. The pieces clattered to the floor along with the tea set which shattered. Jake retreated beyond reach of the puddle of English breakfast. "Do not treat me like a child!"

Derfael turned and laughed. "That is the woman I know!" He clapped his hands once. "The fire is still there." He walked toward me and smartly stopped just short of striking distance.

"So, what? You were provoking me?" I crossed my arms and hugged my elbows to resist the urge to throttle him. "To see if you could get a rise out of me?"

He only shrugged and said, "Just a wee bit."

"That's not an apology."

"I do not intend to give you one."

I growled and let my hands fall back to my sides, fists still balled up and ready to go to work. "I guess I'd forgotten how it used to be with you."

His mouth quirked. "How is that?"

"That you're an ass and apologize for nothing."

"It's good for you to remember that." His eyes twinkled. "And do not forget it." Derfael moved in and clapped me on the shoulder, his firm grip reassuring. That was as close to a comforting gesture as I ever got from him.

He painted a sigil through the air and the tea set and table reassembled themselves. That same set had gone through that process many times before, I almost felt bad for it. He left to get some more water for the kettle, and I took the time to peruse the ancient tomes organized in the same way on the same shelf as they'd always been.

I trailed my fingers across the spines, remembering the hours I had spent memorizing each of their pages. Each of them shuddered a little in response and I smiled as they recognized my touch after all these years.

"They do not forget," said Derfael in response to my unspoken words, coming back into the room with a kettle full of water. He set it on the hot plate and turned the heat to high. "They still ask about you on occasion."

"You guys were always looking out for me."

The books rumbled all along the shelves in reply and a compendium of curses on the end trilled a happy note.

Derfael and I sat and waited in silence for the water to boil. Jake had settled underneath the table almost immediately after Derfael joined the halves back together and was quietly snoozing.

The whistle of the teapot cut through the quiet and it was like the final step in confirming my return to the city. I finally felt completely at ease, back in my childhood home. The whole shop came alive now that I'd let my guard down, full of different energies of varying colors and vibrations. There were all spectrums here. Even the dust motes that got caught in the weak light of sundown took on a golden hue and danced in a breeze that wasn't there.

"Now this is a nice welcome home." I basked in the familiar magick as Derfael poured out some tea for us.

"So what are you going to do first?" He peered over the rim of his cup as he took a sip. "Eat or find some of your friends?"

I smiled. "You know me so well. Have you tried the pupuseria next door?"

He nodded. "Excellent. You can't go wrong."

I rubbed my hands together gleefully. "I can't wait. It's not that I couldn't cook for myself up north, but when the majority of your options are chain restaurants or the local community hall for pasties and a fish fry it really gets old fast." I wrinkled my nose. "Especially when far too many people choose ketchup as their condiment of choice."

"What's that now?" asked Derfael. "Who chooses ketchup over gravy? That's a mortal sin."

"Tell me about it." I sipped my tea. Derfael always brewed his extra strong, more like coffee. "This transition will be a lot easier now that I'll have great food right next door to my apartment."

Suddenly Derfael looked guilty and placed his teacup down. "About that." His long fingers nervously rearranged the saucer. "You'll have to find other arrangements. Your old apartment won't be available."

"What? Why?"

"It's occupied."

"By who?" I was confused by how vague he was being. If he rented it out no big deal, just say so.

"I should have told you before you came, it completely slipped my mind." Another nonanswer.

"Why are you being so secretive?"

He cleared his throat and changed the subject completely. "I suggest you find Adrian and any friends you may still have. You are going to need their help. The sooner you reach out to them the better, I should say."

I slapped my hands to the side of my head. At Derfael's questioning look I said, "Sorry, my head was spinning too fast from that obvious deflection." I narrowed my eyes at him as he visibly blanched, but I let the subject drop for now.

"I don't know if anyone would be willing to help me at this point. I'm pretty sure I burned all those bridges. I cut Adrian off completely. It'll be a total blindside to just show up now."

"You will not know until you talk to them face to face."

"You make it sound so easy."

Derfael looked like he wanted to say something, decided better of it, and went back to sipping his tea.

I was running my fingers over the woodgrain in the table, lost in thought, when he spoke again. "I understand why you are hesitant to return to this life. Truly, I do."

He had my attention. "I can't be that person again. I will never forgive myself for what I did. What if I relapse? What if I kill another innocent?"

"What-ifs will drive you mad, Evyn." He leaned forward and rested his elbows on the table. "Maybe look at it this way. You have the chance to do some good. Not just following the Council's orders. Steering clear of the assassin-for-hire jobs. Turn your skills toward illuminating some of that darkness. Honoring the memory of that little girl instead of just running from the fear."

My eyes burned and my throat was tight as I fought the wave of emotion. I nodded my head jerkily and looked down to hide the tears that threatened to fall. Derfael reached his hand across the table, and I took it. His hand was almost fever hot, and I could feel the layers of scars like a terraform map.

"Emma."

Jake rested his head in my lap and whined.

"I'm sorry?"

"Her name was Emma."

# CHAPTER THREE

Derfael managed to ease my fears, and with reframed purpose in mind I decided to contact Adrian first. Percy would be mad no matter how many platitudes I smothered her with, but there was a good chance that eventually she would forgive me.

Did I mention that Adrian was my familiar? We'd been bound together over a century ago and when I hightailed it out of town I might have, you know... cut him off completely and ignored any attempt at contact.

I drove for about fifteen minutes until I came to a bed and breakfast in the West Grand district that I used sometimes when I was trying to lie low. The older couple that ran it didn't ask too many questions and it was in a beautiful old mansion that had a few bootlegger-era hideaways just in case.

When I walked in with Jake slowly plodding along beside me the same man that ran it twelve years ago was still behind the counter, smiling at me.

He came around the desk and gave me a hug. "Evyn! It's been so long since I've seen you."

"Hi, Mr. Cooper." I returned his hug, albeit a bit stiffly.

He bent down and offered his hand for Jake to investigate but apparently Jake didn't need to be swayed. He put his paw in Mr. Cooper's hand and the older man was delighted, shaking Jake's paw and giving him a scratch under the chin. "And who's the gentleman you brought with you?"

"This is Jake. I'm sorry, I don't know about your policy on animals, but—"

Mr. Cooper waved me off. "For you, he can stay." He moved back around the counter. "Where have you been all this time?"

"I moved to the U.P. and I'm back in town for a while. I need a place to stay for a couple of nights, and I thought of you."

He smiled and tapped the registry in front of him. "You're in luck. Just had a cancellation."

In no time I was checked in and headed up to my room. You may be wondering how it's possible that someone who knew my former monstrous self would receive me with such warmth. Short answer is that I'm an expert with compartmentalizing, especially with humans.

I entered the tidy little attic room and Jake settled in a comfy-looking chair, immediately falling asleep. He wasn't used to keeping Stranger hours yet, but I was sure he'd adjust. I slung my bag off my shoulder and went to the bathroom to clean up.

As I was splashing water on my face the replica 1930s lightbulbs with the giant filaments reflected in the basin. I watched the light dance and wave in the water, and I got an idea.

Filling the sink with water I dimmed the lights until they were just a dull orange glow and then unscrewed all but one bulb that was directly over the basin.

I stared into the water and settled into an alpha brainwave state. I was out of practice, so it took a little while, but eventually my thoughts calmed, and I could feel the weight of the etheric realm like a blanket wrapping around me.

I softened my gaze and deepened my concentration on the water, focusing on Griselda. The surface churned, blurry but still identifiable as Moreno. Once I knew I was on target I cast about for answers as to why she was here.

Slowly, like an old black-and-white movie with a shoddy projector, images began to form. I could tell that something was attempting to keep them occluded, so I didn't pry too much. I didn't want to set off any alarms and forewarn Moreno that I was already coming for her.

A chamber swam into view, dark, possibly underground. A large pool in the middle with steam rolling off it. I got the briefest glimpse of eyes staring in my direction from the darkness and then the image clouded over, and another appeared.

A crate full of carefully wrapped items. The ones that I could see looked ancient, like artifacts from a dig site. I pulled my vision back to get an overhead view and saw dry arid land all around, maybe some farmland. A lot of rocky hills and a nearby pit with large T-shaped pillars exposed.

That image too was swept away before I could get more detail. Suddenly a face loomed up in the water, tight brown skin stretched over a skeletal face more like a mummy than a person, and yet the solid black eyes blinked at me from the expressionless skull. Small tattoos were visible, sigils of some kind, written over every inch of available skin. I got the feeling that this person couldn't see me as much as it knew someone was peeking around and giving a clear signal to back off.

And then the water cleared, and my concentration broke. I blinked rapidly, eyes screaming with dryness. I mulled over the visions as I put the bathroom back together but couldn't make much of it yet. The world was full of artifacts waiting to be dug up that may or may not be connected to the Strangefells.

We weren't always so careful to conceal ourselves from humans. There was a time that we were able to live openly. Relations may have been strained at times, but things always smoothed over, until one day they didn't. There were still ancient sites human history hadn't discovered yet that would raise a lot of questions about humanity's development should they ever be found.

When I reentered the room, Jake had moved and was snoring in the middle of the bed. I hooked my arms under him and scooted him over without any disruption to his snoring at all. Gods, I wished I could sleep like that.

I crawled under the covers and tried to go to sleep but couldn't. I looked at the clock, glowing dimly red in the darkened room. It was only 1:30 in the morning and Adrian would still be awake, at least I thought he would be.

Maybe if I gave him a heads-up that I was here he would have adequate time to cool off before I actually sought him out tomorrow.

I relaxed and opened the channel, the bond that we shared as familiars, reaching out to Adrian and trying to make a connection. I thought I felt him, but I wasn't sure until the resistance fell away and I was flooded with feelings of hatred and betrayal. Yeah, that was him.

After sending as much apologetic energy through as I could, I let the connection drop.

No turning back now.

I spent the day looking for rental properties and getting increasingly frustrated when nothing fit the bill for what I needed. Security was the top priority and not many buildings met the requirements past having a doorman and cameras.

Even the greenest young guns they might send after me were able to disable cameras or disappear outright. A doorman would be at the least a small inconvenience and at most, a snack. More thorough considerations had to be made.

Jake yipped and I looked up, noticing the shadows were getting long on the ornamental carpet. The half-circles of bullseye glass set at three-foot intervals on the west wall began to glow gold with the sunset.

"Too bad we can't just stay here, huh?" Jake cocked his head and I got to my feet and stretched. "Want to go for a stroll before I walk into the hornet's nest?"

He was on his feet and grabbing his leash and harness from the hook on the wardrobe before I even had my toes in my sock.

We passed by Mr. Cooper on our way out. "Oh, Evyn." He turned with a full stack of towels in his arms. "I've been noticing some folks hanging around your car. It could be innocent enough," he said, chuckling, "it is a beautiful restoration job."

I nodded my appreciation, only mildly concerned about the strangers. I couldn't blame them for being drawn like moths to an electric purple flame.

"But then they sort of appraise the house and they end up staring at the attic space for a while before moving on. It's happened a couple of times."

My hackles were all the way up now. I've only been in town for a day, and they've tracked me here.

"Okay, I'll keep an eye out. Probably some old friends that recognized my car." I waved it off, not wanting to alarm him. He and his guests should be safe, no sense in drawing that kind of attention when there would be other chances for them to get to me. Like out for a walk, for example.

Mr. Cooper nodded, looking relieved and went back to his task at hand. "Hold on, Jake. I need to grab a couple more things before we go."

When I stepped out the door of the bed and breakfast it was fully armed with my knife belt, a pistol, and a bowie knife strapped to my ankle, and a couple extra .9mm magazines tucked away just in case. My thick wool sweater hid the extra bulk nicely.

There was a nice breeze steadily rattling the full autumn splendor of the tree-lined street. The damp musky smell of freshly raked lawns was heavy and Jake busied himself for several minutes rustling through the leaf piles on the curb. He found a nice stick that he liked and chose to take that with him but the first time he banged it against someone's car I had to trade it in for a treat.

"Sorry, bubs." I tossed the stick back in the leaf pile and steered him away as he tried to go after it. "You may be cute, but people will still be upset if you scratch up their cars."

We passed a few other folks out for a stroll, made some small talk, and enjoyed the late-evening quiet with most people having settled somewhere for dinner by now.

A couple of streets down from the hotel and the lights were fewer and farther between, houses mostly darkened and the quiet ringing with emptiness instead of indoor gatherings. My senses were heightened. If anyone was looking to catch me out, now would be the perfect opportunity.

The sun was just going down when a porch light clicked on over an otherwise darkened house at the end of the street. The home was a beautiful Queen Anne revival with purple siding and black trim that washed out under the harsh glare of the LED bulb. I paused and evaluated the area but didn't sense anything had changed.

Jake was staring at it too. "Probably just automatic," I soothed.

As we approached the house I noticed neat rows of shrubs, low trees, and vines, all laid out in a patchwork. I could only see a small portion of the backyard, but it looked like it was also full of well-cared-for plants and greenery.

I was still admiring the yard when the front door opened and a small woman stepped out onto the porch, chunky-heeled boots thudding loudly on the wood.

"Fuck." I turned on my heel and enticed a confused Jake to keep up. He kept trying to look over his shoulder to see what had me spooked. I was fishing around for a treat to regain his full attention when a voice pulled me up short and my head snapped up to see another woman standing right in front us.

"You turned tail as fast as you beat-feet out of town. I can't imagine what's got you so scared."

Jake immediately plopped his butt down and stared up at the newcomer, starry-eyed.

"Are you stealing people's dogs now, too?" the woman asked, crossing her arms. Her bronze-black skin seemed to glow of its own accord.

"Do you ever get tired from holding up that glamour?" A question for a question, but the only response I received was a quirk of her mouth. "We were just heading back, actually."

I tried to step around her, but she stepped in front of me and put her hands on her hips. "Uh-uh. You're not going anywhere until we have a few words."

"Does it help matters if I say I'm a changed woman?"

"No." She nodded her head in a quick staccato back toward the house where the other woman was now standing at the low wrought-iron gate. "Go on."

The atmosphere wasn't overly murder-y so I turned and walked toward the house, Jake glued to my side and the necromancer, Vivianne Rollins, close behind.

Or at least that was the name she gave people. Those that work solely with the dead are more careful to keep their real names to themselves, even more so than the rest of us.

Her sister was the woman at the gate. Lorraine Rollins was all of five feet with the chunky heels on, but I was more afraid of her than I was of Vivianne.

"Seer," I greeted her. True seers were rare and Lorraine was one of the best. She was so accurate she had a hard time getting people to listen to the predictions. Folks were a lot less interested in their futures if the outcomes were set in stone.

"Mage." Her bright blue eyes bored into mine, the irises shifting color to cloudy gray and back again. My stomach bottomed out; she'd just read me.

Her face betrayed nothing as she opened the metal gate with a shrill note that shattered the silence before dying off again. As I walked toward the door I could hear them conversing lowly behind me. Vivianne's voice took on a hint of anger, but I couldn't tell who it was directed at.

"Should I go in, or are we just going to talk out here?"

"Are you refusing our hospitality?" asked Vivianne, her fingers flexing toward the small bags that ringed her belt. Each one would contain dried, ground, or fresh specimens from the poisoner's garden paradise all around me. Plants that could kill me, control me, or punish me severely.

"Wouldn't dream of it." I opened the front door and stepped inside. To Jake's credit he didn't hesitate to follow.

An earthy aroma of incense and musk surrounded me, and I closed my eyes and breathed in, detecting a slight hint of blood from somewhere secluded in the house. The magick in this place was luxurious and deep, a warm comforting embrace from a mysterious stranger.

"The instant comfort of a real home, am I right?" A man's voice to my left.

"Dominic." I turned with surprise to the man leaning casually against the doorframe. "I thought you were moving to the Caribbean full time?"

"I thought you were dead, so..." He shrugged.

I bowed my head. "Fair point."

His poker face was excellent. I couldn't tell if he shared his sisters' anger at me. Technically I didn't double-cross *him*.

A gentle hand at my elbow made me jump. Lorraine looked up at me, amused and asked innocently, "What are you afraid of?"

She led me into the family room and all of us took seats on various over-stuffed furniture, Dominic joining me on the couch. Well, everyone except for Vivianne who went to the kitchen to make tea.

The room was decorated with lavish tapestries, ritual garb, drums, and the family shrine for their ancestors. The Rollins family were Strangers, but they'd left for the human world centuries ago and never looked back.

Over the years the family's power had waned considerably from cutting themselves off from the Strangefells, but this generation was different.

"May I?" I gestured toward the small history museum in front of me. Jake had been inching his way toward Dominic, trying to seem uninterested, but Dom knew his game a mile away. I could tell it took a lot of effort for him to resist Jake's puppy fluff.

Lorraine nodded, not moving, only her eyes following me. I saw a flash of gray clouds wash over them again and shivered, keeping my fingers crossed that she would keep any details to herself.

I walked slowly around the room, black-and-white photos I hadn't noticed before showing family gatherings, grand outdoor Vodou rituals around a blazing fire, smaller indoor congregations with healing ceremonies, and even one of a rite of exorcism.

"Thirteen generations in this room," said Vivianne, handing me a steaming cup of tea. I took it but didn't drink.

"This was my mother's." She caressed a carefully preserved and maintained ritual dress, simple white fabric with tiny embellishments only the wearer would notice. The lace collar and hem also looked handmade. "She was a manbo in Port au Prince." Vivianne adjusted the white starched handkerchief wrapped carefully around a wig stand.

"One of the longest serving and most respected," agreed Dom. Jake was lying on his back at Dom's feet, tail thumping as he got some belly rubs.

Vivianne moved to a chair and sat, crossing her legs idly and propping a fist under her cheek as she lounged back. "It was her killer's head you were supposed to bring us."

If I'd been sipping the tea, I would have spit it out. "I-I don't—" I stammered, desperately trying to come up with an answer that would be acceptable. Was there one?

"Granted you didn't know that, but it doesn't change the fact that you took our money and gave his head to another bounty that paid you more." Vivianne still hadn't moved. All the siblings were still, appraising. Waiting to see what the scared rabbit would do.

I swallowed heavily, heart pounding, and said the only thing I could think to say. "I'm sorry."

Vivianne blinked rapidly and her mouth parted in surprise. Dominic's eyebrows were in his hairline. Lorraine, though, looked like she expected nothing else. Although I guess that was also to be expected.

The three of them looked between each other just as the grandfather clock began to chime. As the last chime signaled 6 p.m., the doorbell rang.

"I'll get it." Dominic hurried from the room and Jake followed his new best friend.

"She wasn't lying, Viv," said Lorraine.

"How does a leopard change its spots?" Vivianne's eyes narrowed like she expected the charade to drop at any moment and the candid camera crew to come rolling in.

"She went a step too far, even for her," said Lorraine. "Didn't you, Evyn?"

I nodded.

Lorraine turned to her sister. "You were actually at the crime scene. That Stranger family that was slaughtered in Creston." She leveled her eyes at me with cold indifference.

"That was her?" Vivianne drew herself up in her chair and leaned toward me. Her hands were moving, fingers stretching and twisting like she was constructing something from the air.

"Do you know what my specialty is?"

I shook my head.

"People call me in to raise the dead that were killed suddenly and brutally." The judgment in her eyes was intense but not undeserved. "Most of the time any parts of the soul that are still intact are half-crazy. I specialize in putting all"—she motioned her hands in a wide circle—"the pieces together so we can find out what happened and who is to blame."

Dominic poked his head through the doorframe. "Dinner's on the table."

"We'll be right there." Lorraine lifted her hand dismissively.

Dominic's face pulled into a frown, but he said nothing. I heard low music start to play in the dining room.

"So what did you find out?" I knew exactly what happened but hearing it from someone else would put a clear edge on a night that felt like—that I wished had been—a bad dream.

"Nothing." Vivianne cut her hands in a sharp motion and sat back into her chair, sniffing. "By the time I was ready to start the raising, the cleaners had found evidence the family was involved in the recent robberies and homicides of Stranger families, that their murders were payback. Brokered by Aldous Kildaire." My ears perked up as she sneered. "That man actually had the balls to show up at the victim's house to get proof of the job. Seemed the merc they contracted disappeared."

"Even though the hit was ordered by a bloodsucker mob boss the Council decided it was warranted." Lorraine was clearly not of the same opinion.

Vivianne nodded. "They cleaned the scene, and I was told to fuck off." She absentmindedly started to toy with the ornate orthodox gold cross around her neck. "Makes a lot more sense now that I know you were the one involved."

Great. Any points I may have earned with the unprompted apology were evaporating before my eyes.

"A dog does what it's been trained to do. She was the Council's pet, and the leash broke a long time ago," said Lorraine.

I raised an eyebrow. "You guys know I'm standing right here, right?"

"Are you going to deny it?" asked Lorraine.

"Yes?" For better or worse I had a lot more control of my life than just being the Council's attack dog.

"So you take responsibility for your actions?" Lorraine almost looked hungry for the answer but for the life of me I couldn't figure why.

"Yes. I won't deny what a monster I was. I took those jobs for fun. I didn't need the money, I certainly didn't need the reputation. It was a way to pass the time."

Jake, having sensed my change of mood, came back in the room and sat on my feet, pressing against my legs. I stroked his ears and avoided looking at the sisters.

"I've spent the last twelve years trying to figure out where it all went wrong and vowing never to go back."

There was a silence, but I didn't dare raise my head. I knew my words were unbelievable, especially to people I'd betrayed in the past. I didn't need to see their faces to know they'd call me a liar. As long as I was moving in the tides of my old life, I'd be running into this situation a lot.

Again, I couldn't blame them. I wouldn't have believed me either.

Dominic popped his head in again. "Seriously. Food's getting cold. I set an extra plate, just invite her to eat already."

"Oh, I don't want to impose. We'll just—"

"Just eat the damn food," said Vivianne, more annoyed than angry, waving me toward the dining room. "I didn't poison it or anything." On her way past me she took the teacup out of my hands. "This however..."

My hands snapped closed on reflex and I laughed weakly. "Yikes."

"You'd have been fine. Eventually."

On the table was laid out a nice spread of dishes and my mouth immediately began to water. "Smells delicious. Where'd you order in from?" Jake excitedly sniffed at the table and sat at Dom's side expectantly. I had a sneaking suspicion Jake had been using his powers of cuteness for evil.

"Tuesdays are Filipino," said Dominic. At my curious expression, he explained. "We have a standing order at the same restaurant for every Tuesday at 6 p.m. Wednesdays are Mexican. Thursdays, Jamaican. You get the idea."

"Huh. Makes meal planning easier."

"We like what we like." Dom loaded up his plate with savory lumpia and pork sisig.

"Is that kare-kare?" I pointed to the crock steaming away on a warming plate.

"Sure is," said Vivianne. "Best in town."

"The only in town," Lorraine corrected.

I filled a soup cup with the oxtail stewed in a savory peanut sauce—after watching Lorraine eat some. It was more on the brothy side, so all the flavors were spotlighted.

"Oh, my gods. This is amazing." I swooned. "I was just telling Derfael how much I was looking forward to getting a good meal again that I didn't have to make myself."

"Where have you been this whole time? Alaska?" joked Dominic.

"The U.P."

All three of my hosts groaned.

"So it might as well have been," agreed Vivianne.

I dipped the lumpia in some adobo and almost cried from the deliciousness. "Options are limited, and spice is nonexistent."

After a little while of casual conversation and a sampling of everything on offer, it was Dominic that started talking shop.

"Why'd you come back?"

I looked at Lorraine, figuring she would have told them everything already. "I told them you'd be walking through here tonight, but I didn't look into it further." She took a sip of her wine. "I still like to be surprised, too."

"It's interesting that you mentioned Aldous Kildaire earlier. The new head of the Briste had him send a 'messenger' my way."

"Griselda Moreno." The name clearly left a foul taste in Vivianne's mouth.

I nodded. "She's an old nemesis of mine. If she rousted me out of hiding it was for a reason." At their looks of incredulity, I raised my hands. "Not just because she hates me. She wouldn't waste her time with messengers, she'd have just hunted me down and tried to kill me herself."

"So you need to find out what she's planning before you step into whatever trap she's laying," reasoned Lorraine.

I nodded. "Since I'm here anyway." I scraped out the last bite of stew in my bowl. "Would you know anyone who could help me with that?"

Lorraine didn't miss a beat. "For $25,000, sure."

A piece of sisig lodged in my throat at my surprise and I coughed furiously trying to clear it. Dom laughed and thwacked my upper back with his giant palm and the chunk of meat dislodged.

"The fee that you paid me with interest?" I asked, spitting the meat into my napkin.

"No interest. The rest is my fee."

I nodded. Despite my reservations it would cut down on a lot of legwork if I could just get it all out of the way now. Maybe this would end up just being a quick job after all, and Jake and I could be back home in Copper Harbor before the week was out. "Deal."

Her eyes began to swim with the most intense gray I'd seen yet and then she began to describe her visions.

"There's a dark cavern. She wants something there. No... she already has them. Most of them."

"Them?" My thoughts went to the crate that I'd seen in my own scrying.

"Items. Artifacts. The archaeological team didn't know they were there until one of the researchers fell through the floor. Moreno had them all killed. It's a high conflict area, the authorities blamed it on extremists."

"Does this place have a name?"

Lorraine's head tilted with interest. "Göbekli Tepe."

My eyes widened. That site had been dug up a decade ago in Turkey by the Syrian border but they kept finding layers underneath layers, going back further than ten thousand years.

Some of the iconography was common to the Strangefells but as far as I knew it was nothing more than the usual rubbing of elbows between communities.

"Oh, hell no," said Lorraine. Before I could question her, she held up a finger.

"She's running into roadblocks." Dominic got to his feet and retrieved a censer from a cabinet, lighting incense that wafted in thick smoke tendrils around Lorraine. I smelled copal and tobacco.

"Someone doesn't want me to see what they're doing with those statues." Sweat was beading on her forehead, and she was straining to breathe normally. "I'm moving to something different."

Vivianne wiped a cloth over Lorraine's face and looked at me grimly but said nothing. I was beginning to wonder if this was a family that mostly spoke in glances and glares and company wasn't a common occurrence.

"You're going to make a new ally. Themistokles." Her eyes darted around like she was choosing between several options, possibly several different outcomes. "He's reckless, but trustworthy. He's the catalyst that kicks everything into overdrive. You'll attempt to keep him safe, but he will feed himself to the sharks if it means saving you."

I jumped as she slammed her palm on the table. "Why can't I see more detail?"

Lorraine's gaze went wide and distant like she was seeing a train hurtling toward her at full speed. "Moreno is hungry for power, and she's placed herself to get it. You are a key player in her domination."

"I'm going to work for her?" I was incredulous. Normally there wouldn't be a chance in hell that I'd do anything at that maniac's bidding, but Lorraine was never wrong.

"Not willingly," she clarified.

I nodded, mulling it over. Griselda was a master manipulator. It would stand to reason that she would be pulling strings and setting up her marionette show.

Lorraine suddenly hissed and grabbed her head in her hands. There was a low buzzing noise rising in volume filling the room and the feeling of being watched settled heavily on me. Jake yelped and crammed himself under my chair.

"Who are you!" she exclaimed. She began to tear at her hair, braids fraying as she scratched at her scalp. Like she was trying to wrench something out of her skull.

Dominic rushed to her, placing his hand on her forehead as he began to chant in a low, melodic rhythm. Vivianne was adding some of the herbs from her pouches onto the censer and an acrid odor began to overtake the warm comfort of the copal.

Dom's voice rose, commanding with a mixture of Haitian Creole and Taíno as he pressed Lorraine back in the chair. He dripped a thick oil on her forehead and drew a series of overlapping symbols with it as he massaged it in, all but shouting now to be heard over the chainsaw-like buzzing.

Vivianne lifted the censer, dropped a few more herbs onto the burning charcoal disc and after a final command from Dominic both siblings blew the roiling smoke over Lorraine.

The noise cut out entirely, leaving deafening silence in its wake. The feeling of being watched ebbed slowly away until suddenly the muscles in my shoulders I hadn't even been aware I'd been clenching relaxed.

"You need to leave," said Vivianne.

"Wait." Lorraine placed a hand weakly on her sister's arm. "It's not her fault." She sipped some wine and wet her lips. "I pushed too hard. I knew someone was trying to conceal this shit, but I tried to bust past them anyway."

When it became clear Vivianne wasn't going to insist I leave, I asked, "Could you perceive anything about the magick used to keep you out?"

Lorraine shook her head and took another sip. "The only thing I know is that it's old, old magick. Wielded by an old, old soul." She stared hard at me. "You need to watch your back, Evyn, because these clowns are not playing around."

She shakily got to her feet and motioned for me to follow her to the door. "There's something else involved here that I couldn't get close to, but the fact that it's being guarded that heavily only scares me more. Griselda isn't working alone, it's not a simple power grab, and for better or worse you're in this whether or not you're ready for it.

"She needs you for something and there's nothing you can do to avoid it. She has fifteen backup plans for every backup plan."

I hooked Jake back up to his leash before we stepped outside. "Thank you. I'll leave a check in the mailbox tomorrow."

Lorraine smiled sideways. "No you won't." And she closed the door in my face.

# CHAPTER FOUR

The walk home was brisk; I didn't want to risk running into anyone else I knew. I kept thinking about what Lorraine could have meant. Did she think I just wasn't going to pay up, or was she not sharing something that she managed to see before someone tried to explode her brain?

Tired from his ordeal, Jake was all too happy to curl up and watch some TV. He barely registered while I changed and psyched myself up for what was supposed to be the only task of the evening and was asleep when I quietly shut the door behind me.

The bar was about four blocks away, so I decided to just walk there. It was a Strangefells hangout but it wasn't hidden by any means, so humans did make their way there occasionally. For their sake I hoped there weren't that many in attendance. There was at least one very drunk and soon-to-be-angry demon in the place.

The stench from the dumpsters on the side of the building made my nose wrinkle, and I stopped myself before I could wonder what was in there. It wasn't necessarily anything nefarious. Sometimes the kitchen catered to special "tastes" of all kinds and the basement was owned by a succubus that ran a fetish dungeon to shame all others. Old me had been a regular, on both floors.

I pushed the door open and stepped into the dim interior. I was immediately engulfed in a cloud of pipe smoke belched up by the old man sitting in the corner of the small coat room.

"Evyn?" he asked, adjusting his glasses to no avail.

I lifted the glasses off his nose and wiped them on my sleeve, placing them back on his face. "These work a lot better when they're clean, Gus," I tsked.

"Haven't been touched since the last time you were in here," he said, this time blowing elaborate smoke rings just to show off.

"You are a terrible doorman." I was trying not to laugh, and he leaned forward to study my smile like he'd never seen one before.

"Maybe my eyes are worse than I thought."

I clapped him on the shoulder. "Things change when you come back from the dead."

His wheezing laugh followed me into the bar. A quick scan of the standing-room-only crowd, thankfully with only a few humans, found Adrian pretty easily. "Damn."

He was sitting at the end of the bar, leaning on his elbows, and clutching a half-empty glass. His black hair was longer than I remembered, sticking out at odd angles like he'd just rolled out of bed and sat directly on the barstool.

He had a beard now, decently groomed compared to his hair. It was cropped close to his face and the mustache was longer on the ends with evidence that someone had attempted to twist them but abandoned the venture.

I crossed the room slowly, doing some quick math to figure out if there would be much collateral damage should things get nasty. Or rather, should he get nasty... which he would.

Adrian looked skinnier now, almost deflated. His once wide, muscular shoulders drooped and his tall frame was lanky instead of built.

*Not deflated,* I thought. *Defeated.*

Preparing myself for the shitstorm, I subtly *encouraged* the person in the seat next to him to move on, sat down before the many people already eyeing the barstool could move in and motioned to the bartender.

"Well, shit, look who it is," he said. "I thought you were dead."

"A lot of that going around," I said. "Old Fashioned, please, Tommy." He nodded and started grabbing bottles.

"Since when does a bitch like you say 'please'?" slurred Adrian, not looking at me.

I winced. "Hello, Adrian."

"No, you know what? How about you don't speak. That okay with you?"

I didn't answer and he approved of that. He turned to me and looked at me through bleary eyes, rimmed with red and bloodshot from drunkenness.

"Jesus, Adrian." The words slipped out on reflex, and he slammed his hand on the bar.

"Just shut your damn mouth!" Even on a busy night when the background noise was almost deafening his outburst drew quite a bit of attention.

The bartender came over and set my drink down, looking between me and Adrian.

"If you're gonna fight, take it outside."

I put my hand up. "Not a problem."

"Yeah, run along now," Adrian muttered under his breath. The bartender took one last look at me and when I shook my head once he left us alone.

I sipped my drink and waited for him to say something else, more than likely to start in on me with every ounce of venom that he had. Which was a lot.

A few minutes of silence passed before he said, "Do you know how long I looked for you? How many times I tried to contact you?" He glared at me, working very hard to focus his vision. "I don't appreciate it when someone I'm close to just up and disappears without as much as a 'fuck you, don't bother calling.' I didn't sleep for weeks because I was searching and worrying and waiting to hear from you. You couldn't be dead because I was still breathing."

His anger started to ramp up. "So someone had to be holding you somewhere, right? Because there's no way you would just leave, me, behind!" he shouted, slamming his hand on the bar for emphasis.

Almost half the bar looked around this time, but I turned to them and waved my hands in a don't-worry-about-it gesture. They mostly shrugged and looked away but a couple of them kept watching, expecting a show.

"The other half of me took off and never looked back. So what was I left to do? Drink, drink, and drink some more so I'd forget all about her until I sobered up. Then I started all over again. The bars in this city never met a better customer." With that he went back to his drink.

Was he done? Or just simmering? "When I left, I'll be honest... I didn't give you a second thought." Adrian flinched and drained his glass. He motioned to Tommy for another and the bartender, for his part, was somewhat reluctant to refill it.

"All I cared about was getting away clean, and that meant cutting you out." His shoulders set and his whole body tensed on the barstool, but he let me speak.

"After what happened, I couldn't live with myself. I had to get away from all this and leave everything behind. And everyone." I rolled my Old Fashioned between my palms and tried to find the right words. "I don't think there's any way I can say I'm sorry and have that mean something to you."

"Damn straight," he mumbled, taking a large swig and swallowing loudly.

"Please try to understand—"

"There's that word again." Adrian fought back a hiccough. "*Please.*" He burped sourly and glared at me. "Why didn't you at least tell me where you were going? Say goodbye? Call me and tell me you were safe?"

I breathed deep, regretting it when all the smells of the place hit me at once. "I thought you would try to stop me or track me down and convince me to come back. I didn't want to risk that."

"What scared you so much?"

A switch flipped and it was my turn to be angry. He knew what I did. "I was a monster, Adrian! I killed an innocent child!" Memories of that night roared back to life and my chest felt tight with horror.

"Leaving an orphan behind would have been better?" Adrian asked, genuinely curious.

Angrily I gathered my hair into a ponytail so my hands would have something to do other than wrap themselves around Adrian's throat. "You weren't there." My voice was cold with fury. "That little girl didn't look you in the eyes as she died. I felt remorse for the first time in my life."

My eyes started their familiar burning as tears threatened to fall but I refused to let them. Especially not in front of Adrian.

There was a lot more I wanted to scream at him, but I wouldn't give him the satisfaction of meeting him on the low road. "It made me reevaluate things," I spat. "Maybe you should give it a try."

He set his glass down with a heavy *thunk* on the bar top and grabbed my arm with a vise grip. "So you go into seclusion and cut off all ties?" He was leaning toward me and tipping precariously on his seat. "That's a hell of a reevaluation." He realized where his hand was and let me go before I tore it off him. "Most people would have just made a vow to 'never do that again' and moved on with their life. But you took the coward's way out."

I opened my mouth to protest, but he wasn't hearing it. He stood, wobbled, and clutched the bar for balance. "The lady here is picking up my tab, Tom."

Tommy nodded, relieved that at least one of us was leaving.

Adrian cocked his head to the side, thoughtful. "If you wanted to stay gone you could have just told me that. I would have respected that and left you alone."

"Would you?" I looked him full in the face. "Would you really have been able to do that, in all honesty?"

He shrugged. "Guess we'll never know."

I took his hand, and he didn't pull away. "How can I make this up to you?"

"You can't."

At the crestfallen look on my face, I thought he might actually crack. After a second he downed the rest of his drink, reached over the bar and took a piece of paper and a pen from next to the register. He scribbled away and narrowed his eyes at what he wrote to make sure it was correct before handing it to me. "Here's my address. Give me a couple of days and then come over. We'll finish this discussion then."

He started to weave his way through the crowd but was actually just bouncing off people until they pushed him in the general direction of the door.

I stared after him until the door closed behind him and turned back to my drink. Tommy sidled back over and asked, "What else can I get you?"

"A time machine?"

"Fresh out," he shrugged. "Whisky or rum? How fucked up do you want to get?"

I'd known Tommy for decades, so he knew exactly my reaction to both. I was surprised he even offered rum. The last time I got drunk off it I burned half this building down when I'd suddenly decided my new hobby was fire spitting.

"Let's not get carried away. I'll stick with whisky. Neat."

"Double?" he asked with a sideways smile. I nodded and the glass appeared in front of me like he already knew what my answer was going to be.

I was turning into a whisky witch on my first night back, drowning my sorrows in the corner pub and scrying for a brighter future in the surface of every shot.

I don't know how long I sat there but before I knew it I was ten shots deep, had propositioned and been propositioned by a handful of men—luckily we went our separate ways and I just found myself disappointed and lonely rather than disappointed and sexually unsatisfied—remembered why I loved and hated this city, and unceremoniously made Bob Seger's "Turn the Page" the most played song on the jukebox for the night with a couple appearances of "Old Time Rock 'n' Roll" in between.

Toward the end of the night when things began to quiet down a bit, some of the other regulars all snagged seats at the bar and I was peppered with what I was sure would become the typical questions everyone would ask upon seeing me around again.

Where have you been? I thought you were dead? And my new favorite: "Aren't you Mara's niece that works at the strip club?" Although maybe that was just a one off.

Too late I realized the pixie on the stool next to me was losing the fight against gravity and before I could grab them, they face-planted on the floor.

Tommy sighed and motioned Gus over from the entryway and they each took an armpit and a knee and moved them to a corner. They curled up, and Gus grabbed a pillow from the back and stuck it under their head, the pixie's snoring never ceasing.

"They do that often?" I asked Tommy.

"Often enough," he nodded. "I don't have the heart to kick them out." He looked at me darkly. "They've got reasons for wanting oblivion. I should probably just set up a room for them."

I looked over at the sleeping pixie. Such a childlike face, but that wouldn't change no matter how old they got. The tears falling freely down their cheeks spoke to something more than just a temporary hardship.

"Anything I can do to help?" I asked.

Tommy looked at me sideways. "You serious?"

I splayed my hands. "I'm different now, Tom. You'll just have to take my word for it until I prove it enough times."

Tommy looked back and forth between me and the pixie. "Ro doesn't talk about it in much detail, but I get the distinct impression there are *issues* at home. Pretty sure their partner is a human." The sneer of disgust on Tommy's face showed plainly what he thought of humans in general. He'd take their money, but he was no friend.

"He knows about Strangers, but he's using it as a weapon. Holding the secret over Ro's head to keep control over them. You know pixies. Ro couldn't hurt him if they tried, even if he's making their life hell."

My hands were clenched in anger. "That definitely sounds like something I'm qualified to help with." I wrote my number down on a napkin. "Make sure they get this and have them call me when they're ready for help."

Tommy took the napkin like he couldn't quite believe it was real.

"It's not going to self-destruct, I promise." I winked.

"Actually, I was thinking I'd better test it out, make sure it's the real deal." He aimed a wolfish smile at me.

"I'll let you in on a secret." I leaned forward and motioned him closer. He stepped in close, bracing his giant forearms on the bar top and stopping inches away from my face.

"What's that?" he asked, his grin implying he already knew what I was going to say.

"I'm actually lousy in bed," I said, straight-faced.

Not the answer he was expecting, Tommy backed away with a bark of laughter. "You're full of shit."

"It's true." I made the "scout's honor" sign. "I'm lazy, let my partner do all the work, kick them out when I'm finished." A smile started to crack free.

Tommy indignantly flipped a dirty dish rag over his shoulder, still chuckling. He stopped, struck by a sudden thought, and leaned in toward me again, his face even closer to mine this time. "I'm willing to take a chance."

I couldn't hold back the laughter anymore. Tommy reached over and grabbed the bottle of whisky, pouring us both shots. We clinked the glasses together, tapped them on the bar and downed them.

"I'm going to need at least another twenty of those before I'm drunk enough to make bad decisions," I told him.

"Coming right up." He refilled our shot glasses.

A man that had been one of the last sitting alone at a table sidled up and took the seat the pixie had unceremoniously vacated. I remembered seeing him around here in the past but that was as far as my familiarity went.

"So what brings you back to town?" he asked me.

I looked around at him and gave him more intense scrutiny than I did before. "Do I know you?"

"Kind of. We've mostly just operated on each other's peripherals before now. I think we may have spoken once."

"You don't look like a merc." He was too clean cut, but not in the deadly, alluring, shark-in-wolf's-clothing kind of way. He looked like a nerd, to be honest. I think he might have had a pocket protector in his breast pocket.

"Not a merc. An actuary." He said it almost apologetically.

Super nerd. Got it. "Trying to figure out what my appearance means for the overall risk assessment of the city?"

He shook his head, his cheeks a little pink from embarrassment. "I'm off the clock. It's more curiosity."

"Not much to tell. Rumors and guessing mostly." I still couldn't tell what this guy's game was and was in no way inclined to get chatty.

"Anything to do with Griselda Moreno being stateside?" The man was running his fingers around the rim of his glass, but his efforts at being casual were hampered by the obvious side-eye he was fixing me with.

"Is there something specific you want to ask me about? Because I don't have patience for this hedging." If he was just some sycophant looking to get his jollies off the rumor-mill, I wasn't going to be a part of it.

He chuckled nervously. "Okay." He glanced at the nearest bar patrons to see if they were listening in, but any that weren't half asleep in their seats were in a stupor, lost in their own thoughts.

The man leaned in, and his cloying aftershave made the smell of stale coffee, cigarettes, and brandy on his breath overwhelming.

"I may have heard a few things from my buddies around the office." A slow, lazy smile overtook the paranoia of being overheard. "Interested?"

Great, an "informant." I shot a look at Tommy, who had escaped the man's notice in his appraisal of the rest of the bar and had easily overheard the conversation. Tommy only shrugged and walked around the bar to check on Ro before starting to stack chairs on tables.

"And what would you be looking for in exchange?" I leaned back against the bar.

"Not a thing."

I raised an eyebrow but didn't move. "You're just doing this out of the good of your own heart?"

He ran a hand through his hair and leaned one elbow on the bar, again trying to be nonchalant but only succeeding in looking a bit constipated. "Maybe just don't forget who gave you the information? I'm well placed to get more once you find that this is legitimate."

Just to toy with him I lifted my hand and examined my nails until he started to fidget uncomfortably. "You wouldn't be trying to pull a fast one, would you?" I leaned forward and straightened his tie. "Because you should understand that if that were the case, I'd be quite..." I tightened his tie all the way and he coughed in surprise. "...upset."

I flattened out the knot and his shirt collar and leaned back against the bar. "I can also forget this conversation, if you'd like."

He shook his head. "I-I'm serious." He loosened his tie and took a drink. "There's a couple guys I work with that are more involved with your side of the business than they should be." He blanched and backpedaled. "I'm not saying there's anything wrong with your business, I just mean, um..." He floundered into silence.

My lips twitched but I schooled my expression. "Just say what you want to say."

"Um." The actuary stopped and took a deep breath. "How much do you know about ancient Sumer?"

It was closing time when I walked back out into the cool fall night. I slid my jacket on and zipped it up, taking my time before I arrived back at my hotel.

I was a little tipsy but not drunk by any means. I kept mulling the actuary's information over. In all likelihood he saw a chance to bring some excitement to his life and was making stuff up, or at least embellishing.

It also wouldn't be the first time I'd had "fans" try to ingratiate themselves to me by trying to help, if you could call it that. This guy fit the bill for that perfectly; boring day job, loner-type, probably more than happy to let the women in his life take charge.

I shook my head. Now I was just profiling.

If I had been paying attention, I would have realized that there were several sets of feet approaching from behind.

When a pair of hands grabbed me and shoved me face-first to the ground I was a bit surprised to say the least. "What the hell?" I asked, speech slightly slurred. I flipped over and stared up at a group of human men leering down at me.

"Look at that," I said, pointing to a nondesigner hole in the knee of my pants. "Totally ruined my new jeans."

They snickered at the drunk lady that clearly didn't know what was happening. I took stock of them, each one of them blatantly showing the guns they carried.

Seven guys, seven guns. No problem.

"What I think is, that's going to be the least of your problems," said another of the group, not more than seventeen. I frowned as I realized that not one person among them was more than twenty years, tops.

"I'm actually taking guns from babies," I muttered under my breath. "How about this?" I said, getting to my feet. "I'll give you a chance to walk away and you'll take that chance."

Each and every one of them drew their guns and pointed them at me.

I sighed. "Or not."

For normal people, staring seven guns in the face would start with pant-shitting fear and more than likely end in concussion when they passed out and hit the pavement. For people like me? It's practice.

I dropped the glamour on the garter belt holding my throwing knives and they became visible to the group. Before they had a chance to figure things out, I threw three knives within a second.

Two of them lodged in the hands of would-be assailants. The other went wide and sank deep into the elbow of another guy who shrieked and would most certainly not be pitching for the Tigers any time soon.

Then it was a matter of dodging bullets as they opened fire. They had a hard time following me as I weaved around and through them and started slashing.

The rules of engagement that all mages are bound by prevented me from just blasting them with magick and walking away. Human or nonhuman, if I was in a fight, I could only use magick to defend myself or others. I could enhance my abilities or my weapons all I wanted, but I couldn't start throwing fireballs at someone unless they were directly engaging me in battle. And to be honest, most of the time it was more trouble than it was worth as most magick took precious seconds to conjure that you didn't always have.

Before long I was standing in a body pile. They were all very much alive, but they weren't going anywhere for the time being.

I called the police department and let them know about the sidewalk blockade. I couldn't just let them walk away and hope they'd learned a lesson. The next woman they came across might not be a mage-born assassin.

I retrieved my knives, set their guns on top of a nearby dumpster where they'd be found quickly, and disappeared around the corner as the flashing lights appeared down the street.

I was almost to my hotel, mind set on cleaning the blood off my best knives, when I heard approaching feet for the second time in twenty minutes.

I turned, planning on telling off more people, but they were a lot closer than I thought. A fist shot out and nailed me right in the face. Luckily it was human, so it was like being batted by a kitten.

The fist reappeared and I blocked it, returning the gesture and knocking the man connected to it on his ass.

Another figure, a Stranger, appeared out of the shadows in a blink. I leaned back but he grabbed my arm and tried to throw me. I used the momentum to brace his shoulder and kick his leg out from under him, flipping him onto his back. Before I could incapacitate him, a third attacker launched at me.

The vamp reached for me with blood-crusted claws, and I dodged, too slow to avoid a rake of his nails across my cheek. He twisted his body impossibly at the waist and took another swipe.

I batted his arm aside, snapped my hands to his chest, and blasted him into a brick wall. The vamp was left passed out under a pile of small rubble and brick dust, the occasional moan escaping his throat.

The sound of stiletto heels preceded a voice I never thought I'd hear again. "Very good, Miss Urquhart. So nice to see you haven't lost your touch."

"Havoc," I growled. "Last time I saw you the light was leaving your eyes, and my knife was sticking out of your chest."

"Wishful thinking on your behalf, my dear," said Havoc with a smile, her pearly whites gleaming. "But as we're speaking of people who were assumed dead..."

"Still working for the Briste?" I asked, keeping it conversational. "It's been a while, I'm a little out of the loop."

"Indeed." She walked—well, sauntered—over to me. Her tall, thin frame seemed a little skeletal since last I'd seen her.

"You look like hell," I said. "Stressed out? The sheer thought of my being back in town making you a little less hungry? Or do donors run and hide from you now? You are getting rather old. Losing your touch maybe?"

She was right in my face now. "I would watch my mouth if I were you." She sneered, a look really unbecoming on her pointed face.

"Yeah? What do you suppose you're going to do about it?" I asked, matching her sneer.

She looked behind her and the rest of her posse advanced, two vamps I hadn't seen yet. When I saw the thick, snaking black lines tattooed around their right hands and up their wrists the first inklings that I was truly in trouble started to hit me.

Havoc smiled at the widening of my eyes. "Yes," she hissed. "That fear is what I like to see in you."

I narrowed my eyes in response and brought my predator to the surface. "No fear. Just wondering how I'm going to kill each of you."

She laughed and motioned to her men. "Take her. Her confidence needs to be shattered." She leaned in until our noses almost touched and breathed, "Painfully."

Two white-hot flashes of pain on my neck followed by several thousand volts of electricity seized every muscle in my body and everything went black.

# Chapter Five

I opened my eyes and was relatively surprised that I did, although Havoc did promise a bit of "fun" before the fateful moment.

Wonderful.

The dank, underground room was every bit the cliché as Havoc herself. Stale air reeking of damp and cold, cracked and blackening stone walls covered in a thick green moss that was more poisonous mold and less the stuff that I called "the pillows of the forest floor."

Small puddles were dotted here and there amid the constant *drip*, *drip*, *drip* of water. It took a few minutes of shivering to realize I was lying in the biggest one. I tried to summon up some warmth but discovered that the chamber had been sealed, spells running within the walls that prevented the use of magic.

The connection between Adrian and myself, however, was unbreakable, so I still had a lifeline. They could stop me from hopping a ley line out of here, but there was nothing that would be able to prevent me from reaching out to him for help.

Unless Adrian himself decided to block me.

Like I did to him.

Not that I'd even ask him for help. I wouldn't need to. All I had to do was lie there and hope that I got back enough strength to move and, if I was really lucky, to fight. No need at all.

While I tried to will movement into my body one toe at a time, I read some of the graffiti on the walls and wasn't heartened by what I saw. Although the likelihood that *any* positive mantra was ever introduced to the world through the scratchings of a rusty nail on moldy stone seemed slim.

The tiny slit of a window set deep into the meeting space between ceiling and wall let in the last rays of sunshine as it fell below the horizon. I had maybe thirty minutes before dark and the bloodsucker that would appear with it.

I dragged myself out of the puddle, body still half numb from the stun gun and begging my body to cooperate. I wondered briefly what voltage it was, not that it mattered. Somewhere between Angry Grizzly Bear and Stampeding Rhino should be about right. A human would have been killed instantly, but if Havoc had her way, I'd soon be wishing I was that lucky.

As if in answer to my thoughts, sharp heels clicked on the stairs, excitement evident in the quick descent. The steps stopped and the heavy steel door unlocked and squealed open. Havoc stepped in, stiletto thigh-highs clacking on the stone floor. She was also wearing a leather mini skirt and a leather bustier. I laughed.

"What's so funny?" she asked, setting a bag down on the floor next to her.

I shook my head. "You just never let me down. I can count on you of all people to hold tight to every vampire cliché that's ever existed."

She drew her long blond hair back and tied it in a ponytail. "I just want this to be a memorable experience for you."

"You have succeeded." I raised my eyebrows. "Should I take that to mean that I'm going to be alive after this is over? To carry on the memories and all that?"

Havoc chuckled. I could smell fresh blood on her breath but under that was the bitterness of old rust. A vamp her age could no longer mask the smell of so many meals over so many centuries.

"Oh, heavens no. But we can draw this out for weeks if that makes you feel any better."

I rolled on, ignoring my impending doom. "Would you like a mint? I think I had some in my pocket if you would care to get them out. I can't seem to move very well." I managed a half-assed shrug. "Can't imagine why."

She circled behind me, trailing her fingers across my shoulders. I tried to turn my head to follow her but could only follow with my eyes.

I heard a distinctive clacking sound and then metal as it dragged along stone. She grabbed me by my shirt collar and stood me up.

"Chains? Really?" I asked, looking at them with amusement. "What's the point? I'm not going anywhere." I snickered. "Wait, wait, don't tell me. Even in this state you're still nervous that I'm going to pull a hat trick, recover, and kill you."

I watched her face and saw a small twist of her mouth. I snorted, the sound reverberating in the dead silence and Havoc snarled. "It's true, isn't it?" I could feel that predator rising to the surface again and I bared my teeth. "You'll never stop being afraid of me," I said, low and as threatening as anyone in my situation could manage.

Sick of it, Havoc slammed me up against the wall, an impact that created a few more fissures in the stone and knocked the wind out of me. She held me there by the throat, feet dangling off the ground.

"You are in no position to make threats against me. This is just a last attempt to get into my head. You will not get to me, Urquhart."

"Funny," I choked, struggling to breathe. "Sounds like I already did."

Havoc schooled her expression and said nothing. She simply let me fall to the floor and I slumped over like a rag doll. Chaining my hands, she walked back over to the bag.

"I wonder if you remember these?" she asked, opening it and reaching in. She pawed through it with her claws, and I heard the clashing of metal against metal. Come to think of it... ah, no.

It had been a while since I'd seen it, my old "medical kit." That bag still appeared in my nightmares from time to time, containing all the instruments I'd ever used to torture some of my marks. The bag was even still stained with a few streaks of blood. It's surprisingly hard to get bloodstains out of dragon hide.

"You really are obsessed with me, aren't you? Did you steal anything else from my old apartment when I left? A pair of panties?"

That earned me a backhanded slap across the face.

"So, dirty panties then?" I said, spitting out some blood.

"Your humor is ill wasted on me, Evangeline."

I growled a little, deep in the back of my throat and her only response was to laugh. I tried to raise my arms in an attempt to strike her but failed.

"Oh, that's right. You hate anyone using your full name." She finally found what she was looking for and pulled out a rather nasty-looking blade, eight inches long and slightly curved.

"This was your tool of choice, was it not?"

"You should know." I shifted a bit, trying to ease the jagged pain of the rock digging into my shoulder blade. "You cleaned up enough of your compatriots that I'd torn apart with it."

She smiled. "Have you ever felt the bite of your own tools?" She looked a bit wistful then, as if remembering something from her past. "They turn on you in an instant if you're not careful."

"Speaking from experience?"

Havoc refocused on me, leaving that other time and place to memory. "Things have a way of catching up to you in the end."

"Isn't that a little 'pot/kettle' given the current situation we find ourselves in?"

She sat back on her heels, remarkably well balanced given the five-inch stilettos she teetered on. "Hypocrites make the world go 'round. And now this hypocrite is going to deliver a long overdue dose of penance."

"Penance? For what in particular?"

Havoc chewed her lip. "Many things really." She shifted forward, digging through the bag for anything else that caught her fancy. "But let's just settle on the fact that you've annoyed me for the last time."

"But I was just beginning to enjoy this witty repartee," I said with a pout.

"Repartee is witty by definition." Havoc reached for my manacled hand, and I read the intent in her eyes to start whittling at my fingers.

"Give me a second. I need to file that little English lesson away for my next party—"

"Enough!" shouted Havoc, slashing out with the knife and slicing open my left cheek. I couldn't see the wound, but I'd bet the white glisten of bone was visible as my skin sizzled.

"You poisoned the blades?" I asked. "Even I never sunk that low."

She sliced open my other cheek and chuckled with a sound that could only come from a psychopath. "This is simply insurance. If, somehow, you manage to survive me you will not long survive the poison. You are unfortunately lucky when it comes to a persistence to keep breathing."

"Yeah, I'm like that. Keeps me a step ahead of those who no longer do." I looked at her pointedly and she smiled, flashing plenty of fang.

She wrapped long, thin fingers around my neck in a sensual caress. "I would take every last drop from you right now if I could." She leaned in and I felt her lips brush my carotid. "But I promised my mistress that you would suffer and that is exactly what you will do." A final scrape from her fangs just to make her point and she backed away.

I let out the breath I'd been holding. "Ever the obedient one." That remark earned a swift uppercut from Havoc that sent my head cracking into the stone.

Ears stuffed with cotton balls and stars in my eyes, I heard Havoc say, "Someone should have taught you long ago that when someone is torturing you, you should cease to talk. I will settle for screams."

"Fat chance." I regretted it as soon as the words left my mouth. Anger flared in Havoc's eyes and bloodlust strong enough to make both sets of fangs slide forward ran through her. Without pausing she stabbed the blade through my left cheek and curved it downward, through my tongue and out the bottom of my chin. I tried my best to hold it back, but I screamed deep in my throat.

"We'll see about that." Her self-satisfied grin burned bright in the dim room. "Fortunately for you, I suppose, my mistress has ordered me to keep you intact and somewhat recognizable. We would like a good showpiece left over."

In one swift pull the knife slid out of my face. "No matter."

Havoc plunged the knife into my kneecap as easily as if she were just returning a needle to a pincushion. I was already numbing to the pain—one good thing about the poison—and succeeded in turning the scream into a growl.

"We can still have *lots* of fun." Havoc grabbed a small scalpel from the bag and, in one quick slash, cut my shirt down the middle with barely even a cut on the skin underneath. I admired her precision. She did the same with my bra, peeling them off and discarding them in a puddle.

"If I'd known, I would have freshened up a bit." I'm sure the quip was lost on her, my words mumbled around my split tongue. What a waste.

I felt blood drip down my chin and onto my torso, pooling in my belly button.

Havoc started to carve with sweeping curves. She gouged deeply into my left breast with the C, and I inhaled quick enough that my vision faded at the edges.

"Does that hurt?" asked Havoc, sparing me a quick glance before continuing her work. She never once broke her concentration, like she was an artist working on her masterpiece. "I'm just letting everybody know who it was that ended Evyn Urquhart's life."

I tried to laugh but it turned to a pained growl as she looped the knife along my stomach. She was all but giggling at this point. "I embellished the H with a little curl around the witch mark on your stomach." Placing the knife well out of my reach she sat back and clapped her hands together once, holding them to her face as she appraised her work. "Perfect."

It continued in that fashion for hours, Havoc reviving me every time I passed out from the poison rampaging through my body. When I look back on it all I can remember of that last hour or so is a pool of my own blood, a burning in my veins that made a haze of the superficial pain, and the triumphant smile on Havoc's face.

When Havoc's eyes started to whiten and her skin began to gray and crack like dried clay, I knew dawn was close. I might have a chance after all.

"Dammit," she swore. "As much I hate for this night to end, we come at last to our final parting."

"You don't have to be so poetic about it." The swelling in my tongue was going down. It would be healed already if it weren't for the damn poison.

"On the contrary, dear." She caressed the side of my face. "You were a worthy adversary, once."

"Our story doesn't have to end here," I tried again, needing to buy more time. Panic began to rise in me. It couldn't end like this.

"On your first return to the city I caught you immediately and you barely offered a fight." She sounded almost sad. "Even your familiar has abandoned you, no cavalry is coming to save you." Her thumb traced my lips.

She was grieving my loss. I guess I wasn't ready for this job after all.

Havoc leaned in close, and I thought she was going to bite me, so I braced myself for the end. But instead her lips met mine in a kiss filled with such raw hatred, grief, and love all rolled into one that I couldn't help but return it. Havoc finally wrenched herself away, licking blood from her lips and staring at me with longing. "I'm done with you."

"Wait—" I started, but my words were cut off as Havoc plunged a knife into my stomach and followed it immediately with two more stabs to the gut ensuring a slow and painful death.

Fully confident that I would be dead upon her return at nightfall, Havoc retreated up the stairs without even a backward glance. I slumped over around my pain and felt blood gurgling up my throat as the door closed with a clang that was far too final.

I choked and coughed, and a spatter of red droplets turned into a persistent oozing of blood from my mouth. It wouldn't be long now. I gritted my teeth, hoped that bitch was wrong about the cavalry, and sent out a call to Adrian.

I felt his response, angry as expected. He tried to ignore me at first, but I persisted until he gave in. Once he could feel my heart racing to pump blood it didn't have, it gave him the kick in the ass he needed. I must have passed out for a minute from the effort because a hand was on my shoulder shaking me awake.

I looked around, quite a feat as I was beginning to lose all motor function, and saw Adrian leaning over me. There was a look of not-quite-concern on his face, but I guess I would have to settle for what I could get right now.

"You know, you didn't really have to go this far to get my attention." He crouched down and examined the wounds. "I try to collect my thoughts for a minute and here you are getting yourself tortured."

"You've got to admit that I always pick the best places to meet people." I rested my head back against the wall and he started poking his fingers into the gashes. "Are you searching for buried treasure?" I growled.

"Unless you've got some salves or poultices hidden on you, I'm going to have to cauterize." He looked at me with an impatiently raised eyebrow. "Or did you just want me here so we could die together?"

"Sorry. Do what you gotta do."

Adrian managed a small smile though it was strained. "If this apology thing becomes normal with you, I'm not sure I'll ever get used to it."

Any thought of a retort vanished as his fingertips turned into white-hot irons and the smell of barbecue permeated the dungeon. I hissed at the pain.

"Sorry," he said, voice flat and emotionless.

"How bad is it?" I asked, voice getting weaker by the second.

"A little worse than bad, but better than dead." Adrian creased his brows and looked at me. "Were the blades poisoned?"

I nodded, eyes closed. My head was getting so fuzzy I couldn't focus on his words. He continued speaking but I didn't register what he was saying. Images were flashing through my head at a rapid pace and my heartbeat quickened to an almost painful speed. I heard my name called from a distance, but I couldn't stay awake any longer. Adrian called my name once more, and then I lost consciousness.

My eyes flew open as I was being lowered into a hot bath full of salt water.

"Fucking hell!" I shouted, the room already filling with steam as the poison evaporated from my blood.

"Well, yeah, it hurts. You still remember that, don't you?" asked Adrian bitterly. "Just like old times, right?"

He turned to walk out of the bathroom but I stopped him. "Wait."

Adrian fixed me with a warning glare.

"Can I use your phone? I need to call the hotel and have Mr. Cooper rescue my dog."

He said nothing, but he fished out his phone and tossed it onto the pile of my clothes before turning and slamming the door shut behind him.

"That's just great," I said, lowering myself up to my neck in the water and groaning as it made contact with more of Havoc's "artwork." I smiled ruefully at the closed door. "Just like old times."

I made a quick call to Mr. Cooper, relieved that he'd already saved Jake when he noticed I hadn't come home. After giving him an ETA, I went back to my bath, dunking my head under the water and letting it soak into every nook and bloody cranny until it grew cold. By then most of the steam had dissipated and I felt a great deal better.

Some of the wounds were already closing, the bigger ones just small cuts now. While I was blacked out, Adrian must have set the bones that were broken because nothing was out of place.

There were clothes on the back of the door, and I cringed when I realized that they were clothes I had owned twelve years ago. This was going to be fun.

When I came out of the bathroom, Adrian was sitting on the couch staring at the television. The volume was just a low hum, but I swore I could hear the bickering of housewives before he quickly changed the channel.

He didn't look away from the TV or acknowledge me in any way. I toyed briefly with the idea of just walking out of the apartment but didn't want to take the chance that this was some kind of test of his.

I crossed the room and sat on the far end of the couch. A couple of feet between us might as well have been miles as Adrian barely even blinked, staring at an infomercial with an expressionless face.

We sat in silence for the rest of the commercial and a minute into the next before I cracked. "Are you actually interested in a glove that grooms your pet or are you ignoring me?"

He inhaled sharply and rolled his neck a couple of times but didn't speak.

I nodded. "Okay." I scooted over a small way toward him and we watched another early morning infomercial.

"Want me to order some breakfast or something? That diner on the west side should be opening soon. Or I can run and get Van's."

A small flick of the eyes in my direction. "You can't bribe me with donuts, Evyn."

"Who said anything about a bribe?" I asked, scooting closer. "It's just breakfast."

Adrian lapsed back into his silence. Another excruciating twenty minutes passed as a smarmy salesman gushed about a product to save the poor souls that "can't even" when it came to chopping vegetables.

I moved over one more time, closing the vast distance and sitting shoulder to shoulder with him. He stiffened up and his hands clenched against his legs.

I waited until his hands relaxed before I nudged him lightly with my shoulder. "Thank you for saving me."

"There wasn't really an option in the matter." The tips of his ears were reddening but I couldn't tell if he was embarrassed or mad. Or maybe both?

"How did you get into the dungeon anyway?" I asked.

He sniffed. "It wasn't hard. I was able to portal right outside the building and I only found one guard on the way in." He shot me a quick glance. "Either they weren't worried about you escaping or they never thought someone would show up to get you out."

My lip curled, remembering Havoc's taunt. "Pretty sure it was the latter."

Adrian scrubbed his face and looked at me. "So why are you back?" His eyes kept shying away like he was already regretting the direct contact.

"Short answer, Griselda Moreno."

"Grizz-Mo?"

I nodded. "Not only is she the new leader of the Briste—"

"How the hell did that happen?"

I shook my head. "She's a hybrid fae–vampire apparently. I didn't even know that was possible but if anyone was going to figure it out it would've been her. She killed the old Master in a hand-to-hand challenge and took over the whole syndicate outright."

"No shit?" Adrian ran a hand through his hair, considering.

"And I keep hearing bits and pieces about artifacts having been recovered from an ancient dig site, probably somewhere in the Middle East or Mediterranean."

"People dig up artifacts all the time that Strangers left behind. There's never enough magick left in them to worry about."

I shrugged. "I saw them in my attempt at scrying, and Lorraine got the same thing when she tried to view Moreno's plans." Then a thought hit me like a sack of bricks. "That bitch knew I was going to be abducted."

"Sorry?" Adrian cocked his head in confusion.

"I spoke to Lorraine yesterday—no, two days ago. I told her I'd drop a check to her yesterday, and she said that I wouldn't. Now I know why."

Adrian nodded knowingly and folded his arms across his chest. "I seem to remember you crowing about double-crossing them and giving the proof of death to another bidder. Can't blame her for being that pissed at you."

"Well, you can all get together to form the local chapter of the 'We Hate Evyn Urquhart' club."

We both wallowed in the heaviness of what I'd said.

"Hate is a complicated thing." Adrian said it with a kind of quiet reverence.

I tentatively reached out and took his hand, relieved when he didn't pull it away. "I thought what I did was the best for everyone."

"And you have a bad habit of not giving me a choice in the matter. We were partners. In everything."

That one hurt like only the truth can.

"Adrian, I am truly sorry. Please believe that."

"I think I do believe you," he assured, frowning. "But you have to believe that I was devastated."

"Devastated?"

"Twelve years is a long time to think. You've changed significantly and I've had a few epiphanies of my own."

"Epiphanies like what?" I wasn't sure I was going to like the answer. I suddenly realized just how badly it would hurt if I couldn't fix this. If he wanted nothing to do with me and I never got a second chance.

He sighed. "When you contacted me... I felt a little happy. Relieved, almost. I knew you were alive, I knew you were back, and I knew you wanted to see me."

"Well, that's good news, right?"

"Stop," Adrian said through bared teeth. "Just let me talk." We lapsed into another uncomfortable silence, and I couldn't stop mentally kicking my own ass.

"That little stab of happiness made me feel like I betrayed myself. I thought I was over you, and I hated that I was happy after you fucked me over without the decency to buy me a farewell dinner."

My chest tightened and I dropped my head to hide the telltale pinprick of tears, readying myself for the heartbreak I thought he was about to deliver.

"Just tell me this."

I lifted my head a fraction.

He paused a minute when he saw the tears but his face remained impassive. "Did you even care?"

"Of course I cared." I twisted my hands together in my lap. "After I'd had a chance to calm down and think about everything. I missed you, Derfael, Percy."

He didn't look satisfied with that answer.

"I honestly thought about coming back, several times. I was having a really hard time dealing with it all and I kept coming back to the fact that I needed you."

"Do you mean that?" He was suddenly very interested in the mystery stain on the couch cushion, picking at it with his fingernail.

I nodded. "Yes. I was alone, I was scared for the first time I can remember since I was a child and I just wanted someone I could trust to be with me."

"Then why didn't you come back?"

"Do you have any idea what I did?"

"Yeah. I went to the scene after it had cleared out hoping to find something that would lead me to you." Adrian flinched and his jaw tightened, angry that he'd revealed that little tidbit.

"And you see nothing wrong with the fact that I murdered a child in cold blood?"

"It wouldn't be the first time," said Adrian with a shrug of the shoulders.

I jumped to my feet like he'd tried to bite me, needing distance immediately. "I can't believe you just said that."

"What? It wouldn't."

"And that's supposed to make it okay?" I could feel the familiar dragging sensation of the memories of that night pulling at me. "Let me make something extremely clear to you. The old me died that night with Emma."

"That's the kid, I take it?" Adrian crossed his arms defiantly, not willing to get dragged into my emotions.

"Yes," I snapped. "I was leaving, the job was done." I was pacing now, reliving the moment. "But she started singing, a lullaby, in a tiny voice I could barely hear. But I stopped."

"To finish the job." It wasn't a question.

I snarled the response so harshly it made Adrian flinch. "Yes. I stalked back over to her but something in her eyes . . ." I took a shuddering breath, pacing faster now, almost hyperventilating. "I bent down to her, and she took my hand."

Almost in a dream my hand floated up to my face. "She was getting cold." I hiccuped, choking back a sob. I marched over to the nearest wall and put my fist through it to steady my thoughts.

"Hey! What the fuck!" Adrian jumped to his feet.

The neighbor on the other side of the wall pounded on the thin plaster. "Knock it off over there!"

I rounded on Adrian, and he backed up a step. "She looked at me with such knowing, like she saw exactly what I was, and she wasn't afraid. Like she knew the monster standing in front of her was a broken husk, but just a façade."

I wiped furiously at my tears. "Emma was so young, but her power was already beginning to manifest."

Adrian's head jerked as he turned toward me. "What?"

"Her mother was a Kineseopath. She must have been the same." My voice dropped to a murmur, and I stopped pacing. "She would've been powerful." I stared at Adrian defiantly. "She reached up and touched my face, still singing."

I held fingertips to my forehead. "And then she put her palm right here and something broke loose in me. The weight of everything I'd ever done crashed down on my shoulders." My shoulders slumped in a sympathetic response. "And then she was gone."

Tears streaming down my face, I stood, facing my familiar and waiting for his response. He had to understand now.

A knowing smile twisted his lips and my hope lifted. "That explains it then." He crossed to me and put his hands on my shoulders, a relieved laugh gushing from his chest. "You were blindsided by the kid's power. There's no way you could have expected it, you wouldn't have shielded yourself from it. The minute she touched you she flooded you with emotion as a defense mechanism."

My face fell. "Are you honestly trying to explain to me how Kineseopaths function? That all this was just a magickal boobytrap that I got stuck in?" I stepped back from him.

He shook his head, smile still in place. He closed the gap again and took my face in his hands, caressing my cheek with his thumb. "You said it yourself. The girl was powerful. She hit you with a one-two punch and you were reeling so badly your mind wasn't able to discern between actual emotion and the magick used against you." The look of earnestness on his face, like he thought he would just speak the magick words and break the spell over me, making everything return to the way it was, dashed my hope completely.

"You've got to be kidding me," I hissed, pulling away from him and throwing up my hand to stop him from coming near me. "Why am I trying to talk reason to you! You're a demon in every sense of the word. Compassion means nothing to you."

"Be reasonable!" he shouted back. "This isn't you!"

The guy next door pounded on the wall again. "Keep it down or I'm calling the cops!"

"Fine!" Adrian and I both shouted at the same time.

Our argument moved from noisy outrage to quietly controlled malicious intent. "Even if the initial fallout was from her magick, anything Kineseopaths do is temporary. Emma opened the door, but I stepped through it willingly."

Adrian's elation began to fade as he realized I was speaking truth.

"The old me is gone and I'll be damned if I let her back again."

His disappointment rapidly began to turn vicious. "So you're just afraid? A coward running from your past? From reality? From the life you were meant to lead?" He spat in my direction and went for the lowest blow. He leaned forward and sneered. "You're just as weak as that girl."

# CHAPTER SIX

I struck out and punched him in the face, sending him careening back-ward. "Take it back," I growled.

"No." Adrian's voice was muffled as he held his nose and tried to staunch the flow of blood with his sleeve.

I grabbed his shoulders and brought my knee up for a blow to his gut, but he only laughed in response, so I kicked his legs out from under him. He collapsed to the floor, and I leaped on him, striking him repeatedly in the face and shouting "Take it back!" after each blow.

"That's it, I'm calling the cops!" shouted the neighbor. I paused my attack on Adrian and narrowed my eyes, sending a sonic shock through the wall and waiting until I heard the yelp and thunk of him passing out.

"That was nice of you," said Adrian around the blood in his mouth.

I sat back breathing heavily, still straddling him in case I decided to get a few more punches in but the rage was fading fast.

"I'm surprised you haven't taken care of him before this."

"Oh, he's heard from me." He snorted. "That guy is such a dick." When I still didn't move, Adrian quirked an eyebrow. "Are you going to let me up, or what?"

"I'm debating it."

He sighed. "I take it back." He spat some blood out and half smiled with reddened teeth. "Honest."

I nodded and rose, heading to the kitchen and grabbing a towel which I thrust into his hands. As he wiped the blood off his face, I began to clean up the mess I'd made of the wall.

"I'll run out and grab some patching supplies." I patted my pockets and realized I didn't have my wallet. I rummaged through the discarded clothes in the bathroom and found it in my pants pocket. I was pissed that I'd lost my weapons to Havoc, but at least I wouldn't have to deal with the DMV.

Adrian was scrubbing his blood off the floor when I walked back into the living room. "Which way to the nearest hardware store?"

"Don't worry about it. I've got some around here somewhere." He searched for any spatters he'd missed. "Not the first time someone's busted a hole in the wall. Although it's usually for more... amorous reasons."

Shock zinged through me, and I stopped in my tracks. I hadn't even given a thought to the possibility that he'd find someone else. Not that I could hold it against him. What right did I have to expect him to hold a place for me when I didn't plan to ever come back?

He caught sight of my face and huffed a low laugh. "Something on your mind?"

"No," I said too quickly.

"Nothing at all?"

I shook my head. "No, not really."

"That's strange. 'Cause the look on your face wants to know if I'm seeing anybody." He narrowed his eyes and gave me his best smoldering grin. Even though his face was healed from the light tenderizing I'd given it earlier the wattage was a bit dimmed from the panty-dropper it used to be. But I missed it all the same.

And that smarmy son of a bitch knew exactly the effect it had on me.

"Am I close?"

I tried my best to recover and hide my reddening cheeks by mockingly throwing my hair back. "After me, no one else can compare."

He laughed darkly. "Well, you've got a point there."

I knew he didn't mean it to be a snide comment, but my smile was tight regardless. "I definitely leave an impression."

Adrian nodded his agreement. "I figure if a woman can't make me fear for my life when I make her angry, she's not worth my time." Almost as if he was making sure I didn't get my hopes up he added, "A fling here and there is worth a little home repair. Especially if everyone walks away on good terms in the end."

Thankfully to save us both from continuing this conversation there was a knock on the door. Adrian answered it to find two uniformed officers standing on his doorstep, a big burly guy and a petite woman that carried herself in a more imposing manner than her partner. I moved out of sight before they saw me. Old habits, I guess.

"That asshole really called them," I muttered under my breath. The mess was gone by now, but Adrian still had the bloody rag in his hand which he discreetly put behind his back.

"We've had a complaint of a domestic disturbance. You know anything about that?" asked the big guy.

"Yeah, I kind of got into it with my girl. We've settled it."

"Is she here?" asked the female officer, peering behind him into the room.

Adrian motioned me over with a quick sideways nod. "Babe."

I hid a smile and walked over to Adrian, wrapping my arms around his waist, and kissing his cheek.

"It's okay officers, really. We just get a little... excited, sometimes. Nobody laid hands." I turned and nipped at Adrian's ear before resting my head on his shoulder and smiling at them. "Outside the bedroom, anyway."

The officers were still suspicious, but my little love bite had the desired effect and made them uncomfortable. Since neither one of us was hurt they really had no reason to stay.

"Just keep it under control, okay?" The man nodded at his partner, but she wasn't letting it go.

She glared at us. "If we have to come back here someone's leaving in cuffs." She narrowed her eyes at Adrian before turning and following her partner.

Adrian closed the door and leaned against it. "I'm putting dog shit in that jerk's mailbox." He pushed away from the door and busied himself sweeping up the last of the plaster dust.

"So what were you saying about Grizz-Mo?" He rubbed his jaw and I heard the rough scratch against his beard. "Before things escalated quickly."

I flexed my hand in response. "Um." I cast around in my memory to try and remember where we'd left off.

"Something about artifacts?"

"Right, yeah." I walked over to the small breakfast bar with peeling, yellowed linoleum and leaned my elbows on it. For some reason I just wanted a little distance; whether that was because I wanted to punch his face again or have him between my thighs again, I couldn't tell.

Our relationship was the perennial definition of complicated.

"When I tried scrying for information, I kept getting blocked. And then some spooky mo-fo popped to the surface."

"How spooky we talkin'?" Adrian brought the bloody wash water and rag into the kitchen and dumped them before leaning against the refrigerator. A flutter at the kitchen window caught my attention and a crow was picking around in the bedraggled planter hanging on the ledge. I was starting to wonder if it was just a crow doing its thing or a spy when it flew off.

"Somewhere between a poorly preserved mummy and a scarecrow hunting for blood sacrifice in an ancient apple orchard."

Adrian lifted his chin. "That's oddly specific, but it paints a picture." He nodded. "I like it."

"Lorraine had the same problem, but she fought it. She lost."

"Rollins?"

I nodded.

He whistled in disbelief. "What exactly are we dealing with here?"

That caught my attention and my hopes raised again. "We?"

He shrugged. "It's interesting. Might as well see where this goes."

"Are you sure?" I added, with what I thought was a casual, even humorous tone. "The bars are going to miss you."

His face began to contort with anger. "What's that supposed to mean?"

"Nothing, I—"

"I still took jobs after you left."

"Wait, that wasn't what I meant at all—" I was holding my hands out in front of me to placate him and ward off his anger.

"My life doesn't begin or end with you. I can function fine without you."

"Adrian, stop. It was a joke!"

"You know what happened after you left? Everybody thought I was worthless. 'Without Evyn around you don't stand a chance,' 'without your familiar you'll be too weak to do anything,' 'without Evyn your reputation isn't worth dick.' Well guess what? I managed just fine on my own." His voice dripped with condescension and venom.

"Yeah, it sure looks that way," I shot back, motioning around us. "You really did well for yourself. What's it like living the high life?"

Adrian took a menacing step forward and thrust his arm toward the door. "Get out."

"So I can count on your help, then?" I asked sweetly as I headed toward the door and wrenched it open. "Don't call me. I'll call you." I closed it behind me just as something shattered against it.

That went well.

Havoc had been *very* confident in my demise, so I wasn't worried about having lookouts posted around my hotel. I checked on my baby in the parking lot to make sure Havoc's goon squad didn't key the sides or slash the tires, but she was perfect, as always.

I was only a couple of steps inside the door when an excited bark echoed down the hall and Jake came barreling around the corner.

"Jake!" I held out my arms and regretted it immediately, not realizing just how much muscle he'd packed on. He jumped up at me and I caught him, righting my balance just before I fell backward.

Mr. Cooper rounded the corner as I smothered Jake in kisses; his face lit up with a tired smile.

"Your little friend there has been keeping me busy." He scratched Jake behind the ears.

"Thank you so much for taking care of him. I'll pay you whatever you want."

"Oh, it was no problem," he chuckled. "My grandkids loved playing with him." He cleared his throat. "I noticed you hadn't returned and remembered your companion."

"I can't thank you enough. I'm sorry for any trouble." He knew that I did dangerous work, he just didn't know what specifically. It was no secret between us that when I stayed with him, I was keeping under the radar.

"Not in too much trouble I hope?"

"No, not much," I lied. "I'm going to get out of your hair."

"It's no trouble if you stay."

"I think it's better if I go."

He looked at me with concern. "Should I be worried?"

I shook my head, although I wasn't quite certain. Maybe this game had changed more than I thought. "You'll be fine once I'm gone."

He nodded, patting my hand. "Well, good luck to you. I hope to see you again." His eyes sparkled. "You know our rooms are great to rent for vacation stays, too? Or even just to relax for a long weekend."

I laughed. "That would be a nice change of pace. I'll keep it in mind."

One more squeeze of the hand and Mr. Cooper walked back down the hall, leaving me and Jake to figure out our next steps.

We were all loaded up in the car and just driving around aimlessly. I couldn't stay with Derfael; Adrian was definitely out. I was still striking out with the apartment listings. There was only one more person on the list who I would trust, and I had no idea how much she hated me at the moment.

"Why don't we go for a stroll, and we can think it over. I don't know if I dare to bring you to Percy's place. She's no fan of dogs."

Jake looked up at me, cocking his head like he couldn't understand why anyone wouldn't be in love with him instantly.

"I know. I don't get it either."

We pulled over in a large parking lot in front of an empty strip mall on the outskirts of the city.

"Crazy idea," I said to Jake. "You up for a special trip?"

Whenever I got too into my own head it was an old habit to head to my favorite place in the Strangefells. Now seemed like a great time to head back.

"It might be a bit of a weird feeling, but you'll be able to make the trip just fine."

Jake hopped up on all fours, ready to go.

"Okay." I held out my hand and he put his paw in it. I felt the familiar buffeting of energy, equal parts hot and cold, leaving trails of gooseflesh in its wake. Pressure on all sides and then my stomach bottomed out as I became weightless.

A second later I opened my eyes to the beautiful twilight skies of my true home. I looked down at Jake to make sure he was okay, and he looked back at me excitedly before attempting to run off and explore.

Luckily, he was on leash. "Woah, buddy. You gotta walk before you can run here."

He snorted, disappointed, but waited patiently to get going. I breathed deeply; the cleanest smelling air there ever was. Roses and wild lavender scented the breeze and instantly every knot in my body started to loosen.

Everything in the Strangefells had the volume turned to eleven. The clarity of the distant silver bells of the fae realms was crystal. The colors of the gardens, the shadows, the sky, every raven and owl perched in the trees, every gleaming paving stone and wrought-iron fence capped with golden ornaments was deep and saturated.

The breeze felt like gentle fingers caressing through my hair and the grass under my feet undulated like the tufts of soft winter wheat.

I'd brought us to a stretch of open land, a mix of maintained grounds with flat cobbled paths—most of these roads were built at the same time Rome was making it all the rage—and wild woods that were best explored only by the more hale and hardy.

It was commonly understood that the woods were for the beasts to roam freely, and the lawns were for everyone else. If you wanted to step foot in the woods, whatever happened thereafter was on you.

Since Jake was in no way prepared to face off with something that would make a bear look tame by comparison, we stuck firmly to the trails and paths snaking their way through the verdant green lawns and abundant floral gardens.

Every parkland and wildwood had a patron, and this was no different. I passed the small shrine to Lady Damona as Jake and I entered the gate.

Offerings weren't required, but I always made an effort, and since I didn't have anything else I bit the pad of my index finger and left a drop of blood on the base of the statue. It absorbed immediately into the marble.

"Our Lady thanks you," said a raspy voice. The fetch, in this case the go-between that took the offerings to its master and protected this shrine, coalesced into physical form briefly before zipping off to deliver it.

"Must not be many people making offerings anymore," I said to Jake. All he'd done when the fetch appeared was give it a moment of appraisal before continuing to sniff the new library of smells he was filing away.

"No. Decidedly not." A petite woman wearing blue-and-white-dyed linen had appeared just to my left, next to the shrine. Her ice-blue eyes pierced into mine with no fondness whatsoever.

"Lady Damona," I said, inclining my head in respect. She was what humans might consider a god. To Strangers, these Lords and Ladies were basically like our system of government, powerful people with their own niche and abilities that carved the landscape up among themselves and their families.

"Miss Urquhart. Welcome back?"

"Thank you?" An odd question for an odd question.

Lady Damona gave a tight smile. While I had great respect and a healthy dose of fear of the power the Ætherim held, I was no fan of theirs.

I will give them credit and admit that most of the internal strife and soap opera-style drama that always followed power and influence was kept among them with little bleed-over to affect the rest of us. But when it did... let's just say the polite smiles and apologies were no help during the cleanup.

Damona was standing there, tapping a tiny foot in a blue silk slipper.

"Is there something I can do for you?" I asked.

She smiled graciously. "I appreciate the offer, but no. When you made that offering, I realized it was a perfect opportunity to return the favor."

"Really." I said it completely deadpan, not believing it didn't have enough strings attached to turn me into a marionette.

Jake sat back and put his front paws on her knee, and I flinched. "Jake, get down."

But Damona only cooed and bent down to give him pets. That little heartbreaker can charm anyone. Except Percy. Probably.

"Oh, he is such a dear," she said. Jake flopped backward and offered up his belly, tail thumping on the ground happily. Damona laughed and started to talk to him with a baby voice. "Such a sweet boy."

I hid a smile behind my hand.

"Anyway." Lady Damona sat in the grass and pulled Jake into her lap. "There's a rumor going around."

"Yeah? The weekly Mahjong game all atwitter?"

Lady Damona didn't even blink. "Poker, but yes. It's not often we find gossip good enough to sink our teeth into." She flashed her pearly whites.

I shook my head. "I honestly have no idea what you've been hearing. I've only been back for a few days." And in that time have managed to get into three fights, been tortured in a dungeon, and have potentially ruined my chances at getting my familiar back. But who's keeping score?

"No matter. I'm not one to spread more rumors, especially unfounded." The look in her eye was mischievous and she splayed her hands. "But if there's truth to any of them, well—"

Jake yipped, upset he was being ignored. "I'm so sorry, sweet boy." Damona renewed the belly rubs. "If there's any truth to what that Briste abomination is planning, you'll need help." She inclined her head. "That's what I'm offering."

"So you're offering help for a problem we're not sure there's any truth to yet?" I was really getting tired of all these bits and pieces of information from random sources. Made me more than a little suspicious.

She shrugged. "Take it or leave it, the offer's on the table. No expiration, no stipulation. Just ask for help and ye shall receive."

I looked down and studied my shoes, scuffing them against a weed on the edge of the path. When I looked back up, Damona was gone and Jake was tugging on his leash, eager to get walking and exploring.

Strangefells silence was far different than in the human realm. Besides the constant music of the silver bells there was the thrum of magick all around you. Each type of magick, each practitioner, had their own resonance. If you knew someone well enough you could distinguish their brand of magick by the resonance alone.

It all combined in a harmony of soothing ambience.

I hadn't realized how badly I missed the Strangefells. It was just so good to be home that I lost track of time and suddenly realized we'd been walking for hours, just aimlessly following the paths wherever our feet led us.

There was a bench that sat overlooking the forest and I guided Jake to it. He was still smiling, and his tail was wagging but he'd stopped sniffing everything, and I could see the telltale drooping of his eyes as he fought the tiredness.

I scooped him up and sat him on the bench beside me and he rested his head in my lap. Within minutes he was asleep.

Now that I had a chance to focus on my immediate surroundings, I noticed a few things. One, we'd wandered far closer to the forest than I should have let us. Two, there were suspicious shadows moving among the trees, not beasts but not benign either. And three, we were being stalked.

Without giving any indication that I realized any of these things I wove a silent charm of protection around Jake. Layer after layer I wrapped him in wards, barriers, and concealment charms until I was confident they couldn't be broken by anyone but me.

I lifted his head and moved away from him, gently laying him back down. He stretched and cracked his eyes open a fraction but went back to sleep.

My decision to check out the shadows first was dual purpose in that it would let me know if our stalker was trying to snag an easy meal or if I was the point of interest.

The woods were quiet, no howls or screeching to bely a hunt or a carefree run. The tall oaks and silver birch were luminous in the twilight, and I looked skyward to do a quick calculation. The convenience of telling time in the human world is one thing I do envy.

Time in this world ran in the same intervals as it had since its creation. There were no seasons, just a month of twilight, a month of midnight and a single day of the complete sunrise to sunset in between each cycle. Actually marking that time involves astronomical charts.

We were only about a quarter of the way through this twilight cycle so nothing should have been bleeding through from another dimension. I didn't feel the heavy pull of an open portal anywhere. Maybe they were just teenagers testing their luck where the wild things lurked.

As I got closer to the edge of the forest, I could sense the stalker sniffing around Jake, but it made no move to attack. It quickly moved on and I could see its movement in my periphery.

The shadows were moving deeper into the forest, flitting between trees. Occasionally I'd see a cloaked head peer back at me, and as I stepped into the tree line, I thought I saw a flash of an arm covered with tattoos before it disappeared behind another tree.

A whispering floated to me, an incantation spoken in a long dead language by many voices in the darkness.

I crept closer and the cloaked figures were moving faster now, darting between trees, climbing the trunks. One of them was scratching something into the bark of an oak. The incantation got louder, and I finally pinpointed it. Ancient Sumerian.

A loud growl split the darkness just before the sound of claws raking across the trunk of a tree and splintering chunks of wood.

The chanting stopped and everything was still. The figures were gone. I moved slowly to take cover behind a large maple before peering in the direction the growl had come from.

The pale outline of sharp teeth in a long muzzle was all I could see in the darkness. That, and the muzzle was almost eye level with me.

Werewolf.

"I was just checking something out. No harm, no foul. I'll get out of your way."

The wolf had been stalking, taking its time, calculating. It was fully under control so the wolf's bipedal half should have been able to understand me just fine.

Whether or not they cared was the question, and I got my answer quickly. Another growl pierced the air, punctuated with a snarl and snapping of jaws.

"Werewolf wrestling is not high on my list of fun things to do today. Just let me pass."

Twigs snapped underfoot as it moved closer. It wanted me to know it was coming for me. Challenge accepted.

I want to preface this next bit by saying don't ever try this at home. It's incredibly stupid and should only be attempted if you have super-strength and/or preternatural healing abilities. Preferably both.

I charged the wolf where it stood and I saw a smile stretch its maw before I crashed into it, sending both of us bowling over. I landed on top of it but couldn't get a grip on its fur. It bucked and threw me into a tree, grabbing me with its teeth before I even hit the ground.

My shoulder screamed in pain as a couple teeth sank into the socket. The wolf shook me, and I thought my arm was going to come off. I swung my good arm and landed a punch on its temple, rapidly following it with two more punches to the ear.

That stunned the wolf enough that it released my shoulder, and I stumbled back a few paces. It leaped at me, and I swung a fist to meet it. I connected with its jaw and caught a glimpse of its chestnut colored fur just as the huge forepaws hit my chest and knocked me to the ground.

Giant jaws snapped toward my face and I grabbed them, hissing as my right palm was pierced against the top row of teeth, narrowly avoiding the scimitar-like fangs. I pushed the beast's head away from me, its hot breath rank with a fresh kill as it slavered and spat to get loose.

It wrenched its head to the side in a sharp snap and my hands lost their grip. The wolf leaned down close, tipping its head to look me in the eye. It stood there, chest heaving, each exhalation of breath like fire gusting at my face. A growl started deep in its chest and its lips rippled back to expose teeth.

It leaned closer still until its nose was almost touching me, but it stopped short when it felt the sharp edge of my knife pressing against its neck. I angled the tip of the blade to bite into the wolf's skin.

The growl deepened but it made no move. The rumbling in its chest made my hand shake from the vibrations, independent of my racing heartbeat. I stared into its eyes, waiting for the next move, and something shifted deep within the golden flash of its irises.

Recognition finally dawned on me, and the wolf's mouth twisted into a grin.

"Percy?"

If wolves could laugh, she would've been doing just that. She released me, the sudden removal of a thousand pounds of wolf from my chest causing me to take in a huge gasp of air.

Percy slunk away into the trees and out of sight. I shook my head, wondering if she'd tracked me here on purpose or if it was sheer coincidence, but I don't believe in coincidences.

I walked stiffly out of the woods, working my shoulder in small circles so it wouldn't stiffen up as it healed. Jake was still snoozing away on the bench, completely unperturbed. When I plopped down next to him, he reached a paw toward me instinctively, resting it on my knee while he was still snoring softly.

The wards around him would stay in place for now. We couldn't head back just yet.

A while later Percy walked out of the forest, back in human form and wearing a worn-out pair of sweats and a hoodie. She stopped a few feet away from me and Jake finally woke up. Once he was fully aware he jumped to the ground and stood in front of me defensively.

Percy looked at him coldly. "What do you think you're going to do, dog? Attack me?"

Jake barked in response, and I put my hand on his head. He sat and kept watch, the occasional growl sounding in his throat.

"That's quite the mutt you have there, mage. Just as stupid as you."

I sighed. I guess I knew where Percy stood on the scale now.

"Can I start out by offering an apology?" I asked, knowing full well what the answer would be.

"You can shove your apology up your ass." She crossed her arms tightly across her chest. "Why are you here?"

"Here in this park specifically, or..."

Percy rolled her eyes. "Save your smart-ass comments."

"At least you think my ass is smart."

Her lip twitched in response, and I took the win. "Grizz-mo still has a raging hard-on for me, so I figured I'd come back and face the problem head on."

"That's what she said." Percy didn't even crack a hint of a smile.

I snickered but moved on. If you address it when she makes jokes it just makes her mad.

"I tried to make amends with Adrian, and he hates me. Now I'm talking to you." I smiled at her. "And I'm sure you hate me, too."

"You're not wrong." She looked me up and down like she was checking my foundation for cracks. "Twelve years is way too long for someone in your line of work to be out of practice." She nodded her head back at the woods. "If I'd been any other wolf you'd be dead already."

"Maybe I let you win." We both knew I did nothing of the sort.

"Whatever. Best of luck to you." She turned and began to walk away.

"Wait!"

"What?" she asked, whirling and staring at me impatiently. "I have no interest in helping you so whatever pitch you're about to give me is pointless."

"No pitch. All I wanted was to apologize and tell you I missed you."

That disarmed her but she shook it off. Someone that didn't know her wouldn't have noticed a thing. "Just because you seem to have found a conscience doesn't mean the rest of us have any need to do so."

"I'm not saying you do. I'm just hoping you'll think about it. I don't know what's coming but you've had my back plenty of times before."

"And what makes you think I'll be any different from Adrian?" She looked incredulous that it hadn't crossed my mind. "You did the same thing to me that you did to him."

A pang of guilt hit me in the gut. "Yeah, but when I left him there was heartbreak involved." I gave her a half smile. "I don't think you've ever felt that way about me?"

She returned the smile. "No, I never have. You're not my type." Hesitantly, like she would think better of it at any moment, Percy sat next to me on the bench. "So what else do you know so far?"

I related the story to her with the minimal amount of information I had, plus the run-in I had with Havoc and the subsequent fallout.

"It's not much but it's a start." Percy scratched her chin. "Pretty much the same story the Council has so far."

Percy was second seat to the official head of the Council. The Ætherim were top of the food chain but the Council was the group you had to be worried about. They made the rules, had more tentacles than an octopus, and used mercs like me as their enforcement arm. Covert operations was the name of their game.

"I take it you'll be in town for a while?"

I nodded. "Seems likely. I'll probably just have to find another hotel and hope it's defensible against vampires." I looked at her hopefully.

Percy clenched her jaw and threw her eyes skyward. "Come by my place later." She got to her feet and stretched. "If you and Tara get along you can stay with us until you find a place."

"Who's Tara?" I asked, but she was already walking away.

# CHAPTER SEVEN

A short while later Jake and I pulled up to the curb in front of Percy's duplex in the Creston neighborhood, the faded taupe exterior greeting us with wan interest.

We climbed the creaking wooden steps on the exterior of the building to the second-floor apartment and I knocked on her door, pocked and scarred from who knows what. I even thought I saw a bullet hole, but the door opened before I could examine it further.

Percy didn't say anything, just nodded her head for me to come inside. As soon as I got a full view of the apartment, I stopped in my tracks.

"What'd you do to the place?" I stared around me at the new décor. Percy's apartment had been a real pit; cracked walls, peeling paint, stained and ripped carpet. Her furniture had been on death's door and garbage was always strewn all over the place. I used to throw my shoes in the garbage after stepping foot in here.

But now it was pristine. New everything, repairs and patches and fresh paint, not so much as even a fleck of dust or a granola wrapper... damn.

Percy was a little taken aback by the question. "Oh, that's just, um—"

A sultry voice introduced itself to the conversation. "This is the mage I take it?"

I turned and found a woman coming out of the kitchen. She was gorgeous; tall, curvy, long blond hair. Kind of a Nordic supermodel type, a complete opposite of dark and brooding Percy.

The woman surveyed me with contempt in her eyes; orange eyes, catlike in appearance.

"This is Tara," said Percy.

"A succubus?" I couldn't believe it.

"Does it bother you?" Tara smiled. "Intimidated?"

Percy despised the drama and manipulation that succubi nature demanded. And she was the least sexually driven person I knew.

"Not even a little bit." I shrugged. "It's just a curious pairing."

Tara sniffed. "Would you like some tea?"

Percy looked at me and I shook my head. "I'm good."

She turned back to Tara. "We're set, thanks babe."

"Fine then." She huffed off back into the kitchen.

"Come on, don't be that way." Percy shot me an apologetic glance and followed Tara. They were talking quietly behind the closed door, but I could still hear them.

"Evyn needs a place to stay," she implored. "You're not being very open minded."

"I just don't want you to get hurt when this bitch lets you down again."

My eyebrow hitched up. There was some more back and forth that I couldn't hear over the angry shuffling of dishes and slamming of cabinet doors.

Finally Percy shouted, "Fine!" and Tara echoed it a second later. Percy came out of the kitchen and smiled sheepishly. "She'll warm up to you."

The day was cold and gloomy, perfect for finding a loft in the current real-estate market in metro Grand Rapids. Rain was just starting to fall as I stepped out of Percy's apartment building, closing the door behind me with a slam and a slight kick to get it to stick in place.

I had left Jake behind with much protesting from him and Percy alike. My Camero rumbled to life, and I pulled away from the curb with my real-estate app open next to me, ready for yet another day of searching.

Money wasn't really an issue. Well, I should take the uncertainty out of that statement. Between a couple dozen bank accounts in various parts of the world, accrued interest and at least a dozen high-paying, off-the-books jobs every year for over a century and a half in business... money was not an issue. Most mercenaries never saw that kind of money, but most mercenaries aren't me, and most never do the kinds of jobs I did.

I was never one to live a lavish lifestyle, opting for simplicity over the finer things in life. It makes it easier to move quickly.

If, for example, you don't do enough due diligence before attempting to assassinate a certain faerie queen, I was young and *extremely* overconfident, and you realize too late that she keeps her heart in a separate location, well... you don't want to have a lot of stuff tying you down.

Better to avoid the May Queen's spring clean until you can make a bargain or finish the job. Just as an aside, I'm still looking for that heart.

The first place on today's list was a condo right on the waterfront in the heart of the city. As much as I hated the idea of being beholden to a homeowners association it had everything; open floor plan, balcony, windows that gave me a 360-degree view, private underground parking, and in-house security. The Grand River offered a strong, free-flowing water source for a power boost of the magickal variety, and the cherry on top was a massive convergence of ley lines beneath this part of the city so I could travel quickly.

The building super met me at the door with a surly expression. You'd think he'd be a little more affable when it came to selling an expensive piece of property that's been on the market longer than most. Maybe he thought I looked suspicious. If he only knew, right?

"You the lady who called about the loft?"

"Sure am."

He grunted and led me inside through the small lobby to a service elevator, an old school gate-and-mesh type that was modernized by requiring key access to each floor like in fancy hotels. Sure it could be overridden, but this loft was looking more promising by the second.

Once we reached the top floor and the elevator shuddered to a stop, we got out and stood on the little landing that stretched before the door. Another reason to like this place. I would be able to set up more wards around the loft to stop them not only at the elevator but at the front door should they be able to circumnavigate the previous obstacles.

When we got into the place, I fell in love immediately. Bright and open, easy to clean wood flooring, thick walls to make for a good amount of cover if necessary, and the perfect amount of privacy besides.

"I'll take it," I said.

"What? No tour of the place or anything?" There was a note of pure shock in his voice that didn't make it to his face.

"Never made a sale this easy, have you?"

"Nah." He rubbed a hand over his balding head. "You working with a mortgage company? HOA wants a guarantee before they even think about the paperwork."

"No need. I'm offering cash."

He shrugged. "That'll work."

As I put the check in his hand, he looked at it like it would burst into flames and then his expression turned suspicious.

"This ain't gonna bounce, is it?"

"Absolutely not."

He dropped the keys into my proffered hand and turned to leave, shaking his head in disbelief. Once the door shut behind him, I surveyed the place and smiled. It would do just fine for what I now assumed, and somewhat hoped, would be a decently long stay in the city.

I didn't waste time in setting to work on the wards. I took out the small razor pen I kept in my purse and began to carve sigils in the door and window frames, said all the necessary spells and laid all the proper traps out on the landing that would be the second and third levels of deterrent for would-be bad guys. The likelihood they would find this place was slim, but just in case they did, they'd have a hell of a time getting in. Even Derfael would have had a hard time of it, and he taught me everything I know.

By the time I was satisfied with the work, the sun had begun to set and the whole place turned orange and pink, a direct shot west and several stories up giving me the perfect view. After I called the moving company to get them started packing up my house up north, I reluctantly left and returned to my car, needing to make one more pit stop before I went back to Percy's place.

I was still a bit peeved at Lorraine for not giving me a heads-up and I didn't want to undo any goodwill I may have won back, so I made sure to give myself some cooling-down time before delivering that check.

When I drove up to the house on the corner any hope I'd had of delivering and driving away evaporated. Lorraine was standing by the mailbox.

I pulled up to the curb after maneuvering around a fresh pile of leaves ready for pickup. I rested my hand on the door handle, staring at the steering wheel and trying to psyche myself up. What was she going to throw at me this time?

After a deep breath I exited my Camero and went to face the Seer. Lorraine held out her hand for the check without a word and pocketed the envelope, opening the gate and nodding her head for me to follow.

"I've been doing some more viewing of Moreno." This time Lorraine brought us into a small sunroom full of stained-glass panels and long rows of planter boxes with seedlings starting to sprout.

"More nightshade?" I asked.

She nodded. "And some of Vivianne's more volatile experiments."

"Oo, what kind of volatile?" I started scanning the boxes to see if I noticed anything unusual but my lack of knowledge with herbalism showed.

"The kind that demands harvesting under very specific conditions or it crumbles into a poisonous vapor. Or the one that combusted when the taproot was severed and almost burned this room down." She pointed at the ceiling where some of the exposed timbers were a bit darker than the surrounding ones.

"Are you saying she invented a plant grenade?" My mouth was hanging open.

"More like a molotov cocktail," she shrugged.

I picked my jaw up off the floor. "That's so cool!"

Lorraine looked amused, inviting me to sit down across from her on a bold floral-print wicker chair. The sun was angling in through one of the stained-glass panels, splashing the whole room in vibrant blues, greens, and purples. Despite the autumn chill the small room was cozy with warmth and the smell of fresh earth and greenery.

I rearranged in the chair so my face was bathed in warm sunlight. "How did you get past the blocks?"

"It wasn't easy. I needed Dom and Viv's help to find a backdoor they forgot to close." She frowned. "And even then it didn't get us very far." She started to toy with one of her braids and was biting her lip in worry. That didn't bode well.

"What I found was more than a little concerning. I think the only reason I was able to find it is because their power is too great to conceal completely."

My stomach sank. "That doesn't sound good. What are we dealing with?"

Lorraine's fingers dug into the cushion of her chair. I'd never seen her look this... scared... for lack of a better word. The things she Sees regularly are horrifying enough.

"Lorraine?"

She was still staring off into space, sweat breaking out on her forehead. Her breath was quickening and her eyes closed, but I could see them rolling around behind the lids.

I darted out into the hallway. "Dominic! Vivianne! Are you here?"

"Evyn?" I heard Dom's voice call from upstairs.

"Something's going on with Lorraine!"

Feet thundered as Dominic came running down the stairs and rushed past me. "What happened?"

"She tried to tell me about what she saw but then—" I motioned helplessly.

"Dammit, I told her to wait." He rushed into another room and came back laden with a heavy box. When he opened the lid, I could smell more of the herbs he'd used when she was fighting the block the first time.

Dominic pressed a small burlap bag into her hand and wrapped her fingers around it, anointed her forehead with oil and tied red ribbon around her wrist before beginning to chant.

It was less of a fight to bring her back this time, and when Lorraine opened her eyes, I could see rage within them.

"If I find this son of a bitch, I will kill him!" she snapped, wrenching her hand in a wringing motion to emphasize her point.

"Take a breath," said Dominic, wiping sweat off her brow.

"No." Lorraine grabbed his elbow. "Stay with me. I'm telling her, now, no matter what. Just do your best to keep them off me."

I was looking on with bewilderment and an increasing sense of doom. I sat back down and prepared to hear whatever she was about to say.

"Ancients." She ground out the word like it caused her physical pain.

Whatever I'd been expecting, it wasn't that. I swayed in my seat as the implications sank in. "No." I looked between the siblings, desperate for them to tell me it was a joke.

"Once I broke through all I could see was darkness. My senses readjusted and I could start to see shapes, moving, changing. Then my vision snapped into place, and I was standing in some kind of underground chamber. Some small signs of disruption from recent activity, probably the archaeologists.

"I was looking at two different timelines overlapped on each other. The current day with the excavations going on and far back in time when these creatures were actually residing there. They were watching the dig, and I could feel their anticipation. Then a rift opened up and everything fell away, and I was floating in empty space."

Lorraine clenched her eyes shut but they flew back open as it made the memory even more real. "Massive beings began to close in around me. Abominations." She looked like she might be sick. "Monsters."

Her eyes were pained as she looked up at me. "And then I heard one word resonate through that space."

"Ancients." I buried my face in my hands before scrubbing them down my neck. I was hunched over into myself, hands buried in my armpits, a weak attempt at making myself small. Like I could slink away unseen, and this would all pass over me.

Dominic was grim. "What do you know about them?"

I shook my head. "Not much. Mainly that they should be locked away forever lest the world be destroyed. Classic eldritch horror stuff."

Suddenly Dominic changed, his voice taking on a deeper more musical tone, almost lyrical in cadence. "When the earth finally took shape, it was full of raw, untamed energy. These energies took shape in the form of Elementals, one great being for each such element."

Lorraine gave a weak smile, still a bit shaky. "You just awakened the storyteller in him."

"But there was leftover energy that the Elementals didn't want, ether, smoke, and shadow. Things that fell into cracks and never took solid form. With nowhere for it to go it gradually sinks down from the rest, separated from the fires of creation, and cast off into the cold and lonely places.

"These energies coalesce and over eons they become sentient. But all they gain from that sentience is the knowing that they are alone, trapped in the darkness. The time would come when they'd find another, and another, a small community growing with hateful hearts and venom in their veins, and in the dark they multiplied.

"Many generations were birthed into that miasma of bloodlust, desiring vengeance against the power that made them. Against the Elementals for walking in the sun. Against humans for daring to suppose they were superior."

Lorraine took the reins, not wanting to be left out. Her voice gained strength as she spoke. "Humans arrived far earlier than their history generally tells it. But they didn't stand a chance against Elementals or Ancients and were wiped out time and time again, food for the gluttonous beings that controlled every aspect of the world the humans were trying to survive in.

"Luckily our world functions on the law of diminishing returns.

"Every generation of these once supreme beings became less powerful than the one before, but they did make connections their forebears did not. Taking a form of flesh and blood as they'd observed in humans, they fed off the elements, consumed the physical, and transformed it into fuel for their corporeal bodies. They could find new types of power and a different way to transform themselves and their surroundings.

"The Elementals became the Ætherim and many generations later became the whole host of fae, Seelie and Unseelie. The Ancients birthed the Titans, ancestors of the Infernals. Demon-kind, shades and wraiths."

Dominic stepped in again. "And then came the great betrayal. A rebellion of flesh and blood against raw energy. The Elementals and Ancients were still immensely powerful, but their offspring outnumbered them a thousand to one. The Ætherim, the Titans, fae and Infernals all banded together to force their forebears into captivity.

"Beings that had been in existence since the earth was formed were separated, cast into various dimensions, bound and imprisoned there. Over time, with no other energies to draw upon, these beings lost their sentience and once again became just swirling masses of energy returned to the universe."

Dominic, his face animated and caught up in the magick of the storytelling, hit a wall. He sobered and all the energy seemed to drain out of him. "At least that's what we thought."

That statement brought all of us back to reality with a crash. Lorraine was gripping Dominic's hand, exhaustion washing over her in a visible wave. "What I've Seen contradicts that. The Ancients are still very much alive and waiting. For release, for revenge. And Moreno might have all she needs to give it to them."

My heart was in my throat. "The artifacts?" I swallowed heavily, mouth dry.

They both nodded.

"I hate to ask, but were you able to find anything else out about them?" I didn't want to send Lorraine into another spiral.

Lorraine ducked her head. "They're not from Göbekli Tepe. They're from a site even older, a short distance away. Some of it even runs under Göbekli."

"One of the super cities." Not an official name, but most of those cities were barely mentioned even in Strangefells history.

"Afraid so. Vivianne is actually with one of her connects right now, trying to find a way to track records on the site. There has to be something on paper. Griselda has a long reach, but I don't think she could erase all trace of what they've found."

I nodded. "Especially since nothing will stop archaeologists talking once they've got a site secured. Somebody will have heard something even if the paper trail is gone. It's too big a find."

"We just need to hope we get to them before Moreno has them killed. If they've moved even one of the artifacts before Griselda found out, then we might have a chance. With any luck something will have slipped through the cracks and wound up cataloged in a storage facility as a curiosity."

I was staring at the floral pattern on the pillows. "Instead of put front and center in a museum as Item #666: Key to Armageddon."

Dom cracked a small smile, but Lorraine looked at me with raised eyebrows.

I shrugged. "Humor is my coping mechanism."

Then I remembered what Lady Damona had offered. "This would explain why the Ætherim are already offering help. If they don't know outright that their great-great-times-infinity grandparents are preparing for a long overdue visit, they suspect it."

"The Ætherim? When did they approach you?" asked Lorraine.

"I was in the Strangefells and Lady Damona came calling after I made an offering at the gate shrine. None of them have ever done that before and then she just offered me help. No strings."

Lorraine nodded slowly, thinking through the implications. "It couldn't hurt. Even if there are strings, I'm afraid before all this is said and done, you'll need to call in every favor and offer for help that you have." She shivered and Dom wrapped an arm around her shoulder. "If you still think you can do this. I don't think anyone would blame you for changing your mind."

"What? And miss being front and center for the end of the world? Wouldn't dream of it."

The drive to Wolfe's was short. I'd taken longer at the Rollins's than I'd planned so the roads were pretty empty at this point.

"Derfael, I'm here!"

He poked his head around the corner of a nearby bookshelf and frowned. "Aye, the bell told me as much. No need to shout."

I shrugged. "Sorry."

"Old habits," he mumbled under his breath. "Where is your companion?"

"I left him with Percy and Tara while I searched for a new place. Found the perfect spot."

Derfael smiled. "So you're in it for the long haul now?"

"Seems like. I have all my stuff heading this way from up north. I should be out of Percy's hair in the next couple of days."

Derfael looked at me askance. "And do you find Tara... personable?"

"Tara— Wait. How do you know about Tara?"

"I have been keeping watch on them since you left. It wouldn't do to have your friends killed because you left them open and unprotected."

"Ouch." But I couldn't get mad at him for speaking truth. "You could've at least given me a heads-up about the damn succubus," I mumbled. "I will never stop getting freaked out by those eyes."

"And the wards?" Derfael asked, changing the subject. "Do you need help?"

I scoffed. "I had that taken care of before I left tonight."

"Good." He finished his cursory, once-monthly dusting of the bookshelves and tossed the dust rag back into a corner where it scurried off and left runnels of dust in its wake. "There is much we need to plan." He made his way to the back room and ushered me past the curtain.

"About that." The tone in my voice made him turn. "I talked to Lorraine and Dominic again."

Warily, Derfael sat at the table. "I take it they didn't have inspiring information."

My palms started to sweat just thinking about what they'd told me. I sat across from Derfael and ran a hand through my hair, fingers getting stuck in the tangled waves. I nervously finger-combed my hair while I spoke. "I don't even know how to say it so I'm just gonna rip the bandage off. Lorraine saw the Ancients."

I'd seen Derfael pale before, but his face lost all trace of color so great was his shock. "It can't be."

I shook my head. "That's what I said. But my denials didn't do any good."

The color was returning to his face in a flush. He retrieved a bottle of scotch from a cupboard along with two glasses and poured us both a healthy portion. "Damn," was all he said.

"I'd hoped getting snatched by Havoc would be the worst incident of this whole trip."

Derfael's eyes sharpened to points. "They had you?"

Shit. I forgot he didn't know. "I had a lot of other things on my mind," I said, defensive. "Like not dying. That was really important at the time."

"You take things too lightly," he reprimanded, a spike of heavy disbelief in his voice.

"Adrian pulled me out of there and I've just been going on with business as usual trying to get re-acclimated into the city."

Derfael looked like he was about to interject.

"It was a close call, but I'm fine." I spread my arms to prove my wholeness and disguise the vulnerability I felt as I remembered the knife sliding into my gut so effortlessly. And the look in Havoc's eyes when she told me she was done with me.

"But you should have told me the instant you were safe." Concern and relief broke through the anger.

"I'm sorry. I messed up."

"No, Talulla." Derfael looked at me with bitter disappointment. "'Messed up' is when you ripped a whole between dimensions. This was just irresponsible."

I cast my eyes down. "Sorry, Derfael." I felt like I was a child again, just waiting to get grounded. Although I still think it was partially his fault that I got that workbook in my grubby little hands in the first place. He could have easily put it on the high shelf out of sight: I was only ten at the time.

I smirked, remembering. "All I did was open a small portal with *moderate* potential to rip a hole between dimensions. The likelihood it would've led to a domino collapse of timelines was minimal. And I gained a much more thorough understanding of quantum mechanics because of it, so was it really a mistake?"

Derfael failed to see the humor. "Tell me right now if you are up to this job or not. If I need to find someone else I will, but I must know now before we go any further. The chances of success are small, even for you. And now that we know the Ancients are involved those chances got even smaller." His face fell. "I'm sorry I even dragged you into this. I had no idea."

"No offense, old man," I said teasingly, trying to lighten the mood, "but the younger generation always fixes what the older generation left undone. Worlds weren't built by nice people and fixing them is just as messy." I smiled. "I'm in this to the end. No matter what that end is."

Derfael frowned. "That's a very interesting approach you're taking to make me feel better about this."

I chuckled. "You know I suck with this stuff. Making people feel better has never been one of my strong points. I know how to make people feel a hell of a lot worse though."

Derfael poured himself another glass of scotch and offered to top off mine.

"No thanks. I did all the drinking I need for the year after I met with Adrian."

"Yes, how did that go?"

"He hates me. No, check that." I leaned my elbows on the table and rested my chin on my fists. "He *loathes* me."

Derfael shrugged his shoulders. "To be expected. But he will change his mind and remember what you mean to him."

I shook my head. "I don't know. I've tried talking to him, but it just turns ugly. The cops got called on us when I was at his apartment."

"That bad?" Derfael raised his eyebrows.

"At least I'm winning Percy over again, so that's one ally."

We lapsed into silence for a short while. Trying to wrap my head around what all this meant was just giving me a headache. Without realizing I was even saying it aloud, I asked the question I feared the answer to most.

"Is there any hope here?"

# CHAPTER EIGHT

Derfael's glass thunked on the table and I jumped at the sound. I'd almost forgotten he was even there. He stood and grabbed a book from the highest shelf in the room, the one that housed the most dangerous items and grimoires in the shop. I grimaced when he set the book on the table and the smell of rotten flesh wafted over to me.

I would never get used to that smell. In all my working years I never once dealt with decayed bodies. I was usually the one turning the living into said bodies. On the off chance I had to come into a situation post-murder, I demanded the company ghouls clean up the mess first.

It wasn't really work for the ghouls anyway, more like a lunch break.

The malodorous book was written on faerie flesh in the blood of the fae that were skinned alive to make it. The grimoire was then bound with two heavy iron plates for the front and back covers. I hated it.

The pages were always warm to the touch and the texture was soft as silk. Needless to say, the spells contained therein were some of the most potent and cautiously used in the mages' arsenal. There were only a few copies in existence.

"What are we doing?"

Derfael peered at me over his glasses. "We need to summon a Pit demon."

I groaned. "Seriously?"

"Is there a problem?"

I wrinkled my nose. "All I can smell is sulfur for at least a week afterward."

He was rummaging around the bookshelves collecting various odds and ends while I flipped to the pages of the grimoire we'd need for the summoning.

"A price we shall have to pay, I'm afraid." Derfael jerked his head toward the basement stairs and I followed.

"What are you hoping to get out of it?" Pit demons weren't known for being truthful and only a complete idiot would send one on an errand.

"They are the closest to their ancient brethren and their arrogance always gets them in trouble. With any luck it won't be able to stop itself from gloating."

As good an idea as any, I supposed.

The basement was mostly stone with a rough slate floor, but it had a large patch in the middle that we kept cleared and smoothed for workings that required properly anchored magickal circles. This was definitely one of those workings.

The shelves down here were crammed with the less-used tools and ingredients and not a few ghosts. We also peeled the floor up in a back corner so we'd have direct access to fresh earth as well as a convenient place to stash... things.

"What else do you need?"

He tossed me a thick piece of sidewalk chalk. "Add what we need to the circle. It's just a simple outline."

I looked down at my feet and noticed that there was a rough-hewn circle etched into the floor. "When did you add this? I always had to start from scratch."

"I'm far too old for that."

I nodded agreement. "You certainly are."

Derfael shot me side-eye but didn't reply. I got down on my knees and began to add the sigils that were needed around the different lines and points of the circle. Basic symbols for protection and more complicated sigils for binding and enticement were carefully traced while I tried to keep my hands from shaking.

"This is no time for nerves, Talulla," Derfael chastised.

"Don't worry about it," I assured him.

The circle was done shortly and Derfael turned to consult the book. The incantation was relatively simple but if you got the words wrong, even one word out of place, there could be serious consequences.

We both took our places at the edges of the circle across from each other, Derfael at the east point and me at the west.

In a strong, commanding voice Derfael spoke. "From the Dark I demand you come, rise and meet me." He slit his palm and dripped blood over the center of the circle.

"The Pit, the perilous journey, the proper fortification of all that is undone."

The room began to grow dark and one by one the candles extinguished themselves. All normal procedure so far.

"In the darkest of times, in the failing of the sun, rise and meet me."

A growl issued from the center of the circle and the rest of the candles went out in a gust of wind. We stood there in the tense silence and utter darkness, waiting for it to appear.

Derfael leveled an accusatory finger at the inky black space. "Show yourself, by command of Strangefells law."

"That means nothing to me," said an impossibly deep voice.

"Show yourself!" shouted Derfael, reaching into his pocket and pulling out a vial of powder—dried mandrake root, unless I was mistaken.

A laugh issued from the circle that echoed around the room and Derfael, not one for indulging anybody, took a handful of the powder and threw it into the center of the circle. It exploded in a flash of light but there was no sound whatsoever. The candles flickered once and went back out.

A tense atmosphere built as the demon tried to resist but couldn't. A roar issued from it that shattered glass in the other room and shook items from their shelves. The candles burst into flame and in the new light a huge demon was contained in the circle, oil-black skin slick and cracked in places, oozing noxious fluids. The smell of sulfur was nearly unbearable.

"Druid," it growled. It turned its slitted red eyes on me, and its tone changed to one of delight. "Urquhart."

It smiled, its white teeth standing out so startlingly against the blackness. Venom dripped from its fangs and sizzled as it hit the floor. "There was word spreading that you were alive." The smile widened. "I'm happy to learn that it's true. We've all placed bets on how quickly you'll be killed." All humor left his face in a flash. "Maybe I'll be the lucky one that gets to do the honors." The "s" trailed off into a menacing hiss and a forked tongue poked through its clenched teeth.

"We can put that to the test right now," I offered.

It narrowed its eyes and frowned. "Why don't you let me loose and we'll do just that."

"Remember the purpose of this summoning, Talulla," Derfael warned.

"Yes, Talulla," the demon mocked. "Listen to your keeper."

Derfael sighed, knowing what was coming. My hand shot into the circle and wrapped around the demon's throat and I squeezed, fingers clamping down tight on its windpipe. Its hands wrapped around my arm, the look on its face clearly anticipating the fight it wanted so badly. That look changed as its hands immediately started to convulse, popping at the joints and involuntarily releasing their grip.

A nifty trick I'd picked up in my career; transfigure the energy field of the protective circle into a flexible membrane. It coats things, such as an arm angrily thrust into the circle, like a glove instead of breaking the boundaries.

It choked and I laughed mirthlessly. "What's the matter? Can't seem to find words?" Its eyes widened at my change in demeanor, much like the "My 1st Demon" junior-league version that paid me a visit in Copper Harbor. "Do I have your attention now?" My voice lowered to a harsh whisper. "Don't you ever use that name."

I reached into my back pocket with my free hand and grabbed a knife. "If I hear it come out of your mouth again, it'll be the last thing you ever say." I let go of its throat with a little shove, a last pressure on its windpipe that made it choke again.

The demon rubbed at its throat while Derfael turned its attention back to him. "We called you here for answers."

It shot a glance at me. "Does she know that?"

"You brought it on yourself," said Derfael simply. "We need to know about Griselda Moreno."

"Why?" it asked.

"You do not need to know why."

It sighed, resigned that it would have to do as told. "What do you want to know?"

"What is she planning?" he asked.

"I can't see people's minds, you know that."

"Spare me the ignorance game. There must be talk circulating among the darkness," said Derfael. He reached for his pocket and the demon watched carefully to see what he might pull out of his bag of tricks.

"Give us an answer or I start removing things," I threatened, waving the knife in front of its face. It didn't want to answer us, that much was crystal.

"Rumor has been spreading that she's not content with her takeover of the Briste."

"Anyone that's known her for more than a day can figure that out. What else?"

"She has set her sights on a bigger target."

"Cut the vague shit and get to the point!" I snarled.

The demon shrugged. "She has the means to jailbreak our ancestors." He hissed the "s" again. "The Ancients."

I let fear slide over my face like a mask and backed up a step. The demon smiled and stepped as close to the edge of the barrier as it could. "Yes." It drew a claw down the membrane separating us and a humming filled the air at the disruption, like someone was trying to play a tune with the wet rim of a crystal glass.

I slumped to the floor, really hamming up the performance and the demon lapped it up, its arrogance rolling off it in waves. It wasn't even giving Derfael the time of day and he was probably more dangerous to it than I was.

"She found our last ancient stronghold. Our grandest city. So much blood-shed and sacrifice. The humans built that city on the bones of their enemies and invited us in to increase their power. Elementals, Ancients, generations of their infernal and fae children. Living side by side with humans who thought they were in control."

The slimy laugh that followed made me want to take a bath. I started to shake and looked up at it warily. The demon flicked its tongue at me and winked. "We gave the king a few spells and a fancy golden ring and he thought he ruled over us. Solomon." The demon made a meal out of the name.

"But the timeline is wrong," whispered Derfael. "Solomon wouldn't even be born for thousands of years after the Ancients were cast out."

The demon whirled on him. "Would you really believe the humans history?"

"So what's the plan, huh? Release these monsters with a few spells and destroy the world?" I sat back on my heels, still well away from the circle.

The demon looked at me piteously. "Nothing so average. This kind of thing needs flare." It started to pace around the inside of the barrier, back and forth. "There are some old artifacts. Idols, plaques, statuettes, holy instruments." Its eyes widened hungrily. "Used properly they will open the gates and let my people go."

The demon threw back its head and laughed, a loud booming sound in the small space. It was really proud of itself to be making biblical jokes. I'd hate to be stuck at open mic night with this idiot, but maybe it plays better to a select audience.

"But how does Solomon fit into this?" asked Derfael.

The demon dropped its head and lolled its neck around to look at him. "After things went pear shaped and the city was in flames all Solomon could do was watch as the gods fought and the world shattered. An ice age passed and when it started to thaw, he was eager for a second chance. To make things right."

It rolled its head to look at me. "To make amends for the terrible things he'd done. Leading people to the slaughter. Keeping the Ancients and their kin fat and happy with human blood. That ring we gave him granted him immortality but even after he cast it away, he still couldn't die." Another laugh.

"Cities began to rise again. Göbekli Tepe was built. And Solomon, King of Nothing, came to call. He built a temple to house the artifacts he stole from our paradise and then he sealed it away. But we found it."

"That still doesn't explain—" tried Derfael, but the demon cut him off.

"I'm getting there!" It cracked its knuckles, and I could actually hear it counting to ten under its breath. "Solomon learned some new tricks, human magicks. He used those to seal the artifacts away and made *himself* the key. The prick."

It shook its head. "But it's no matter, we have him. And he's much more amenable to helping us. Being mummified while alive changes people." It guffawed and slapped its knee. "And the brainwashing did the rest." Pride gleamed on its oily face. "We have so many talented demons in the Pit. You really should stop by and visit." In a flash it was at the barrier. "There are many things we'd love to show you."

I stood and crossed to it. The demon growled and rolled its neck, eager to break loose. The humming filled the air again as it raked its claws on the shield.

I smiled. "You are really dumb. But thanks for the information."

"Wh-what?" It looked back and forth between me and Derfael who was also grinning.

I looked at Derfael and he nodded. "Go," he told the demon. "We are finished here."

"No, wait. I didn't mean— I didn't tell you everything! There's way more. I didn't tell you the important stuff!" When it could tell we weren't buying it, the demon roared and vanished with a crack that split the air.

Now that the immediate danger was over my adrenaline rush crashed and I leaned over to brace my hands on my thighs. "Shit, Derfael." I stood up straight and pinched my nose in the space between my eyes. "What did we land in the middle of?"

"This is Griselda's compound."

After taking the day to rest up and really reflect on what it means to be so close to annihilation I was back at Wolfe's. My furniture had been delivered earlier in the day, so I'd left Jake at the loft to acclimate to his new digs.

I could still feel the bruising around my freshly healed nose. Tara had slammed the door in my face the minute I got my suitcases on the landing.

Derfael spread out a pile of blueprints and pointed to a highlighted path that led through several passages and across many pages.

"This is the path that I have determined is the best way to get to Moreno's office. If you make it there you can plant this charm somewhere," he said, handing me a small wood-and-brass plaque with a few runes carved into it.

"A good ol' Eye-Spy. Undetectable, simple, old school." I turned it over, admiring the work. We'd be able to tap into everything that goes on in there. "When did your craftsmanship get so good? You used to laugh at me whenever I put emphasis on aesthetic—"

"Aesthetics instead of effectiveness," he finished his own adage. "Aye." He took the charm back and turned it to catch the lamplight, then gave me a scowl when he caught my knowing smirk. "Everyone needs a hobby in their retirement."

"You won't retire until we're building your funeral pyre." I plucked the charm back out of his hand. "But still, that's it? I just find my way through this labyrinth and plant a charm?"

"If we can find out more about where she has the artifacts hidden it will escalate the planning quickly, but until we have something definitive, we'd just be spinning our wheels."

"Right. I knew that." Patience has never been my strong suit.

"With any luck we'll learn more about her preparations at the same time." He scratched his bearded chin. "What worries me is that I can find no reference anywhere to what these summoning requirements might be. Or what specifically Solomon might've done to lock the artifacts away."

"Have you tried asking Aunt Theresa?" My aunt was my father's sister. After he died, she took over guardianship, but sitting on one of the most respected seats on the Council made me easy pickings for bad guys that weren't powerful enough to get to her directly. Hence why I came to live with Derfael.

Derfael, who ducked his head and looked guilty about something at the suggestion.

"What?" I asked. "Is there a problem between you two?" Granted, I hadn't spoken to my aunt at all over the last twelve years, so for all I knew they'd become mortal enemies in that time.

He shook his head. "No problem. It's been a long time since I've spoken with her, that's all."

It still seemed oddly evasive but I let it drop.

"Moreno will be out of town in a few days, so her compound will be much easier to infiltrate." Derfael rolled up the plans and handed them to me. "Study these and get ready." He bustled out of the room but remembered something and popped back in. "Talulla?"

"Yeah?"

"We must tell no one. Not yet."

I was well on my way home when I decided to ignore Derfael's orders and do recon on Moreno's compound. I was in the neighborhood anyway. Would it have been far easier to wait until she was gone? Definitely. Would it have been better left for the daylight hours when she'd have non-Briste bodyguards on duty? Sure would. But where's the fun in that?

I parked a block away in a hospital parking lot and made my way back, sticking close to the shadows around streetlights.

The house stood behind high walls on the edge of the Gaslight district with a palatial lawn surrounding it. I stalked the perimeter until I found a weak spot in the wall. The protection spells were badly in need of maintenance on this end and the wooded area behind the house was close enough to give me cover once inside.

I hopped the wall and touched down on the other side, sprinting for the woods. There was a small boom somewhere up in the house and I swore under my breath, although I'd be disappointed if she didn't have second-level security.

I eased back into the shadows of the trees and cast a concealment cloak about me just as two Hulk-sized Briste vamps wandered outside to check out the intruder situation. They stared out into the yard for a good two minutes but didn't come down to investigate. When the coast was clear I took a few steps toward the house and almost fell on my face when a sentient potato vine tried to bring me down by wrapping itself around my ankle.

I kicked at the vine but it was in no mood to let go. I ended up having to stab it like a Kraken tentacle that was chasing me up to the crow's nest. They had cameras facing the walkway right in front of the door but with my concealment cloak there should be no way a camera could see me--or the kickass victory I just scored against the vine. Knife still clutched in my teeth and keeping my eyes peeled for anymore landscaping guard dogs I put on a skintight pair of leather gloves and touched the doorknob, twisting a small fraction to test the resistance. Why weren't there wards on this door? Then I answered my own question.

"Because nobody would be stupid enough to intrude though the front."

I backed away, gingerly releasing the doorknob and going around the south side of the house to check out the window situation. I circled around carefully, looking for the best place to enter that didn't have a camera facing it. I finally found a blind spot on a window on the west side positioned right under the only camera on that side of the house.

"Entry point secured." I was still speaking to myself.

Now turn around and leave, right? Well, I was going to. But just as I was about to leave, I caught sight of someone walking through a back hallway. Aldous Kildaire.

It was just too much of a temptation. At this point I didn't even want to question him. I just wanted to exact some vengeance on the man that blew up my life twice.

I ignored my better judgment and walked into the lair of the woman who wanted me dead without any plan whatsoever and no backup, just a small number of the weapons I usually carried and without the charm that Derfael wanted me to place in the office. Other than that, I was good.

I spelled the lock open and slid the window up, pulling myself through and landing softly on the sleek wood floors. A quick appraisal of my surroundings showed elegance without opulence, just a classy vibe that wouldn't tell you anything at all about who lived here.

It kind of reminded me of a hotel I visited once in Mexico City. It had been a cute little villa, very nice bathrooms, spacious and well lit. Easy to make sure you've got all the blood off you and hang up some clothes to dry. Discrete maid service too, the kind that didn't even need to be paid off to forget what they'd seen.

The floor creaked in some places and all I could do was hope it didn't draw attention. There was next to no movement in the house as I made my way through, following best guesses as to which way Aldous went.

What I didn't notice until it was way too late were the cameras following my every move. They toggled their positions to follow my steps all over the house, whether on their own or from an astute security guy, I didn't know. She must have had some witches on payroll that enabled the cameras to see the unseeable.

Again, it would have been a great point in the evening to just bow out and leave but no. Apparently in all my time away I'd come to believe my brain knew better than my gut instinct.

I was about ready to head up the stairs when I heard another boom close by and felt myself start to melt. It was like hot sugar was being poured over me as some ward she had on the staircase forced me to shed my concealment cloak. A door banged open down the hallway and running feet came in my direction.

They were on me before I had time to react and I only just avoided the club-like fist of one henchman and narrowly missed being kicked in the chest by another as I dove away, jumped to my feet and booked it for the door. I blasted it off its hinges to get it out of my way and raced toward the gate, vaulting it with some enhancement from my magick. I sprinted down the sidewalk, the vamps still breathing down my neck.

When my car was in sight, I cast a cherry bomb jinx behind me and held my breath as all the air pressure in a twenty-foot radius was sucked into a sphere and fell toward the earth, detonating in the sidewalk like a small mortar. Concrete went flying, giving me a lead on the Briste bodyguards. I charmed the ignition and hopped into my car, peeling off in time to avoid the raking claws that would have done a hell of a lot of damage to the chassis.

They tracked me for a couple of minutes before I hit a stretch of open road and gunned it. I drove around for a half hour to watch for tails and circled my building multiple times before pulling into the underground lot. Derfael was going to be pissed.

I darted to the side door of my building, keeping a careful watch on my surroundings and my .45 ready at tactical carry. Nothing out of the ordinary, my skin wasn't even prickling. I made it up to my landing without incident and I could hear Jake scrabbling around on the other side of the door. I tucked my gun away, and as soon as I opened the door he bypassed his usual mugging and burst out onto the landing, hackles raised.

He moved into a guarding position as he scented something and tried to herd me backward into my apartment. Then I noticed it, taped to the wall opposite my front door. A note.

I maneuvered around Jake despite his insistence and plucked the note off the wall. A simple sheet of white printer paper, folded in quarters with *Hello* written on the front. I flipped it open.

*Evangeline,*

*I know you were at my compound and I wanted to let you know that I don't hold it against you. The only thing that has me feeling insulted is that you didn't stop to say hello to me while you were intruding upon my property. You had my entire household riled up and caused enough disruption that I had to shut everything down for the remainder of the day.*

*I think that you owe me an apology, one that I will only accept in person at my compound. Tuesday evening you will meet my staff at sundown. Use the door that we'll have to replace because of your visit. This offer is nonnegotiable.*

*If you fail to do this, I will order an attack on your familiar. A drunkard demon is no match for my men, and I could do things to him that would have him begging for your help. I give you my word that, if you comply, I will not harm you or your friends. I will see you Tuesday.*

*Your old friend,*

*Griselda*

"Fuck."

Jake jumped up and snatched the note out of my hand, tearing it to pieces.

The only course of action I could possibly take at this point was to fess up to Derfael about my massive blunder. The next morning, I shouldered Wolfe's door open with a foreboding groan. He might actually take me off this mission now. *I* wasn't even sure I knew what I was doing anymore.

"Derfael!" I called, Jake hot on my heels as I moved through the shop. He was sniffing everything within reach, and I kept an eye on him to make sure he didn't eat anything he shouldn't.

Try explaining to a vet that the egg-shaped rock in your dog's stomach was indeed moving on its own and the basilisk that lived in it was about to hatch. Not only would they have to remove it immediately, but they'd also need to clear the area for the exterminators to come through.

"Derfael?" I asked, pulling the curtain to the back room aside. The front door was unlocked, he had to be here somewhere.

"He's not here," said a quiet voice behind me. I pulled a knife and whirled around, grabbing the speaker and holding the knife to his throat. Jake was still sniffing around and showing no sign of concern for this stranger.

"Who are you?" I questioned.

"Easy," he said, putting his hands out. "I work here."

"Bullshit," I hissed, pressing the blade against his neck.

"Name's Tristan. I'm Derfael's apprentice." He laughed nervously. "Nice to meet you."

I eyed him suspiciously but lowered the knife. "Where is he?" I asked, not quite ready to believe him. Since when did Derfael take on apprentices?

I didn't count; Aunt Theresa didn't really give him a choice.

"He stepped out for a minute. He's meeting a supplier that's supposed to have gotten some dragon's blood, the good stuff. One hundred percent genuine." The "apprentice" smirked. "Derfael didn't want to meet him here just in case the guy brought the actual dragon with him."

"Sounds like something he would do." I sheathed my knife.

Jake's nose finally led him to the stranger's feet. He looked up curiously to see who the feet were attached to but still didn't react like I would've expected him to. He sat and stared up at the apprentice, tail silently dusting the floor with happy contentment. The apprentice reached down and scratched Jake's chest.

"Cute dog. What's his name?"

I was still staring in flabbergasted silence while Jake reveled in the attention, a huge smile on his face. The man looked at me.

"W-What?" I asked.

A smile spread across the apprentice's face, a genuine smile that lit up his eyes. They were a shade of gold that was unusual, and I got caught up in their glint. He wasn't human, that was obvious, but I couldn't figure out what he was. "What's his name?"

It took a minute to process the words and I blinked out of my trance. "Oh. Jake."

"Bernese mountain dog?"

I nodded. "A little over a year old, now." I couldn't help myself, I had to ask. "What are you?"

The apprentice laughed, but it wasn't cold or derisive. It was so out of place to hear real laughter not tainted with hidden meaning or threat. "That's a bit forward, don't you think?"

I opened my mouth to answer but Derfael's voice cut in before I could. Neither one of us even heard him come in. "Please excuse her lack of manners, Tristan. Tact has never been one of her gifts."

"Rude," I muttered.

"Did you get it?" asked the apprentice, turning to Derfael but giving me a wink.

Derfael set down his bag and I heard a clinking of several bottles rattling together. "Aye." He sighed. "He brought the actual dragon with him. I will never understand why people insist on doing things the hard way."

Derfael moved into the sitting room, intent on making tea. "Why expend all that energy to cloak the thing in invisibility when a simple test will prove if the blood is real?"

"Can't beat the showmanship," I said.

"Very true," said the man. I corrected myself in the face of Derfael's acknowledgment. Tristan.

While Derfael busied himself with the kettle he said, "So you have met each other. The secret is out."

"Uh, not quite," said Tristan. He looked down at Jake who was sniffing away at the bag Derfael had brought back. "I was too distracted by that little guy."

Jake trotted over to him for more pets and Tristan sat down on the floor to play with him. Jake was beside himself with excitement and immediately attacked.

"So who is this guy, really?" I asked Derfael while the mystery man and Jake rolled around laughing and yipping, respectively. "Since when do you take apprentices?"

"Since someone else needed my help like you did when you first came here." He held up his hand to fend off the questions he knew were coming. "That is all I'm going to say, it's not my story to tell."

I nodded and turned back to the wrestling match which was now just Jake pouncing on Tristan and chewing on his hair. His golden-brown curls were already soggy in several places.

Tristan rolled Jake on his back, who yipped in surprise and then started to kick his feet from some belly scratches. "So you know my name. And I know Jake's. Who might you be?" He flashed me another one of those genuine smiles and I swear I saw Derfael frown from the corner of my eye when I smiled back.

"Evyn."

# CHAPTER NINE

Tristan got to his feet and Jake started pulling on his shirt, trying to bring him down.

"Jake. Time out."

He backed down and walked away, laying down with a heavy sigh and a pout.

Tristan laughed. "Aww, she's no fun, is she?"

I snickered. "Whose side are you on?"

Derfael cleared his throat loudly. "You didn't just come here to interrupt a day's work?" he asked me.

That brought the mood down real quick. "About that." I took a breath. "Just for the record, I honestly thought it would be simple recon."

"Talulla," he warned.

"Right. I was casing Moreno's compound and things got a little out of control."

Derfael huffed. "You mean you immediately did the thing I told you to wait a few days to do?"

"Yes. I was only planning on doing exterior recon, but I saw Aldous Kildaire and I couldn't help myself. I entered the house and tried to track him."

"What else? Were you seen?"

"Yes?" I offered. He looked at me expectantly and I continued. "I found an entry point at a side window. I know I should have walked away. But I couldn't resist."

"So what happened?"

"I didn't make it very far. Once I reached the stairs there was a jinx that melted the concealment cloak off me and I was out in the open. I made a break for it and drove around until I was sure they weren't following. Then I went home."

Derfael sighed. "It could have been worse."

I must've made a noise because Derfael narrowed his eyes. "What else?"

I fished the note out of my pocket. I'd pieced it back together as well as I could after Jake had gotten hold of it. "This was waiting for me when I got back to my apartment."

Derfael snatched the note out of my hand so fast I got a paper cut. He read it through, and his brows furrowed so tightly they were practically touching. "Dammit," he swore, crumpling the note in his fist. He handed it over to Tristan who read it in much the same fashion.

"I know I'm stating the obvious, but it's clearly a trap," said Tristan.

"However she does not have much of a choice," said Derfael.

"You're not sending her in there?"

"Derfael's right," I said. "If I don't go, the war hammer of the Briste will be pointed directly at everybody around me. There wouldn't be much anyone could do except wait for Moreno to catch up with them."

Derfael locked up the shop and we moved upstairs to his apartment to talk. Everything was the same except for a plush new sofa that I threw myself onto just to see how deeply I would sink into it.

"Where did you get this couch?" I still had my face pressed into the cushion.

I heard Derfael chuckle. "Sorry? Your voice was a bit muffled."

I sat up and ran my hands over the soft velveteen fabric. "This couch is heavenly. Did you give that old one the Viking funeral it deserved?"

Tristan cleared his throat. "I actually took it for my apartment." He nodded his head across the hall.

"So you're the one living in my old place." Derfael must've been serious about training this guy if he gave him the apartment.

"Your old place?" Tristan nodded thoughtfully. "That explains a lot."

I rolled my eyes. "Ha ha."

Tristan sat down a couple feet away leaving enough room for Jake to settle in between us. Derfael went to make tea and some snacks, less because he wanted to be hospitable and more because he still needed time to cool off from my blunder.

I turned to Tristan. "I bet you didn't realize an apprenticeship with Derfael would come with hazards quite like this."

Tristan waved it off. "Not the first time I've been in the crosshairs. My family has its share of enemies. I'm a target by association."

"Mind if I ask what family?"

He hesitated so long I almost told him to forget I asked. Was it that bad?

"Iraklidis."

"Oh." It was that bad. Tristan frowned and I winced. "Sorry, I didn't mean it to come out that way."

He shook his head and sighed. "I'm used to it. Part of me hopes that at some point I'll finally find a place where people have no reaction to my family name at all. But now you can understand why this doesn't faze me. We have long standing enemies that have been doing a great job hunting us down. I'm one of the last."

"And I just added Moreno to that list." I cringed. "I'm so sorry."

"This might be a boon for me, I'm not complaining."

I looked at him quizzically.

"I've got Evyn Urquhart personally invested in my safety."

"So you knew who I was the whole time?" I asked, not sure how I felt about the deception.

"No, not until you told me your first name. I've found quite a few books in his personal library with some colorful commentary written in them, and you signed your work."

I barked a laugh. "I forgot all about that." I swiped at a tickle on my nose, an errant dog hair flying into my face as Jake scratched an itch. "But having me watching your back is not as much of a boon as it might've been in the past, I'm afraid."

"Talulla." Derfael sighed, setting down a tray laden with hot tea and finger foods. "I am upset at your carelessness, but I don't doubt your abilities. A thousand years ago you would have been guarding the royal families, I have no doubt."

Tristan fidgeted uncomfortably. "Although even you would have had a hard time defeating the Council's rebellion and subsequent takeover."

My ears perked up. "Were you around to witness that?"

"I've only heard stories, but I'm certainly glad I wasn't. My grandmother told me everything she could before..." He trailed off.

I would've left that one alone even without Derfael's firm shake of the head. Tristan's bloodline founded most of the great families in the human world and the Strangefells. That much history and that much power led to a lot of enemies scratching at your door. How he ended up last man standing was probably a story the likes of which Hollywood couldn't fathom.

Tristan's face cleared and he smiled, like he knew what I was thinking. "I've got about three-hundred-years worth of stories so there should be a few bottles of booze to go around before we settle into those."

"You look pretty good for your age," I joked. "I'm not used to being the youngest one in the room."

"Thanks. A little nip and tuck goes a long way."

Derfael cleared his throat. "Now that the basics have been established, I think we should discuss the problem at hand. We can find a way to use this visit to our advantage."

"Always looking on the bright side," said Tristan.

I choked on my tea. "Derfael? Bright side?" I asked. I rounded on Derfael with a beyond-the-pale quizzical look. "Did I fall into opposite world?" I held out my hand and put the other to my forehead like I was a sideshow psychic. "No, wait. You have a grumpy twin that handed the happy twin the keys to the shop the minute I left. Probably retired to Boca Roton. Making the homeowners association rue the day they tried to enforce the rule about nonapproved colors for the front door." I flung my hand out toward Derfael. "Did I get it?"

Derfael chuckled and Tristan just looked confused. "I handle him a little differently than I did you. He does not give me nearly as much trouble and I haven't had to mix a headache remedy at any point during my time training him."

"Hurtful."

Tristan was still trying to figure out the two of us. "There were a lot of selling points when I decided to ask Derfael to train me. But he never mentioned training the Mercenary's Mercenary."

"He never mentioned he knew nobility, either," I said. We both turned to Derfael and waited for an explanation.

He sighed. "Do I really need to explain how it could be detrimental to the health and well-being of the two of you should you be questioned? Neither of you are small targets."

"And by 'questioned' he means 'tortured,'" I clarified with air quotes.

"Aye, thank you."

"Fair enough," said Tristan. "So how did you end up training with him?"

At this point reliving my family history had far less impact on me, if any. What made my stomach drop is the memory of how many other families I'd put in this same situation. "Derfael took me in when my father was killed and my siblings were taken. I never knew my mother. Derfael's the only family I've ever really had besides my aunt."

"How old were you?"

"Eight. My aunt brought me here and I was raised and trained by Derfael until I was old enough to start guild training."

"At least I had time with my family. I'm sorry, Evyn."

I shrugged. "It happened a long time ago." I changed the subject. "Now, about this Moreno thing?"

Derfael straightened his robes. "At the very least it will be an opportune time to plant that charm in her office."

"Assuming we meet in her office," I countered.

"Bright side, Talulla," he said with a sideways smile. "And while you are planting the charm *in her office*, you will have a chance to ask some very direct questions and hopefully get some very direct answers."

"Why would she tell me anything?"

"Oh, she assuredly will tell you nothing," Derfael agreed. "But it's what she doesn't say that will give us the best chance at figuring out what her plan is."

After a little more halfhearted "planning," Derfael went off to his study, mumbling something about research.

Jake was now almost fully in Tristan's lap, his eyes getting heavy. "Are you missing it yet?"

I looked at him. "Missing what?"

"Your solitude?"

I exhaled a soft laugh. "Copper Harbor was a paradise for a hermit. Only a few friends to speak of, some friendly faces whenever I went into town. Most of the time, though it was just me and the woods. And dogman, on occasion. Lots of old magick, lots of dark places to recharge and hide away."

I reached over and scratched Jake lightly behind the ears. "I miss our hikes in the forest preserves. But there are a lot of things I missed about the city. Namely the food. But the people too."

"The wilderness certainly has a draw. I spent a lot of years completely off the grid."

"Whereabouts?"

"Arizona, Colorado, the Yukon."

"So you like fighting big cats and bears for resources?"

Tristan shrugged. "They usually left me alone. Only a couple of close calls."

"Do you move a lot?"

He nodded. "Usually every few months. That's part of the reason I came here. I'd like to be able to stay in one place for a while, but I need a lot more experience with defensive and concealment magick. That part of the equation was always handled by one of a handful of people in our little family caravan."

Sadness came off him in waves and his gaze became distant as he was lost in his thoughts. Quietly he spoke. "We would travel around as a group, safety in numbers. My family has holdings all over the world that are off the books. When I was a kid, I thought it was great. Moving house to house, always seeing new sights, exploring. Like a big extended vacation."

"Your family must've done a really good job of normalizing everything for you."

"They did." He smiled but it didn't break through the sorrow. "It wasn't until I was older that I started to figure things out. That we were constantly running. When my grandfather was killed, they finally told me the whole story."

He dropped his head and hid behind a cascade of curls. "When I found out who we really were, what my grandfather and the other nobles had done, I honestly couldn't blame our enemies for wanting him dead. My grandmother wasn't much better. She always held on to the belief that her rightful place had been taken unjustly by upstart peasants."

He swept his hair from his face and leaned back, staring at the ceiling. "What was your family like?"

I blinked rapidly. My body had involuntarily jerked back at the unexpected question.

Tristan noticed my silence and sat up. "You don't talk about them much, huh?"

I shook my head. "I never talk about them. Not even with my aunt." We were heading into deeply uncomfortable territory and every cell in my body was screaming at me to rabbit. The best way I've dealt with my personal tragedies is to keep them firmly locked away. "The last time I dragged up those memories it was to try to find my brother and sister. It only led to more questions."

Tristan wasn't offering up any more conversation, so I allowed myself a peek into my family memories. A small smile played on my lips. "I grew up with two equally rambunctious siblings in the Highlands in the early 1800s. We got into a lot of trouble."

Tristan laughed. "Waylaying travelers like the bandits of old?"

I chuckled. "Not quite. My brother probably would've though. He was definitely the kid the whole village watched keenly wherever he went." I laughed at a memory that came back as clear as if it was yesterday. "Mrs. Johnson at the bakery caught him stealing a sweet bun and she smacked him over the head with her broom. The bristles exploded everywhere and tangled up in his hair so bad my sister and I had to pick them out one by one."

Tristan pulled a pained face. "You don't mess with old ladies with brooms. Rule number one."

"He never did it again, that's for sure. He felt so bad afterward that he left a whole brace of rabbits that he'd hunted on their doorstep. Mr. Johnson had been injured recently and couldn't hunt just yet."

"So he was a troublemaker with a heart of gold."

I nodded. "Yeah, he was. My sister was just an annoying little sister, though."

"Aren't they always? I had two little sisters, and the rest were all older. They were always underfoot. I'd even try to sneak away but they'd be there every time."

"And then they'd tattle on you if you didn't let them come with you." A tale as old as time. "There was this wolf den near our home. We became kind of a safe haven for wolves after they were pretty much wiped out. But I'd made friends with the mom, and she'd just recently had pups."

Jake, lulled to sleep by Tristan's constant stroking of his fur, lifted his head at the word "pups."

"Not you, sorry bud." I reached to scratch his ears again and wound up with my hand pinned under Tristan's.

He started and looked down, pulling his hand back quickly. "Sorry. I was kind of on autopilot. He's still got so much puppy fluff."

I gave Jake a few pets and leaned back into the couch, my hand tingling where we'd touched. "No worries." I tucked some hair behind my ear and tried to remember where I was in the story.

"So I take my sister to the den and all the puppies come running out to play and she loses it. Terrified, just because they were wolves. Tiny, adorable baby wolves. And when the mom showed up, my sister really freaked out. Although momma wolf was none too happy that I'd brought someone else around her babies. Even I was nervous for a minute."

Tristan's eyebrows knitted together. "Was your sister mundane?"

"No. Her and my brother were both on their way to developing solid power." I gave a sideways grin. "They actually thought I was going to be a mundane."

"Really? I never would've pegged you for a late bloomer. You seem more the type that was born wrapped in lightning and being heralded by a murder of crows."

We both dissolved into laughter and Jake jumped off the couch, disturbed by the shaking and noise. He lay down with an indignant huff on the other side of the coffee table and that just made us laugh harder.

When we finally petered out, I looked at the clock. "We'd better get going."

Tristan's face fell just a fraction, but he recovered quickly. "Of course. Let me walk you down."

Jake got a second wind on the drive home, so I didn't even bother going up to the loft. My boot heels clacked in time with Jake's nails as we headed out in no set direction. The air was bitter tonight and I wished I had grabbed a jacket on my way out, but what's the point of having magick if you don't use it, right?

I spoke a quick incantation and my body warmed. It didn't use enough power that would make it apparent to any Stranger that may have ill intentions but still kept me nice and toasty. Refraining from giving up your location like a damn beacon in the night was preferable.

After living so long in relative seclusion, only a handful of friends and Jake to keep me company and the sounds of the forest and Lake Superior around me, the rumble of Grand Rapids in the early hours of the morning was kind of soothing.

Jake jerked his head up and stared into an alley behind a cash checking joint. I followed his gaze expecting to see a human skulking in the shadows, but it was actually another shadow... in the... shadows.

One of the cloaked figures was hovering in the mouth of the alley, arm outstretched and pointing at us. Jake was already trying to pull me across the street, so we hurried toward the opposite curb and squeezed between a couple of SUVs charging at the public ports.

The cloaked figure glided backward into deeper darkness and I checked Jake to stay behind me as we moved hesitantly forward.

"Okay, cool. Just wandering into a dark alley after a mysterious shadow creature. Not a bad idea at all." I stopped. "Back up, Jake. We're not doing this."

We moved back out onto the street, keeping watch for any more shadow friends, and continued our walk.

A Stranger bar up ahead was still rather rowdy, even with last call coming up. Some drunks weren't going home quietly, and my mind immediately went to Adrian, followed by the familiar pang of guilt.

A *thunk* on the door and its subsequent forceful opening stopped us in our tracks as a body came flying out the doorway to land with a loud scraping sound across the pavement in the street. That guy really caught some air.

Jake and I kept walking, both of us keeping an eye on the man as he picked himself back up clumsily. He turned and spotted us. Well, speak of the demon.

"What are you doing here?" asked Adrian, rearranging his coat which had gotten tangled up around his shoulders.

"Just taking a nighttime stroll. I'd ask you what you're doing but I think the answer is obvious."

"Don't lecture me, Evyn."

Jake growled and I put my hand on his head. "It's alright. He's always an asshole, this isn't unusual behavior."

Adrian snorted. "I can make it unusual. Give me a couple minutes for the alcohol to wear off some and I can really dial the anger up."

Jake started to snarl, and I crossed my arms. "Keep it going. Fighting you will be one level up from his favorite plush toy."

"Fucking bitch," Adrian snarled.

That was that. Jake launched into an attack, knocking Adrian onto his back and scratching and biting him until all I could see were flailing limbs and fur.

"Call him off! Call him off!"

"Jake, enough," I said halfheartedly. I was actually enjoying watching Adrian struggle.

Jake stopped and moved back to my side, his fur still raised and a snarl on his lips like he was just waiting for another turn.

"Dammit, Urquhart," grumbled Adrian. He wiped some blood off his face and within a few seconds his injuries were gone.

"You got a little something," I said, rubbing at my nose.

He looked at me scathingly and wiped off the remainder of the blood. "What do you want?"

"Like I said, we were just out for a walk. I didn't intend to run into you."

Out of the corner of my eye I could see a cloaked figure skulking under a dark bus stop shelter and another a little ways down the street.

"Ah, good. I'm out." He turned and started to walk away but I called him back.

"Hey! Since you're here."

Adrian stopped in his tracks and turned, hands shoved in his pockets and shoulders hunched. "What?" He said it in a manner that expressed all too well where he wanted me to go. He noticed my distraction and turned to see what I was looking at. "Do you see something?"

"Uh, no. I thought I did." I wrenched my gaze from the shadows and focused on him. "I've been invited to meet with Griselda at her compound. I might've gotten a bit overconfident in my recon and she busted me. She said she wouldn't go after anyone if I showed up, but watch your back just in case."

Adrian's anger faltered a bit. "You're just going to walk right in there? Give her exactly what she wants?"

"She's always been good with her word. I'm sure she's played out every possibility already on that giant chessboard in her head, so this is probably just another trick of hers to manipulate me."

"Ol' Domino back at her scheming."

My body relaxed now that he was in a conversational mood, and I dropped my defensive battle-ready stance. Jake followed suit.

"I always knew she'd grow up to be a supervillain," I said.

"I'm surprised she grew up at all. The way you two fought... every training session turned into a battle royale."

That was an understatement. We used to be friends when we first met. Both of us had big goals and the drive to get there. The problem arose not just from competition and our skills being relatively evenly matched. Griselda had a bad habit of playing games and eventually people got sick of it.

But the worst of it came after her family was caught in a Wild Hunt-style escapade with humans as prey. They would be far from the first to do it, but they got caught. Yes, it was hypocritical, but what about the fae wasn't?

Griselda's bitterness toward her own kind after that grew and her hatred for humans was extreme, even among others in this line of work. She was a fierce adversary but her judgment was easily clouded.

It allowed me to pace ahead of her in the rankings and naturally she was super understanding about it. Wait, did I say understanding? I meant she turned into a conniving, underhanded snake that would go to whatever ends necessary to bring me down a peg.

Keeping an eye on her and her few associates was one round after another of spy games.

"At least I learned some neat tricks about surveillance and strategy. I've always been better at hands-on learning."

"Is that why you were so 'hands on' with her fiancé?" The jealousy in his voice was unmistakable even though it had been over a hundred years ago.

"That wasn't my finest moment. But to be fair, he was just her boyfriend, and he started it."

"So it was his idea to splay you out and bang you on the War Room table just before Griselda and her cronies walked in?"

I looked down. "No. But—"

"Did you tell him to scream your name when he finished or was that his idea?" Adrian's movements became agitated again and the tips of his ears began to turn red.

"That one was all him. But I didn't—"

"Were you also planning on having me and Percy find you like that so we could help you fight Moreno and her team when she came at you?" He said it quietly, like he was afraid of the answer. He'd never asked me about that part of it before.

But I'd be lying if I said that hadn't been the plan, so I avoided his eyes and said nothing.

"Seems like you learned a lot more about manipulation from her too."

It felt like the air got sucked out of my lungs before my own anger took the lead. "I said it wasn't my finest moment. I've already apologized for everything else." I was almost shouting at this point. I did a lot of things I'm not proud of, but I couldn't take it back so what was the point of ruminating on it?

All I could do was make amends and move forward. "What more do you want?" My eyes flicked again to the figures that were closer this time, and another two friends joined their party.

"Nothing you could give." He whipped his head behind him and back to me. "What the fuck are you looking at!"

I pointed right at them. "Those cloaked assholes standing right there!"

Adrian looked again and turned back to me with fire in his eyes. "There's nothing there! What kind of shit are you trying to pull?"

"You honestly don't see them?" I screamed back at him. How was this even possible? They weren't just in my head. Right?

"You're really losing it, aren't you?" His sneer twisted his face.

I took a step toward him. "Stop being a prick."

He pointed a finger at himself and looked at me like I'd sprouted a second head. "Demon."

Adrian turned to walk away but I grabbed his arm. "Wait, please!"

"Dammit! What the fuck, Urquhart!" shouted Adrian, trying to wrench his arm away from me. He went stumbling backward when he broke free and fell hard. Surrounded by a tangible cloud of outrage he stalked over to me, stopping inches in front of my face.

"Adrian, I just wanted—"

"I don't give a damn what you want," he said, hissing the words. He stuck his finger in my chest and pressed down hard until I could feel his fingernail biting into my skin. The area began to heat up and a little smoke rose from the cloth until it actually caught fire.

Jake began to bark like mad but I silenced him. "It's alright, Jake. Let him get it out."

"Leave me alone, Evyn. We're done." He removed his finger from my still-smoldering shirt and stalked off.

I looked after him while I patted my chest to get the flame out. When I looked there was a nice hole in the fabric and burned flesh beneath it.

Jake whined and came up to me, licking my hand. "I'm fine, really. It's already healing." I watched as Adrian turned the corner and disappeared, the figures turning their heads to follow him until he was gone. As one they all turned back to face me and then they disappeared.

We returned home just before 4 a.m. to find a note taped to the front door.

"What now?" I asked. "Something else unpleasant, I presume?" I unlocked my door and stepped through the enchantments, locking it behind me as soon as we were inside. I took a seat at the bar and unfolded the note.

*Evyn,*

*Change of plans. Our meeting will take place tonight. There is a car waiting for you outside.*

*See you soon,*

*Griselda*

"Shit." It was only halfheartedly that I said it, not able to feel any one way about it right now. The impending threat hanging over my friends was in the back of my mind, but I was tempted just for a moment to let her have Adrian in exchange for the others.

"Who needs sleep."

# CHAPTER TEN

There was indeed a car waiting for me when I stepped out of my building. Son of a bitch must've been watching me, and I didn't even notice. A vamp in an Armani suit pushed open the door from inside and beckoned for me to get in.

Before I left, I'd shot Derfael a text explaining the situation, grabbed as many weapons as I could conceal comfortably and hoped she didn't find all of them, and slipped the Eye-Spy into my ponytail tie. Jake tried to shoot through the door before I could close it behind me.

"You have to stay here," I said, picking him up and setting him back inside. I crouched down in front of him and gave him plenty of scratches, hoping it wouldn't be the last time I saw him.

"I will be back, Jake."

I hesitated, staring into the dark interior, and Armani hissed at me. I wiped a few flecks of spit off my jacket, took a deep breath, and climbed into the car.

We drove through the city back to Moreno's compound and Armani reached around me, opened the door and pushed me out while the car rolled past the curb.

I stumbled upright and shouted after him. "Eat a bag of dicks, you leech!" He was definitely out of earshot, but it made me feel better anyway.

The gate swung open silently as I approached. The whole compound was eerily quiet. My hackles were fully raised by the time I knocked on the door, noting the fresh paint around the hinges and the shiny new brass fittings.

Heavy trundling footsteps introduced the doorman before I saw him. At first I didn't know if I was staring at Kilimanjaro or a person. He smirked at my notice of his size and nodded his head in a quick motion for me to move past him and go inside.

I tried to be conversational. "You guys get a lot of visitors? You really know how to roll out the red carpet. That driver was top notch."

A grunt was the only response. He grabbed a metal detector from near the door and turned back to me. "Weapons check."

I went through the motions, raising my arms, feet apart, watching as one by one I was divested of my weapons. But he didn't get them all. No, I will not tell you where I was hiding them.

We walked through the house, growing closer to the source of the sandalwood incense that permeated everything. He escorted me through a back hallway and past a narrow door. It was open just a crack and I could see stairs leading downward.

There wasn't enough sandalwood in the world to cover the smell of sulfur, fresh blood, and a catastrophic dose of fear.

"You sure you guys don't get a lot of visitors?"

Instead of a grunt I received a toothy grin.

He led me to a room at the back of the house and knocked on the door in a staccato of taps.

"Enter." I recognized the smooth alto voice even though it had been at least fifty years since we'd had a run-in.

The man-mountain opened the door and stepped back, allowing me to pass through. As soon as I was inside, he shut the door quickly behind me.

"Afraid I'm going to run?" I asked the chair in front of me, turned so that I could only see the back of it. "If you turn around with a cat in your lap, I'm going right out that window."

A fat white cat jumped down from what I could only assume was Moreno's lap and went sprinting off out another side door.

Griselda swiveled around in her chair, picking absentmindedly at cat fur on her expensive cashmere sweater. "Always so critical."

She appraised me with bright eyes and rosy cheeks. She'd just fed.

"One of your many character flaws. I'm sure the others haven't improved either." A sneer twisted her perfectly painted bow of a mouth and I caught a flash of fang.

"And you've still got all your arrogance and holier-than-thou posturing. There's just a little more dried blood on your teeth now."

Her lips snapped shut and I knew she was resisting checking her teeth in the mirror behind her.

Vampires do have reflections, I'm not sure where the idea came from that they didn't. Their eyes are giant black orbs when reflected though so it certainly makes them easier to pick out if you're unsure.

"Please," Moreno said, motioning at the chairs facing her desk, "take a seat."

I checked out the cushy black chair across from her and didn't see anything suspicious about it, so I sat down. It was so plush that I sank into it to the point of my feet not touching the floor.

Moreno watched my struggle to free myself from its grip with catlike attention until I finally succeeded, perching myself on the edge.

I readjusted my twisted jacket and brushed hair from my face as I tried to maintain my dignity from that classic power move she'd just pulled.

"Just for the record, if you threaten my friends again, I won't be so civil about our next meeting." Nice, Evyn, way to play it cool.

Griselda just laughed with a light sound that made you wonder if you even heard it. "I had no intention of any ill will. I was just giving you some incentive to show up." She rested a hand on the desk in front of her, nail tips down. They were filed to points and painted an acid green that set off perfectly against her light-brown skin and silver hair.

"Right."

She drummed her nails once against the desk before she sat back and steepled her fingers under her chin. "Now, I want to get this out of the way before we get started." Griselda cleared her throat. "When my dear Havoc played... *host*... to you, it was not on my orders."

"Funny. That's not what she said." I rubbed my chin like I was trying to remember the very vivid memory of her words. "I believe she said 'I promised my mistress that you would suffer and that is exactly what you will do.'" I shrugged. "Or something like that."

Moreno tried her best at an apologetic smile. It looked painful.

"I assure you, I said no such thing."

"Oh. Well, that settles it then." I stared at her, face impassive.

Griselda growled low in her throat before doing a 180-degree turn. "Would you care for a drink? This is a special tea blend I just received from family. It's very good."

"I figured your family would've disowned you after your transformation. I thought they hated vampires just as much as they hated humans?"

Her face faltered and she fought with her rage, eyes blazing. I shifted my weight and prepared to move quickly.

"They were less than pleased, but they've come to realize it was a good move on my part." She motioned to the tea set. "Now, would you like to try some?"

I looked at her, dubious.

"It's not poison, I promise."

"But it's from Faerie. I'll pass. I'm more of a coffee person anyway."

"Oh. In that case," she said, motioning to her left behind me where a person melted out of the shadows that I hadn't even sensed. Moreno noticed my unnerved expression and smiled, less tooth and more vindication. "Chester, would you bring us some coffee?"

"Happily, madam." The Lurch-like character stalked away out a door that I hadn't seen either.

She took another sip of her tea and got very still and stared at me with the unblinking, unwavering eye contact only the dead, and undead, are capable of. Thankfully her porter came back with a tray of coffee and fixin's about then and broke the tension.

He set the tray next to me and I reluctantly poured myself a cup. A sniff and tentative taste revealed nothing more than just plain coffee.

"Thank you."

"You're very welcome."

I shook my head. "Cut the shit. Why are you being so pleasant? You already sent an assassin after me—"

"A messenger," she clarified.

"Right. Whatever you want to call it, you reintroduced yourself by blowing up my quiet life and threatening violence. You didn't just bring me here to chat."

"Can't I just want to reconnect with an old rival? Talk about our younger selves?"

"No. If you wanted to do that, I would have settled for one of your creepy handwritten notes. We could've been great penpals. But now I'm here, you're up to something and I'm not fooled by any of this." I waved my hands at the tray of coffee.

Derfael wanted direct. I can do direct. A small movement in the corner of my eye caught my attention, something outside the window. Guards?

Griselda noticed my gaze. "Did you see something?" She was disinterested. If she was that unconcerned, it must have been guards.

"My eyes are playing tricks on me I guess."

"Since you want to get straight to the point"—she rose to her feet and crossed to a display cabinet—"I'd like to address the rumors going around. I know you've been looking into things."

"Like you wanted."

She licked her lips and smirked. The cabinet she stopped in front of wasn't filled with weapons like the others. The shelves were mostly empty except for a few items that looked like she got them from a cheap knock-off retailer of "old world" decor.

She motioned for me to join her, and I cautiously moved across the room, positioning myself beside and slightly behind her at least three arm-lengths away. It wouldn't give me much time for defense if she attacked but it would be enough to block most anything.

"What have you heard so far?"

"A dig site, artifacts of interest, the slaughter of the archaeological team, and something about wanting to release the Ancients." I lingered on that last bit.

"Ancients?" She turned to me with absolute disbelief on her face and she really sold it. "What kind of ridiculous bullshit is that?"

"Word on the street."

"Worthless. The more sensational the better, that's how it is with rumors." She batted a hand at the air and turned back to the cabinet. "Although I wish it were possible. It would certainly make things easier."

"Then how did those rumors get started?"

"Haven't the foggiest. I may have said something in indiscreet company, wishful thinking that planted the seed for that nonsense."

"Then what are your plans?"

"The same as they've always been. Securing the future of the Strangefells."

"Gross." I pulled a face. "There's never been a reasonable word uttered after someone says a sentence like that."

She laughed darkly. "Evyn, I've never denied who I was. What my aims are. If anyone here needs to take a step back and examine their life, it's you."

I raised my eyebrows and invited her to go on.

"You used to be a force of nature. I was actually jealous of the kind of power you commanded the minute you walked into a room. The fear people felt. The pressure they were under to impress you, to make themselves useful."

She folded her arms and popped a hip out to the side, leaning against the cabinet. "You miss it. Whatever you're trying to do with this charade won't work."

"It's not a charade." I shook my head. "This conversation isn't even about me. Let's get back to the important topics."

"Don't sell yourself short, Evyn. I think you are far more interesting than anything else we might talk about tonight."

Her green eyes drew me in and I could feel myself falling under her thrall. I ripped my eyes away and turned my head.

"Evyn?" I could hear the smile in her voice. "What's the matter?"

I was breathing hard, fists clenched as I tried to collect myself.

"That shouldn't even be possible."

"What—"

I whipped around and punched Griselda in the face. Her head barely moved and the self-satisfied smirk never wavered.

"I found there were a lot of enhancements after the change. There's something very potent in the mixture of fae and vampire blood. Many rules no longer apply." She bobbed her head around trying to catch my gaze again. "Including the thrall gaze not being effective on mages."

She ducked her head close to peer into my eyes and I put a little extra sauce on the uppercut I threw at her. This time her head snapped back and she snarled, stopping herself from lunging at me.

"Keep trying that shit and I'll gouge your fucking eyes out," I hissed.

Like watching a body snatcher put on its new skin, Moreno rolled her neck a couple times and her body language changed from the feet up, ending in that pleasant hostess mask sliding closed over the monster that lurked underneath.

"My, we do have a way of riling each other up, don't we?" She walked stiffly over to her desk and ensconced herself in her wingback chair, gripping the chair arms.

I stayed on my feet, ready to move at the slightest provocation. My eyes wandered to the window again and I saw a shoulder covered in a deep black shirt, so black an untrained eye wouldn't have seen it. Whoever it was, was hiding just out of sight watching our interaction.

"Look, I don't think it's a secret that my organization dabbles in some things with questionable legality. No matter how this shakes out I don't see that changing in the slightest. But the things we've been discovering at these archaeological sites"—she motioned to the cabinet—"they are truly fascinating. There are so many things we can learn from them. Maybe even make a regular deal out of reclaiming lost artifacts from Strangefells history."

I studied the artifacts in the case a little closer up, and not one of them actually looked genuine. There was a price tag still stuck on the bottom of a little figurine of a coiled cobra. "There are lots of people, especially on the Council, that would like those things to stay buried and forgotten."

"Correct. But since I'm inclined to disagree with that, I'll be going forward with my plans regardless. If they won't approve, maybe just looking the other way would be a compromise. There are great mysteries that could be answered, long-lost magicks to rediscover, maybe things that shouldn't have been forgotten in the first place can reframe issues in the current times."

"You're just a veritable historian now, is that it? Nothing to do with using those artifacts for your own gains, certainly."

"Research shouldn't be a crime. Curiosity, study, seeking answers, that shouldn't be a crime." She leaned forward. "Everyone thought alchemists were insane until they discovered the secret to immortality. There's great knowledge out there just waiting to be found."

I waited for her to say "ta-da" with jazz hands, but I was to be disappointed. "Does that conclude your TED talk?"

She sniffed and sipped her tea. "By all means, keep your enthusiasm to a minimum."

"You've never been the philanthropic sort. If you're studying these things, it's not to reveal long-lost knowledge. You've always had an eye on the same prize. Eliminating humans. So how does this fit in? And don't think I've forgotten about the Ancients."

Griselda's jaw ticked as she ground her teeth together. "Humans are a scourge upon this earth. That we should have to hide from them is an insult."

"We're coexisting. Not hiding."

She spat. "We are hiding!" Moreno shoved out of her chair. "We cower in the shadows while they go about their days so confident of their place in the universe. They have no idea! We're right in front of them and they don't see us!"

"Do you want them to?" I asked. "Isn't it easier to hunt them when they're not on the lookout for ghosties and ghoulies?"

"They aren't hard to hunt now, and knowledge of our existence would probably make it even easier." She gnashed her teeth. "Scared animals make stupid mistakes." She stalked a few steps toward me. "I want them to realize their arrogance and feel true helplessness before they all die terrified and screaming." Her face changed again. "If we're talking these hypotheticals of yours, of course."

"And then what? Strangers start preying on other Strangers? Without humans to breed with, the fae will dwindle in numbers even smaller than they are now. Vamps will have to change their feeding habits unless they want to risk their prey taking a bite back. And all of us will have nothing left but to focus on how much we can't stand each other and the sideshow of humanity won't be there to distract us from warring amongst ourselves. Even more than we already do."

"Think what you want." Griselda circled back around to the display of fake artifacts and stared at them intently. "It won't matter."

"So it's still all about the world domination for you." She may have gotten a few, very frightening, upgrades, but ultimately, she hadn't changed a bit. Control freak, power hungry, narcissist. Psychopath.

"Did I say anything about world domination?" she tsked. "I simply outlined my wishes for the future of the Strangefells. I don't fancy myself some sort of empress."

"You're right, I misspoke. You're a simple demagogue that's never known when to cut their losses and fuck off." I resisted the smirk that wanted to rise to my lips as she struggled. A direct hit.

"Again, think what you want." The teacup in her hand was starting to form spidery cracks in the porcelain from her carefully controlled grip starting to waver.

Movement and another splash of color as a face peered around the windowpane. Dammit. No need to call her attention to that.

"So is this all you really called me here for?"

"What's that?" she asked, batting her eyelashes.

I grimaced at her, disgusted. "What are you hoping I do with this information?"

I could see the story that she'd practiced cueing up in her mind. "I'm assuming you'll take this to the Council. You'll have some less than flattering descriptions of what transpired tonight, I have no doubt. But they don't harbor the same vendettas you and I do. Cooler heads will prevail, and they'll see the truth behind whatever you try to sell them."

She threw her head back with a lofty movement, like she was divulging something important, and I should prepare to be impressed. "Then they'll get off my back and I can continue doing the work I'm doing. For the benefit of all of us."

The smell of that pile of horseshit she was shoveling at me was overwhelming. "Is there anything else you want to talk about, Dr. Strangelove? I'm feeling a little worn out from this conversation. Long night, unexpected meetings." I raised an eyebrow. "Borderline abductions."

I stretched and played with my hair, pulling out the Eye-Spy and concealing it in my fist with another stretch. "That feeling you get when you realize some bitch interrupted your whole life just to make you a messenger girl."

The cup in Griselda's hands shattered, but she kept her composure even as the servant melted back out of the shadows to clean up the mess.

"That is all I wanted to discuss with you, yes." Her eyes were full of rage and promises to do great bodily harm next time we met. "From this point forward, if you would keep your nose out of my business, I would greatly appreciate it. I really would hate to cut it off."

I shrugged. "At least those threats are aimed at me this time."

"Oh, I guarantee they'll remain that way."

I tapped my hand on her desk in a sharp rap. "As long as we understand each other."

I spied a piece of the broken cup and saw my chance. I bent under the desk to pick it up and when I stood, I slipped the plaque into the underside corner where it immediately disappeared into the wood grain.

"You missed one," I said, placing the shard on the tea tray and smiling sweetly at her. "You should be more careful, porcelain is so delicate. It doesn't do well around angry people."

Her face contorted and she hissed. "Hector will show you out." At the mention of his name the man-mountain opened the door and stood aside. As soon as it closed behind us, I heard what must've been the whole tea set shatter against the wall as Griselda shrieked, "Bitch!"

Hector returned my weapons and ushered me out of the house.

"I don't suppose I can get a ride home?"

My only reply was a door slamming in my face.

The lights on the porch went out a second later which would make this next task much easier. I checked carefully if I was being watched and cast the concealment charm on myself again, making my way around the house until I came to the window outside Griselda's office.

He couldn't see me, so I walked right up behind him, cast the cloak over his dumb ass, and dragged him by his shirt collar out onto the sidewalk. He was so shocked he didn't even make any sound until I released his collar.

"How stupid are you?" I hissed at Tristan.

"Evyn!" he exclaimed. "I thought—"

"Not a word." I grabbed his arm, pushing him along in front of me until we were several blocks away.

I shoved him so hard in the chest he almost went down. "What the fuck do you think you're doing!"

"I wasn't going to just let you walk in there alone."

Breathing hard I schooled myself and stood there, shaking silently. "Did you have a momentary lapse in memory and forget that you aren't trained for this?"

He continued to meet my gaze, not backing down. "Derfael told me about your text and he seemed worried. I thought I could at least try to back you up if things went sideways."

I considered him for a second, but "it's the thought that counts" doesn't go far in this business. I just threw my hands in the air and walked away.

My anger was fueling my pace and I realized I'd been jump stepping so I'd traveled several city blocks in the last thirty seconds. I looked over at Tristan who'd been keeping up but was obviously not used to the technique; he was a bit green around the gills.

I tried to keep the smile off my face. "You don't flash-step very often, huh?"

He just shook his head and regretted it instantly. Tristan leaned over and vomited into some scraggly bushes, an angry raccoon bursting out with loud chittering as it waddled off toward a dumpster.

A deep laugh behind us caught me off guard and my hand went to the holster concealed in my waistband. Incidentally, magick is the only thing that'll make a holster fit *inside* the waistline of a pair of skintight jeans. There's your fun fact for the day.

I turned slowly and watched two figures move slightly out of the shadows behind an old gas station, but not enough to get a good look. They weren't human but that was all I knew at the moment.

"Forget the chump, sweet-cheeks. Come on over here and we'll show you a real good time."

I was hoping they could see enough of my face in the weak illumination of the streetlight we were standing under to know how nonplussed I was by their invitation. I added a middle-finger salute just in case.

"Aw, come on." The shapes moved closer but remained obscured.

Tristan straightened up and wiped his mouth on the back of his hand. He peered around at the newcomers but looked no more worried about them than I did.

A stiff breeze heading in our direction signaled the displacement of air as someone appeared instantly in front of us. I had my .45 out and aimed directly at their gut before they stopped inches away from me.

There was something familiar about his face and I squinted like that would solve the problem, all the while pressing my gun barrel into his belly. Side note, I will highly enjoy using that phrase as a euphemism the next chance I get.

The stranger, almost head and shoulders taller than me which put him easily over seven foot, stared at the gun with an easy smile. His face was almost hidden by a wild, muddy brown beard and equally unkempt hair. "You really don't recognize me?"

I searched my memory. Then it dawned on me. "Barry?"

He nodded and chuckled, backing up a step now that he'd had his fun.

I punched him in the arm. "What the hell, you dick? I almost shot you out of principle." I holstered my gun and punched him in the arm again for good measure. "You should know better."

"I thought you knew who I was." He was still laughing. "*I* would never forget *you*." He put his giant hand to his heart and pulled a sad face. "That's truly hurtful."

Tristan was standing quietly, watching both the interaction and the man that was sidling up next to Barry. This guy was even taller than Barry and twice as broad. His sandy blond beard was well groomed, and his long hair was pulled back into a tidy topknot. I also knew for a fact that he couldn't fit through the average doorway without contortionist skills.

My face broke into a huge grin at the sight of the second giant. "Moshe." I wrapped my arms around his middle for a hug and I was swallowed up by his puffy jacket when he returned it.

"You threaten to shoot me but hug him?" This from Barry.

I shot him a look as I emerged from the giant's cocoon. "I tolerate you. Moshe's like a brother to me."

"It's good to see you too, Evyn." The rumble from Moshe's bass vibrated in my chest. "I never believed you were actually dead."

Tristan cleared his throat and I started. I'd forgotten he was there. "Tristan, this is Moshe and that asshat is Barry. Moshe, Asshat, this is Tristan."

"Nice to meet you. I'd shake your hand but—" He held up the hand he'd used to wipe his mouth.

"A chump with manners," chuckled Barry. "Where'd she find you?"

"Someplace he wasn't supposed to be," I said before Tristan could reply.

"Big mistake, pal," said Moshe, clapping a massive hand on Tristan's shoulder. His knees almost buckled and this made the two giants laugh even harder.

"Guys, ease up." I stifled my laughter, but Tristan still caught it.

"We were just heading to SkullDug's. Want to join?" Barry asked.

SkullDug's was one of the roughest merc clubs in the city. The *under* underground where most people didn't dare tread for fear of never walking back out. It was all the worst parts of a biker bar, sex club, opium den and MMA ring rolled into one. I looked at Tristan. Looked at Barry.

"Damn right I do."

"Yes!" Barry slapped his hands together and rubbed his palms in anticipation. "I'm sure there will be plenty of folks happy to see you."

"Oh, yeah, we can make it a real homecoming!" Moshe boomed. He draped his arm over my shoulder and pulled me into a side hug. "You bringing the chump?"

"I think he could use a little scared straight right now."

Tristan was following us, walking with Barry who was already talking his ear off like they were best friends. His eyes pleaded with me for help, but I smirked and shook my head.

I tilted my head up so Moshe could hear me but noticed him looking at me with curiosity.

"What?"

"Nothing. You just seem different is all."

"Seriously? Is it that obvious?" I was starting to get worried. There'd be a huge target on my back if people could pick out my weaknesses from a mile away.

"You've been gone for a while. Changes are easier to see." Moshe shrugged apologetically. "It's probably not what you want to hear. Maybe it's just because I know you, but . . ."

Moshe had seen me in more vulnerable states than just about anyone. I don't think Adrian had seen as many facets of my personality as the giant walking next to me. Moshe was terrifying in battle, but he truly was a teddy bear otherwise.

Even at the height of my reign of terror he weathered it like it was nothing. Just listened when I needed to vent and talked me out of doing really awful things more than once. He'd never given me a reason not to trust him and that's a hard quality to find.

"You okay?"

I blinked and looked around at him. "Fine." I glanced back at Tristan, who was still looking miserable. "Just help me keep an eye on that one tonight, okay?"

# CHAPTER ELEVEN

SkullDug's was already hopping, a fight spilling out onto the street as we walked up. Music was blasting so loud I could feel it through the concrete of the sidewalk before I actually heard it.

There were no bouncers on these doors; we tended to self-police if things got too extreme but that was a very high bar.

On the outside it was an unassuming abandoned furniture factory on a deserted block of the city. Once we walked through the heavy steel doors it became the Shangri-la of no-man's-land.

The music echoed down the hallway and out the double doors like a trumpet blast, an assault on the ears. Once you adjusted to that, the smells hit you. Blood, booze, the lingering smoke, sulfur, and plenty of sex, pheromones, and fear.

Various side rooms branched off the main hallway that were shielded to deaden noise going in and out. Moshe immediately steered me toward one of the larger anterooms and roared for people to quiet down.

I was mostly concealed by his puffy-jacketed arm so people couldn't get a good look at me. I could feel Tristan at my back and apprehension was rolling off him.

The crowd was clad almost exclusively in leather. It was almost funny after you'd been away from it for so long. You don't realize you're essentially wearing the company uniform until you take an objective step back.

And here I was in comfy casual wear. I felt so overdressed.

I knew almost every face in that room, some friends, others decidedly not. But other than rivalries I didn't see anyone that would want me dead on the spot.

Once every pair of eyes in the room was turned to us Moshe moved his arm and pushed me forward like he was feeding hungry lions. "Look who I found! The prodigal child returns."

There was silence and the four of us started to fidget until a grizzled woman with a heavily scarred face stepped forward. Her hair was dark gray and streaked with white and long-healed burns ran up her exposed shoulders, neck, and chin.

Queenie had been in this game for less time than most, but she was mortal. For her to have survived at all was a miracle and the fact that she'd been so grievously wounded on more than one occasion made her a fucking badass.

She was half dwarf, half human, and as such she didn't heal like the rest of us either. But she was still kicking. And she had the best stories.

"You finally made it back, huh?" Her voice was raspy from inhaling fire while hunting down a rogue baby dragon from a breeding operation.

I nodded, silent.

Her face pulled into a grin, and she grabbed me in a rough hug, using her dwarven strength to squeeze me like a lemon slice. She slapped me on the back and grabbed my wrist before hauling my arm in the air, victorious.

A round of cheers rose up from the crowd. They must've been good and drunk; I can't imagine that kind of welcome otherwise.

"Next round's on me!" I called. That really got them going.

Queenie leaned in so she could be heard over the raucous crowd. "Before you leave, come see me." I nodded and she moved back into the sea of black leather.

"See, I told you they'd be happy to have you back," Moshe grunted.

"Barry actually said that, but okay," I teased. "I bought them liquor, of course they're happy."

Moshe shook his head and chuckled as he gave me that big brother "bless-your-heart" look. "You may have been terrible, but look around. You're our kind of terrible." He clapped his hands on my shoulders and shook me. "This is a family. We're all mad here."

He blundered off to the bar to get drinks making a large wake as he went, the people filling back in behind him like an undertow.

"This is an interesting place." Tristan had come up beside me, hands shoved deep in his pockets probably wrapped around a knife and ready for action.

"Isn't it? You can't beat the atmosphere."

"I'm sure when some of these people get drunk enough, they try. To beat the atmosphere, I mean." He wobbled his head back and forth, trying to decide on his wording. "Like, in a fight— Never mind. Forget I said anything."

I patted his cheek. "At least you're pretty."

He puffed out a laugh. "Thanks. That means a lot."

"Just a word to the wise. Stay in this room unless me or Moshe is with you. Shit gets crazy fast and new faces draw unwanted attention."

A loud squeal equivalent to the feeding frenzy when the strippers show up at the bachelorette party pierced through the music. "Evyn! It *is* you!"

"Gods, no," I moaned to Tristan with a stricken face before turning to the new arrivals and plastering a smile on instead.

Two short women with greenish skin pushed their way in from the hallway, their burly, well-built physiques accompanied by rotund beer bellies and round, fleshy faces. They each stood about a foot shorter than me.

"Tina, Trina, it's been a long time!" The enthusiasm I tried to infuse into my voice sounded a bit too saccharine, but they took no notice.

Trina gave me a broken-toothed smile that mirrored her sister's. "Someone mentioned your name on the dance floor and we had to come check it out!"

"Come on, let's go!" Tina grabbed my arm and dragged me toward the pool tables. "You are going to tell us everything about what you've been up to!"

Trina clapped her hands excitedly and grabbed my other arm. I was officially stuck between two boulders rolling downhill. Resistance was futile.

I threw a look over my shoulder at Tristan who returned my earlier gesture of smirking and shaking his head in a refusal to save me. Bastard.

Once we got started playing pool it turned into quite the competition, more and more people joining in until we had a little bracket going among all the tables.

In order to stave off the more uncomfortable questions I made a bet that I would only answer questions if I missed a shot. Did I mention I was a pool hustler in all but name?

An hour or more had passed when I finally looked around to see what Tristan was up to. I didn't see him but I didn't see Moshe either, so I figured Moshe might've taken him on a tour to increase the intensity of the scared-straight tactic.

We kept playing another couple rounds when Moshe tapped my shoulder. "I was going to head out, I wanted to say goodbye."

I propped my stick against the side of the table and gave him another hug just as someone at the bar cracked a bottle over someone's head and started a multi-person brawl.

"We should probably be going too, seems the wildlife is getting restless." I looked around. "Did you deposit Tristan into a corner to shake off the horrible things he's seen tonight?"

Moshe gave me a puzzled look. "What do you mean?"

The bottom dropped out of my stomach. "Hasn't Tristan been with you?"

Moshe ducked his head and avoided my gaze. "I kind of got caught up with a lady friend of mine. Last I saw the chump he was with you."

"Shit." I dropped the pool stick and raced out into the hall, opening my Sight all the way and pushing past the sensory pollution to try to locate him. A fifty-foot radius was the best I could do in this place, so I stalked heavily through the building, throwing open doors, interrupting illicit deals, disturbing all the "do not disturb" signs.

Nothing. Moshe was following behind me ready to take action when needed but following my lead in the meantime. I was projecting a repellant force that made people scatter out of my way as I approached.

Once we reached the dance floor my already limited Sight range was cut in half by the sheer press of bodies and everyone's magick intermingling freely.

Towering above most of the heads in the room Moshe yelled over the music. "I think I see him. Three o'clock."

I headed in that direction, most of the people here too high on their drug of choice to heed the warning to get out of the way. I shoved my way through the crowd and the closer I got the more I could feel his presence. It was Tristan, but he was being influenced, his essence dimmed.

I finally broke through the last of the living wall that surrounded my quarry and felt rage light up inside me the moment I laid eyes on the perpetrator.

"Yuki," I growled, grabbing her jacket collar and hauling her away from a dazed Tristan.

"Hi, there. Fancy meeting you here." Yuki's jet-black hair shone blue under the club lights. The self-satisfied smile on her face plumped and reddened from the life force she just stole.

I jabbed my finger at Tristan and yelled back to Moshe. "Get him and leave."

Moshe nodded and picked Tristan up like a baby doll. The stark veins in Yuki's face thrummed under her deathly pale skin as her meal was carried away out of range.

They couldn't have been more than a few steps away when Yuki wrapped her ice-cold fingers around my neck. A sensation like thousands of ice crystals forming under my skin blistered with searing pain. I stared into her eyes as all pretense of humor disappeared from her face.

"You take one of mine, I take one of yours," she hissed.

I gritted my teeth against the burning cold. "I understand why you'd be upset." Her grip faltered a bit. "But he was feral. I had no choice." Yuki's grip tightened more aggressively.

"My brother wasn't feral! I could've gotten him back!"

"The Maou disagreed. And since he was on American soil it was at the High Council's discretion." I inhaled sharply at a new stab of pain.

Yuki stared, eyes bloodshot and wild, pupils dilated to saucers. Her mouth was open revealing razor-sharp rows of teeth that I had no trouble imagining tearing into me. Just like her brother's had before I beheaded him. Except there was nothing in his eyes at all except pure, unrelenting hunger.

"I made it quick. He didn't suffer."

She searched my face for lies and found none. Slowly her grip relaxed until she released me entirely.

The dancers around us never took notice or slowed their pace during the entire confrontation. Even as Yuki shoved the nearest couple out of her way and sent them sprawling into other dancers, they merely continued on like it was a planned interruption.

The soul eater disappeared without another word, and I rubbed my neck, wondering how many more of these I'd have to survive before this job was over.

Tristan would be fine now that he had some space between him and Yuki. Moshe wouldn't dare leave him alone until I got there, more to protect his own hide than Tristan's.

I remembered Queenie's request and stopped back by the room where this party had started.

After scanning the room, I didn't see her anywhere, so I asked the people still sober enough to string words together at the bar. They pointed me in the general direction of the factory floor above us; I paid my tab and headed off.

The bass could still be felt through the floor, but the sounds by and large were sealed off as I stepped onto the massive expanse of the broken and decrepit leftovers of a former furniture mecca.

Several walls were crumbling, most of the floor above this one had collapsed leaving giant chunks of concrete and rebar in haphazard piles; thick cobwebs and bird's nests were everywhere. I could hear the far off chitter of bats and stray cats on the prowl. But I didn't see or hear Queenie.

After looking around a bit more I figured she must've left, and I was about to do the same until a shadow moved into the frameless doorway ahead of me.

Reflexively I stepped back behind a boulder of fallen concrete and peered around at him. A man, average build, but that's all I could tell in the low light. I heard him sniff the air.

"Why don't you come out and play a game with me, Urquhart?" he taunted.

Assassin? "You're not gonna like it," I called back. "I play dirty."

"That's why I took this job." He chuckled and a wash of coldness swept over me. So much for run-ins with grieving family left behind or old enemies; the stakes just went up.

"And who would you be working for?" I asked.

"You put his mother in the ground when he was a child, came back for his father years later."

That didn't narrow it down, but I asked the obvious, just for clarity's sake. "So you're here to—"

"Kill you? Most definitely." He took a few steps forward, sniffing the air again. "Not that you're surprised, I'm sure. You returned to the one city with more people per capita that want to kill you than anywhere else on the planet. Seems like you have a death wish to me."

"What is it with you assholes always trying to blame the victim?" I asked facetiously. "You think I ever said that to any of my contracts? No. I told them who they could thank for this, and I shot them in the head. End of transaction."

"Then let's get on with it."

I did a quick inventory sweep of my weapons before I moved out of my shelter. A quick glance at the windows showed the first light of dawn starting to creep through the jagged glass teeth hanging in the iron frames and I suddenly felt every ounce of tiredness I'd earned up to this point.

I was facing a tall man with an angular face and dark blond hair. He was in all ways completely unextraordinary. Just a guy in a well-tailored suit that could be a local CPA or the perfectly unassuming murderer-for-hire.

"So how do you want to do this?" I asked. "Old-fashioned battle to the death?"

"Do you know any other way?"

I shrugged. "Not really. Just thought maybe you had something with more flare in mind. Those cufflinks say boring, but that pocket square..." I shook my finger at him. "That says you're a guy that's full of surprises. Maybe the kind of guy that likes to change things up every once and a while."

"Afraid not. But you know what did change? There was a lot more money to be made by the rest of us with you out of the picture. It would be a shame for the brokers to fall back into the same habit of hiring you all the time."

"Then you can all breathe easy, my friend. I'm just here for one job and then I'm gone again."

That actually piqued his interest. "Really? Say that's the truth, what could be important enough for you to come back here?"

"Continue this fight and you'll never find out."

The man chuckled. "Was that a plea for your life?"

"I was actually implying that you would be the dead one, but... You know what, never mind."

I was trying to stay positive, confident. The sparring with Percy and Adrian were never high stakes, we would have never actually killed each other. At least I don't *think* Adrian would have.

The run-in with Havoc would have most certainly ended in my death, and the brief fight that I was able to put up before they captured me did not leave me with a whole lot of confidence.

The best odds put a sixty to forty shot that I wouldn't walk out of here.

Suddenly he disappeared and I felt a rush of air behind me. I had milliseconds to shift out of the way before a blade aimed at my neck only nicked my skin.

I rounded on him, threw a punch and was blocked, aimed a kick and was blocked again with a side arm that he circled around to grab my calf. He could have easily snapped my tibia but settled for throwing me several feet where I landed in a cloud of dust and rusted metal.

Picking myself up I charged him, magickally boosting my momentum and dropping down to slide on my knees through gravel and broken glass. The assassin stepped to the side and grabbed a large metal pipe, swinging it at me.

I flattened myself to the ground as the pipe barely missed me, threw my weight into a spin and popped to my feet in a runner's starting-block position.

He was still completing his swing and I dove at him, taking him down with a shoulder to the gut. He landed on his back with a thud, and I sprang away, repositioning in a crouch. While he was still bent forward trying to get to his feet, I grabbed the back of his neck and smashed my gravel- and glass-studded knee into his face. He screeched and fell back with glass shards in his eye.

He swung wildly at me with the knife in his hand, losing all composure. I grabbed it and snapped his arm, not wasting the opportunity that he himself wasted earlier.

This was only going to end one way.

I drew my gun from my waistband and he lunged at me, knocking it from my hand and hitting me with a cinderblock fist under the chin with his good arm. I momentarily saw stars and staggered away.

We moved to opposite ends of the room, recovering. I saw him pick the glass out of his eye and watched as the burst and oozing ocular fluid melted over his cheek.

Eyes didn't regenerate but his arm was regaining its strength and he flexed it carefully, popping it into place at the shoulder and forearm. The crunching of bones grated on me; that sound had always been like nails on a chalkboard.

My gun was lying off to the side, no way for me to reach it before he was on me. I only had a couple of knives and I reached into my boot to grab one just as he retrieved another one from a sheath on his arm.

He passed it back and forth between his hands, testing out which was the better. His muscles tensed and he hissed angrily. When he sprang across the room it was almost too fast to follow.

I barely avoided him, his passing leaving me with a deep cut on my abdomen and him with a slice across the shoulder. He rounded on me and poised for another attack.

He sprang again and we exchanged a flurry of hand-to-hand that injured both of us and left neither with the clear advantage. I finally caught him with an elbow and when he fell, I pounced, punching him in the face and neck repeatedly.

I was trying to crush his windpipe or invert his nose, but the nose was steel, and his windpipe was oddly flexible. An adder, a giant snake shifter; that was the only explanation.

He found an opening and threw me several yards. I landed on something that was oddly warm and leathery. Pulling away from it I saw that it was a body. Apprehension distracting me from the fight, I moved my gaze up the body and was met with the bloodied, mostly decapitated head of Queenie, her dead eyes staring out at nothing.

The adder grabbed my legs and dragged me backward, attacking with blinding speed. I pushed him back enough to draw myself to one knee and threw up my arms to block kicks. Several stab wounds appeared before I even felt the first one and I was soon bleeding profusely.

I grabbed his right leg the next time it came near me and dislocated the knee following up with a strong drive of my palm into his femur. A little trick utilizing sonic resonance added a blast of energy of the strike and his leg broke with a wet, snapping sound as he crashed to the floor in pain.

He was only out of the game for a second. This guy was tough, struggling up and favoring his left leg. I was breathing heavily and waiting to see what he would do as he finally drew a weapon, a .45 much like my own.

I looked at my gun, lying a good ten feet away. Might as well have been the Grand Canyon of a distance. He noticed the look of concern on my face and smiled.

"Don't tell me I caught you without a weapon?" His smile faltered a bit as he stepped too confidently and pain shot through him.

I gave him a sideways smile as I raised my hands in the air. "This is awkward."

We both stared at each other, waiting for a move. If there were any tumbleweeds, they would have been rolling. There was no cover to hide behind so I was in a little bit of trouble, but then again, so was he.

I watched his body language closely. A dog barked nearby, and it caught his attention. It wasn't outwardly apparent unless you watched his eyes which flicked out of focus for just a moment.

In that moment I reached under the back of my sweatshirt to the small Derringer in my waistband. I drew the gun and fired before I'd even finished steadying my aim, the explosive round nailing him right between the eyes.

After that everything went in slow motion, just like in the movies. The look in his eyes changed from hatred and intent to utter surprise as the bullet found home. A small spurt of blood landed in a rain of droplets on my shirt, and he crumpled in on himself. I watched as the life left his body, his final breath an almost inaudible hiss of air.

I did what triage I could with what I had before struggling back over to Queenie.

A quick glance confirmed that she was beyond help. I couldn't imagine that she tried to set me up and was double-crossed. More likely she was in the wrong place at the wrong time. The adder had seen a perfect opportunity and then disposed of the unknowing bait.

I pulled a couple of bronze coins out of my pocket, a habit I'd never given up. I placed one over each of Queenie's eyes and spoke our prayer for the fallen.

"Swiftly 'cross the Bridge of Swords, a warrior's rest awaits. Though you go before me now, find glory with the Fates."

I bowed my head and paid my respects before calling for the cleaners. They would gather Queenie's body and ensure it was disposed of according to any wishes she may have made known.

I looked at the adder's body and couldn't have cared less what they did with him. He'd killed my friend for nothing.

The dawn light was cold, and I didn't have the energy to make myself warm. I was covered in the adder's blood and my own. While I was walking slowly and painfully toward the nearest portal I was cursing the events of the night. I hated using jump portals when I was weak, it was too easy for someone to intercept your intended destination and send you to one of their choosing.

Luckily that didn't happen today, but I had to jog about a block to my home from the nearest portal exit and try to avoid being seen by the early morning crowd. This wasn't New York; people would notice a woman covered in blood and at the very least call the cops.

Once safely in the building and heading to my floor, I leaned back in the elevator and stared at my reflection in the recently shined metal that lined the walls between faux wood paneling.

Most of the wounds were healed, bruises just visible now. I looked at my sweatshirt and the droplets of blood from the adder's head wound standing out starkly amid the rest of the mess. I popped the emergency stop button and the elevator stuttered to a halt with a small alarm screaming somewhere far off.

Queenie was dead because of me. She'd survived so much and the night I came back into her life was the last she'd see. I was poison, death to everything and everyone. Tristan almost died tonight just because he'd been unfortunate enough to be in my presence.

A burst of anger and frustration came bubbling to the surface and I smacked my reflection with both hands. Something snapped and I starting beating on the doors, fists pummeling dents into the metal, not stopping until the wall began to groan under the onslaught and the elevator felt like it might jump off the pulley.

I pulled my hands to my sides and caught my breath. This would not get the better of me, not again. This had to happen eventually; it's not like I was going to make it out of this mission without a body count.

That guy was just doing a job at the behest of someone else, same as me. I know he would have killed me if he could have but I couldn't help but feel disgusted at myself for taking another life when I wasn't protecting somebody else or within the confines of the mission.

And it brought the fact crashing home that I was back now. I was a target again, people wanted me dead for one reason or another. The life I had tried so hard to get away from had caught up to me within a day and more enemies kept lining up at my door.

I didn't know if I would be able to get out of it a second time.

I slammed the emergency stop button again and the elevator continued up. I slid the gate out of the way after taking a last glance at the damage to the wall. Maybe the landlord wouldn't notice.

# CHAPTER TWELVE

Much to my surprise, the landing was already occupied.

"Tristan."

His wan smile was quickly replaced with horror as he took in my appearance. "What happened?"

I took in an exhausted, shuddering breath. "Assassin."

His genuine concern elicited a shuddering breath of exhaustion as the weight on my shoulders doubled. "Are you okay?"

"I almost got you killed tonight and you're asking me that?"

Tristan approached and gently lifted my chin to examine the lingering bruising. "I didn't walk away from the encounter covered in blood."

"Queenie's dead. It's my fault."

With a lingering brush of his fingers on my cheek he leaned back. "Queenie?"

"The woman that greeted me first tonight." A wave of nausea rolled through me, and I bent over, resting my hands on my knees.

Tristan was next to me in an instant. "What's wrong?"

I tried to breathe through it but images came unbidden, flashing in rapid succession. Queenie's dead eyes, the assassin's confident smile, the bullet wound in his head, the laser-focused details you pick up when you're in a fight for your life.

The coup de grâce came when the fear, pain, and reality that I might not have survived this night overwhelmed me. My stomach heaved and I barely made it to a potted plant before coughing up bile and blood.

Cool hands at my nape pulled back my disheveled hair and a calm stroking up and down my back helped ease the spasms as my stomach emptied itself. I could hear Jake barking and whining on the other side of the door.

I spat, fished my keys from my pocket and Tristan offered to take them to help me out. I shook my head. "If you try to open that door without me programming the wards first you really will end up dead tonight."

He stood back as I unlocked the door, Jake pushing his way out the moment it opened. He circled me worriedly, sniffing and nudging, trying to herd me into the apartment. He spared a brief instant to greet Tristan before resuming his fussing over me.

I held out my hand, a small hat pin that I kept secured on top of the lintel in my grasp. Tristan offered up his pointer finger and I stabbed it quickly, guiding his hand to the door frame and running his finger along it. The smear of blood was absorbed and there was a slight blue tinge to the sigils before they disappeared back into the wood grain.

"Come on in." I stepped heavily through enchantments that usually were nothing more than a flutter against my skin. I felt defeated in so many ways.

Tristan followed and made a beeline for the sink, grabbing one of the glasses sitting on the counter and filling it up. "You know you didn't have to vomit just to make me feel better about puking earlier tonight." He handed me the glass and I gratefully drank, clearing the foul taste from my mouth.

I laughed weakly. "Thanks, but it was the least I could do." I motioned to the couch. "Make yourself at home. I'm going to clean up."

Jake whined and stuck close to my side, following me step for step. When I came back out in the living room Tristan was texting someone and there was a steaming hot pot of tea on the coffee table. I could smell the ginger from here. I smiled despite everything.

"Keeping Derfael abreast of the situation?"

He nodded, reaching over and pouring me a cup. "He's been trying to get a hold of you. He thought maybe Moreno kept you as an unwilling guest."

"Fuck. That happened tonight too." I crashed down onto the sofa. "Amazing how time flies." Jake jumped up next to me and smooshed himself as close as he could get. I wrapped my arms around him, taking comfort in the furry warmth and he put a paw on my shoulder to give me a hug back.

Jake finally settled down when he could feel my tension easing up. I sipped the tea and was delighted by the strong spice of the ginger. "This is delicious. Thank you." I wrapped my hands around the heat of the cup. "And I'm sorry."

Tristan grinned wryly. "You have nothing to apologize for. Moshe explained the scared straight idea and that you were both planning on keeping an eye on me."

I closed my eyes and sighed. "Not that that worked out. At all."

He shook his head. "Shit happens. I also should have known better than to get hypnotized by a soul eater. It's not the first time I've met one." He ran a hand through his hair and smiled, embarrassed. "I guess I got cocky trying to impress a girl."

Suddenly the fuzz pilling on my sweater seemed a whole lot more interesting and I busied myself picking at it. "Did Derfael ask how you ended up with me?"

Tristan looked guilty. "I might've said that I ran into you while you were coming back from your meeting."

I frowned. "If he finds out he will be none too pleased." I took a sip. "But he won't hear it from me."

"Thank you."

"Thanks nothing," I scoffed. "I'm protecting my ass, too."

"You've got a point." He propped his right foot over his knee. "So do you mind if I ask what happened with the assassin?"

I picked a few more sweater pills before I answered. "Adder shifter. Still haven't pinned down who hired him, there are a couple of candidates. When I went looking for Queenie, I found him instead. We fought, I won. Not much else to tell."

"Maybe not much, but something," he pressed.

The nausea came back but it was far less severe. "Only realizing that I'm a danger to everyone around me." I tucked my feet under me and huddled into my sweater firmly avoiding Tristan's gaze. "I can't go back after this no matter how much I want to. I'm trapped in this life until I die, which I was fairly sure at one point was going to be tonight." I flicked my eyes to his. "I don't think I've ever actually considered my own mortality until now."

He moved from the chair and sat next to me on the couch. "What are you really worried about here?"

"You mean besides the terrible things I just listed?"

"Humor me."

I thought, trying to sort through the angst-ridden feelings and self-serving hyperbole. "My worst fears are coming true. Once the initial alarm subsided and the fight was on, I felt right back at home. I never stopped being a hunter, I just convinced myself I was a vegetarian for twelve years. But that joy in the hunt, in the fight, in the kill…"

The micro-expressions of surprise on the adder's face when I got the upper hand. The feel of his bones snapping, the sound of viscera, the grunts of pain. That rising bloodlust when you know the fight is almost over.

"In the moment, I felt free. Once it was over and the threat was neutralized I felt…" I searched around for the words. "Disappointed. And then I felt guilty about the disappointment. And Queenie's unnecessary death just made me feel more guilty because a part of me has been wanting the assassins and death squads to come for me and she got caught in the crossfire."

I was on a roll now, the thoughts tumbling from my mouth almost faster than I could process them. "I was the thing everyone feared in the night. I want them to remember that. I want everyone to know that's still true. I just don't want to be that monster anymore."

I shook my head, at a loss. "But I can't have one without the other and I'm afraid I'm going to lose myself to that desire to be feared and respected. That's who I was, the only reason I existed. What am I without it?"

I started when Tristan's hand clasped my knee, warm and reassuring. "Why can't you be both?"

I blinked at him. "How do you mean?"

"You clearly detest everything about the person you used to be. You want to help people, I don't think that's just something you invented during your 'vegetarianism' to make yourself act the part. You can be every bit the unholy terror whose name makes people shit themselves and still be a good person."

His hand squeezed my knee before he released it. "I've only known you for a few days but from the way Derfael talks about you I'd say you've always been good. You just had to compartmentalize to deal with the shit the Council put you through and you leaned into it harder the tougher things got."

"I didn't know you were a psychologist. Are you going to charge me for this hour?" I joked.

"I'm not and I won't. But I honestly don't think it's impossible to merge those two things. The bloodlust is necessary to survive and thrive in your part of the world. The empathy makes you a better hunter."

I looked at him dumbly. "Huh?"

"You see a true monster and destroy it before it does more harm than it already has. Embracing both is what's going to keep you sane."

"Where'd you learn to analyze like this?"

"I did study a lot of psychology," he admitted. "But after the last of my family died, all I wanted was vengeance and I didn't care what I had to do to get it." He scratched the back of his head. "It got real dark."

His hand was resting between us on the couch and without thinking I took it, twining my fingers with his, but even as I gave him a sympathetic smile the exhaustion was settling in hard. Despite my best effort I couldn't keep my eyelids from drooping.

"I better get going, you're exhausted. I don't want to keep you up." But he didn't make any move to release my hand.

I nodded and reluctantly let go, yawning for good measure. "It's been a long day. Thanks for the pep talk, I needed that."

Tristan got to his feet and stretched. I was about to walk him to the door when my phone rang. I fished it out of my pocket and saw a number I didn't recognize.

An explosion of sound answered from the other end of the line.

"Hello?"

Crashing objects and two people screaming back and forth, one of whom sounded like they were pleading and terrified. Running feet and a slamming door could be heard before a small voice whispered into the receiver just as banging started up on the other side of the door.

"Who is this? Can you speak up?" My questions went unheeded as the voice kept repeating the same thing over and over again. I motioned Tristan over and put it on speaker so we could both listen.

Almost simultaneously we both understood. "It's an address," said Tristan, scrambling for a pen and paper.

"We've got the address, can you tell me your name?"

"Ro," the voice whispered before hanging up.

Tristan's eyebrows knit. "Did I hear 'row'?"

"It was their name." I sprang to my feet and grabbed my jacket. "I've got to go." I was hitting the back stairs out of the building before I realized Tristan was with me.

He cut off any objections at the knees. "I'm not letting you go alone."

We reached my Camero and jumped in. I peeled off toward the address Ro gave me, hoping we weren't too late.

With the way I drive normally it would've taken us about five minutes to make the ten-minute trip. That morning it only took two. We pulled up in front of a duplex and the sounds of chaos coming from the one on the left were audible from the street. I grabbed a couple of plaques from the center console and handed one to Tristan.

"These will keep us from being identifiable if there are any cameras. We'll be pixelated blurs."

Two voices were still screaming, so Ro was still alive. As Tristan and I approached the house a man sitting on the front step of the adjacent duplex just shook his head and took a drag on his cigarette.

"They're at it again. He doesn't know how to control his temper."

"I can see it really concerns you," I said, disgusted at this man's apathy.

"None of my business what happens between a couple in their own home."

"Now I'm making it my business." I sent a scatter pulse of energy at him and he hurried inside, cigarette still dangling from his mouth.

Most of the houses on this street were quiet, whether they'd left for work already or were still asleep. I was grateful either way. This would already be difficult to keep under wraps in the daylight, let alone with neighbors around. Although most of them could probably hear what was going on and possibly shared this man's apathy.

I handed Tristan my backup pistol and told him to circle around back. "Give me a few minutes to make silent entry before you kick the back door in, okay?"

He nodded and ran around the side of the house, ducking under windows.

I spelled open the door and winced as the door creaked. The noise inside paused for a second before starting back up again. The thick carpeting, littered with shattered picture frames, torn magazines, and broken side tables dampened my footfalls. The large coffee table, a solid pane of thick glass, was broken into terrifyingly large shards, one of which was covered in still-wet blood.

I crept toward the source of the noise in the back bedroom. That bastard had Ro cornered. They were crouched down, trying their best to shield themselves from the blows and kicks he was aiming at them while calling Ro every name in the book. They were pleading for their life.

He didn't have any weapons on him besides a broken leg from the coffee table. I rushed him and before he even registered I was there I'd grabbed his throat and pinned him to the wall. Even though there was no doubt he was human I had to remind myself how easy it would be to kill him by genuine accident. Not that that would be any great loss.

While he choked and struggled against my vise grip, I turned to Ro. "Do you have any wounds that need immediate attention?"

They shook their head, tears streaming down their face. They were still guarding their body with arms up. They looked so frail and small and the tremors shaking their body made it worse. They were so childlike, my heart broke.

And my grip on his throat tightened. Before I crushed his windpipe, I threw him across the room into a pile of bedsheets that had been ripped to shreds. He stumbled to his feet and took off running, me close on his heels. I was toying with him now.

He headed for the open front door, but I jerked my hand and it slammed closed in his face. He ran into it, bounced off and headed for the back just as Tristan kicked it in. I saw Tristan register that this scum was human, and he tucked the gun away, pulling back his fist and delivering a nasty uppercut to his jaw.

Tristan kicked his legs out from under him and pinned him to the floor, hands behind his back. I heard him mutter words under his breath and an opaque shimmering thread formed from ether and wrapped around the man's hands.

I nodded to him and went to check on Ro, still shaking and fully fetal now. I crouched down next to them, making sure not to get too close.

"Ro? I'm Evyn. We've got him restrained, you're safe."

"Not safe. I'll never be safe."

"You are safe," I said firmly. "I promise you."

Ro looked up at me with wary, tired eyes. "You actually came."

I nodded with a sad smile.

Their face broke and a new cascade of tears poured out as they realized their ordeal was over. "He was really going to kill me this time."

I swallowed heavily, tamping down my emotions. "You'll never have to deal with him again, I'll make sure of that."

"How?"

I stood and offered my hand. "I'll let you decide, if you like. Otherwise we can walk him out of here and whatever happens happens, but it won't be on your conscience."

Ro nodded and slowly got to their feet. They wiped their face on their sleeve and smeared some of the blood from several facial lacerations.

"I didn't see any wounds on him, so you're the one that must've been hurt by the glass on the broken coffee table?"

They nodded, putting their hand to their side.

"Can I take a look?"

Ro nodded again and peeled the bloodied shirt up. It was soaked and sticky with coagulation and the stain continued down the side of their pajama shorts where it dripped onto their leg.

They gasped as the shirt that had been acting as a bandage pulled away to let loose a stream of blood. Their eyes rolled up, but I caught Ro before they hit the floor.

"Tristan, I need some help here!"

He appeared in the doorway. "Shit. What happened?"

"They have a deep stab wound somewhere near their kidney. I need you to grab the kit in my trunk. Is the human secured?"

Tristan grabbed the keys I tossed to him. "He's tied to the chair, and I knocked his ass out for good measure."

He took off for the car and I grabbed the nearest cloth to wipe away the blood. Tristan returned with the kit and popped the lid open. "What do you need?"

"Grab the forceps."

He handed me the forceps and I extracted a large piece of glass still lodged in their kidney. The odd discoloration on the glass caught my eye.

"The fuck? How did iron oxide get on the glass?" I tossed it aside. I rummaged through the kit for the poultice, adding some additional calcium powder, charcoal, and ground coffee that would draw out the iron.

I packed the wound and spoke the activating words that would set it to work quickly. "This won't heal without stitches, not with iron in the wound. Grab a suture pack with the silver needle."

Tristan handed me the small packet with cotton thread and a fine silver needle. I couldn't even thread it. "Dammit."

"Here." Tristan took the needle and thread and deftly began to suture the wound. Within seconds he was done and then we waited.

After a few minutes the bleeding had stopped completely. The sheen of sweat on Ro's skin began to dry and I was confident that they were stable. I draped a blanket over them, found some clean clothes and set them nearby so they could change when they woke. I left a note within their eye-line so when they woke up and found themselves alone, they wouldn't panic.

I joined Tristan in the living room where he had tied the human to a chair, one of the few that wasn't broken. The man had blood on his lip and brow, a black eye, and a scowl that turned his already mean face into a caricature of villainy.

"Who are you?" he spat.

"Friendly neighborhood cleanup crew," I said, smacking him in the face casually as I walked by. "Heard a disturbance, thought we'd check it out."

"Quite a vermin infestation here." Tristan, who had been sitting forward purposefully invading the man's space, leaned back. He'd taken his jacket and sweatshirt off—possibly to keep any bloodstains at a minimum. I took a second to admire his defined, well-muscled shoulders. They looked tense and, if he was feeling anything like I was, ready to tear this guy's head off if he sneezed the wrong way.

"Explain something to me..." I trailed off, motioning my hand for him to fill in the blank.

"Jimmy."

"Explain something to me, Jimmy." I sat next to Tristan. "I've met that pixie before. In a bar. Drowning their sorrows. Sweet, innocent, couldn't hurt a fly."

Jimmy scoffed. "Innocent? None of you Strangers are innocent."

I blinked and smiled sweetly. "Have a lot of experience with Strangers, do you?"

"Enough." A cocky smile played on his face, marred by the fat lip.

"What did Ro do to earn all this, then?" asked Tristan.

"That bitch is always trying to use magick on me. Controlling me."

I narrowed my eyes. "So Ro made you do this? They brought this on themself?"

Jimmy shrugged. "You said it, not me. I gave it a home, companionship, didn't even make it pay any of the bills—"

"It?" Tristan's voice was dangerously low, his expression equal parts stone and ice.

"Well it's not human, what the hell else should I call it?"

"You, sir—" I chewed on the word. "—are all too human."

The cocky smirk grew. "Thanks."

"That wasn't a compliment." My cold tone and equally cold glare made him realize the precarious situation he was in.

He was sitting across from two Strangers, both far more dangerous than his kindhearted pixie-turned-punching-bag and both glaring at him with nothing but contempt. All while he was tied securely and helplessly to a chair.

"Look," Jimmy began, looking for all the world like he was about to divulge a huge secret and we should think him very brave for doing so. "Ro and I met at a shelter while I was doing community service."

"Shocker," said Tristan.

Jimmy sneered at him. "Like you're so much better than me. You're probably planning on killing me, aren't you?" He scoffed. "At least I ain't a murderer."

"You were about to be." I motioned to the coffee table. "How did iron oxide find it's way onto that glass Ro was stabbed with."

"That coffee table is also used for recreation imbibing of substances. Ro snorts iron oxide to tamp down the magick."

"Ro's choice, or with heavy 'encouragement' from you?" I was horrified at either prospect. The pain that would cause would be excruciating.

"Like I was saying," Jimmy continued, "we met at the shelter. Ro was fucked up on drugs and started talking about being a pixie and all that shit. I thought it was all the drugs but then Ro kept talking about that shit sober and demonstrated the pixie magick."

I could see Jimmy's fingers waggling behind his back.

"So you saw an opportunity?" I asked.

"I'm nothing if not an enterprising gentleman. At first I was planning on using Ro as some kind of freakshow but then I caught feelings, you know?"

"No."

He ignored me. "Ro wanted to be more human. The pixie thing was wearing 'em down. So I offered to help."

"And just like that you found a hapless victim." Tristan rested his foot on his knee, the casual gesture not covering the clenched fists and reddening of his ears.

"You guys keep making me out to be the bad guy. I was trying to help."

"I never wanted your help."

Ro's small voice came from the hallway and we all turned. They had changed into the clean clothes and attempted to wipe the blood from their face.

"Babe, come on. Tell them."

I threw my hand out and Jimmy's head snapped back as a magickal gag slapped over his mouth.

Ro took some tentative steps into the living room. "I'd just been abandoned by my clan, left behind at the annual move and told not to follow. He found me and got me to trust him, kept plying me with human drugs which were nice for a while."

Ro shook their head like they were clearing away cobwebs from the memories. "I confided in him and then he used me to enrich himself and his buddies. He kept me prisoner by threatening to expose all of us. He had tapes, too much proof for people to ignore. Whenever I wasn't performing prosperity or luck magick or jinxing his enemies he"—Ro choked back a sob—"used me for unspeakable things."

Jimmy started screaming against his gag and thrashing in the chair. Tristan was on him in a second, punching him in the gut and face several times until Jimmy was slumped over and quiet again.

"What do you want us to do with him?" I asked Ro.

"I know what my heart wants."

Jimmy looked up, hopeful.

"Revenge. Pain."

Jimmy looked rightfully terrified for the first time since we got there.

Ro sighed. "But my conscience won't let me. Despite everything he did I just don't have it in me to harm anyone." They wrapped their arms around themselves, guarding against the decision they had to make. "That's why I'm going to let you decide."

Ro gathered their coat and keys, stopping once to look Jimmy in the eye. "I hope you get everything you deserve."

Jimmy slumped, defeated as Ro walked away from the house of horrors. "I'll come back to collect some things, maybe in an hour?"

I nodded.

"Then I'll disappear." Ro chewed their lip. "Thank you both." And they were out the door.

Tristan and I waited until we heard their car pull away. Double-checking that all the window shades were down and there were no neighbors finally becoming interested in everything that had happened here, Tristan and I removed the threat that Jimmy posed to Ro and the entire Stranger community.

I called a cleaner team for the second time that day and told them to wait until Ro was cleared out. After that, everything must go.

"Do you need a ride back to Wolfe's?"

Tristan nodded. "That would be great. I've got a bit too much blood under my cuticles for a cab ride."

We drove off in the direction of Heartside, taking some detours around the late season construction.

Tristan was fiddling with the radio, looking for a good station. Don't worry, he asked first. "That's exactly what I was talking about, you know."

I met his gaze before turning back to the road. "What was what?"

"An avenging angel."

I barked out a laugh. "Have you lost your mind?"

"Maybe that's a bit hyperbolic—"

"A bit?!"

Tristan laughed. "It gets the main point across. You weren't using your gifts to cause pain." He held up his hands to stave off my retort. "You saved someone's life. And while someone else died in the process, that guy made his bed. You just enacted accelerated justice."

"That seems like a skewed way of looking at it."

"It is. But you recognize the complicated morality. Would you have seen it that way before?"

I considered. "Definitely not."

"You weren't following orders, you didn't get paid for it. You did it purely out of a desire to help a person in trouble. That was your motivation. And you didn't even hesitate to jump at the call despite how exhausted and mentally worn out you were."

Tristan finally found a station that he liked. "You're worried about that monster taking hold again, but I think you've changed in ways you don't even recognize yet."

A new song started up on the radio and Tristan turned it up. "I love this song."

I smiled at him and turned it up louder. "Me too."

# CHAPTER THIRTEEN

After arriving home I finally slept the afternoon and most of the evening away before Jake started getting antsy. The night air was particularly brisk as Jake and I stepped outside for a walk along the riverfront. The recent cold snap made for some icy spots along the path, but I'd take that over an assassin any day.

I was focusing on the river, the rapids surging once again after the water breaks had been removed years back. To have such a wild source of water energy in the middle of the city spoke volumes for the draw Strangers usually felt to this area.

A collision with something short and angular brought me back to attention. I blinked and watched a young kid that was all limbs and skinny as a beanpole hurry away. I patted myself down and realized my wallet was gone.

"Dammit, kid, get back here," I said with more than a touch of warning.

The youth showed no sign of slowing down so I dropped the leash. "Jake, if you would."

Jake barked and the kid broke out into a run but only made it about twenty feet before Jake caught up.

"Jake, release."

Jake sat back and the teen scrambled up, aiming to run again. "Do you really think that's a good idea?" Now that I was up close, I noticed the kid was actually a pixie so as usual there was no good way of telling age other than asking outright. And that's never not rude.

A deep frown creased the pixie's face and they leaned sourly against the wall.

"Hand it over." I stretched out my hand, palm up.

"Hand what over?" they asked.

"We're not playing these games." I flexed my fingers. "Give it."

The pixie reached into an inside pocket of their coat and produced a wallet, handing it to me. I looked at it. "Not my wallet. Try again."

They became markedly more upset as they retrieved my wallet and slapped it in my hand.

"Thanks," I said with a frown. "Next time you pick someone's pocket, make sure they don't have a dog."

"I could have outrun it if I wanted."

"Get out of here. If I catch you again, I'll hang you from a telephone pole by your thumbs."

"Sure thing," they grumbled. "If Evyn Urquhart tells me to do something, I better do it."

Ready to turn my back on this incident and walk away, I paused and appraised them.

"Who are you?"

The kid's face broke into a grin as they apparently got the reaction they were hoping for. "Nobody important."

I scowled. "Want to try again?"

"Consider me a friend."

"A friend? If you know who I am you should know what happened to the last person that told me that." I looked at them hard, daring them to flinch, but they didn't.

"You're trying to get a reaction out of me. It won't work."

"What do you want?" I was more curious than angry now.

"Like I said, I'm a friend. A very valuable one."

I sighed and decided to play along. "In what way?"

"I'm privy to certain bits of information that others are not."

"Fine. Tell me something good or I'm walking."

The pixie knew they had me and they smirked. "Do you know why Moreno came back to the States?"

I raised an eyebrow. "The big picture is a bit mercurial right now, but we've got a pretty good idea."

"Is 'pretty good' something you're happy with?"

I crossed my arms. "You're really starting to test my patience."

"Moreno mentioned the archaeological sites when you spoke, right?"

I looked at them sharply. "How do you know about that?"

They ignored me. "The Ancients taught a type of magick that no one, human or Stranger knew at that point. Now we have refined magicks to harness the chaos of dark matter. What the Ancients taught those people was pure and unbridled. Extremely unstable and supremely dangerous. That's what they trapped in those artifacts."

"So from what you're saying it sounds like a grand ol' time."

The pixie frowned at my attitude and then gave me the single best piece of information I'd received yet. "The only thing that's slowing her down is figuring out how to activate it. Without destroying the world." They shrugged. "Before she can conquer it anyway."

"Since you seem to know everything else, do you know where the artifacts are being kept? Or how close she is to figuring out the key?"

"Not yet." The pixie clearly hated to admit they didn't know something. "If I hear anything I'll let you know." They raised an eyebrow. "I'm assuming you do want me to keep you informed?"

I inclined my head. "I would. What's your price?"

They shook their head and their face softened. "Ro is a friend of mine. They told me what you did to help. So I decided to help you."

Surprised wasn't a strong enough word to describe what I felt at that answer. "Thank you."

The pixie nodded. "It's clear you need a lot of help, so I'll do what I can." They smirked, not unkindly.

"Ha ha." I realized they hadn't given me a key piece of information. "What's your name?"

They considered. "Most people call me Grimm."

"Because that's the nature of the news you always bring them?" I joked.

Grimm huffed out a laugh. "You're about to have a hell of a fight on your hands, Evyn. Get ready."

Jake and I had barely stepped foot back in the loft when my buzzer rang. I cursed. Couldn't I just get a breather to maybe read a book or watch *Judge Judy*?

"Hello?"

"It's Percy, let me up."

I pressed the button to unlock the door and waited on the landing to repeat the same ritual I'd done with Tristan. Jake walked up to Percy hesitantly, tail wagging. He was respecting the cantankerous wolf's boundaries.

Percy reluctantly put her hand out and he danced over for some pets, victorious.

"Resistance is futile. You're not the only one to fall under his spell."

"Are you sure he's actually a dog? And for the record, I don't hate dogs. They usually don't like me either." She eyed Jake. "That's why I'm suspicious of this one."

"Pretty sure, but hard telling." I brushed it off, although I'd be lying if I said I hadn't wondered the same thing.

Percy cut right to the chase. "I had a contact reach out, wanted to set up a meeting with you."

I knit my brows together. "Why not just come to me directly?"

Her response was glib. "Because he doesn't trust you."

I nodded. "Cool."

"I'd actually contacted him first because I wanted to check in on a fluctuation we've noticed in High Order ceremonial sorcery."

What fresh hell was this? "Since when have you been part of the monitoring teams?"

"I'm more oversight."

Before I could ask her any more questions she breezed on by.

"This contact has a penchant for running in those circles so I figured if anyone would know anything..."

"Where do I fit in here?"

"Well, he had a bunch of reasons that made sense in the long run for the uptick in activity. Something to do with thousand-year cycles closing out." Almost offhand, Percy added, "He seemed pretty excited about that and a ten-thousand-year cycle, but he goes down a nerd rabbit-hole and I don't have the patience for it. I've already set up the meeting, just ask him. I honestly don't care."

"You set up the meeting—"

"Right, so he reached out a couple days ago and says he needs to talk to you. He's been hearing some rumblings about an old order of some priesthood or other that's got eyes for you. Wouldn't say much more than that so I said you'd meet him tomorrow night."

"You did, huh?"

Percy shrugged. "What, like you've got anything better to do?" She turned and headed for the door. "I'll text you the address when he decides on it." And she left.

Jake, who was lying on his bed, looked at me and sighed heavily.

"Ditto, bud."

I was up early the next morning, so I stopped at one of my favorite bakeries on Fulton Street on my way to Wolfe's.

Fifteen minutes later I hit the door with a box of still-warm donuts, licking some remnants of orange glaze from my hands. Derfael was usually up by now, but Tristan was just coming up from the basement stairs when I walked in.

"Hey." He noticed the box in my hands. "You brought Van's?"

I smiled. "You've been?"

He gleefully pulled out a classic glazed and bit into it with relish. "Best donuts I've ever had."

"Sorry, your mouth was a bit full, what was that?" I teased.

He polished off the donut and was eyeing the box for another. I opened the lid and held it out. "Might as well. They're still warm."

He shook his head. "I'll pace myself."

"Suit yourself." I grabbed another orange twist and dug in.

"Fine, if the cool kids are doing it." He tucked into a second donut as Derfael came down the stairs.

When he saw the box, he broke into a grin. "You always were my favorite, Talulla."

"What brings you by so early?" asked Tristan. He had glaze on his cheek, so I reached over with a napkin and wiped it off, ignoring Derfael frowning over his bear claw.

"A fitful night's sleep and an impending meet-up with some kind of nerd sorcerer."

Both men stared at me blankly. "Is that some kind of new VR game?" asked Tristan.

I just sighed at the dad joke as he snickered. "Percy came by and let me know she was setting up a meeting tonight with someone that knows of a group of High Order priests that have me on their radar for some reason. And she mentioned something about thousand- and ten-thousand-year cycles that he would be much more eager to explain than she was."

"A brotherhood with a vendetta is hardly new." His mustache was twitching at the ends like it did whenever he was connecting the dots. I learned that tick very early on in my childhood. "The cycles, however."

He bustled off, his robes flowing behind him in the current. Derfael climbed the stairs out of view, and I heard his apartment door creak open and shut.

"We've lost him to the library." I wandered into the back room and set the box of donuts on the table. I looked toward the stairs. "How much of my little existential crisis have you mentioned to Derfael?"

Tristan pantomimed locking his lips with a key. "Not a word. As a certified armchair therapist, I'm obligated to keep our sessions confidential."

I sighed with relief. "Thanks."

What was I doing? I barely knew this man and I was already confiding in him my deepest fears and personal gnosis. Sure, the guy seems genuine and Derfael clearly trusts him, and I can't imagine what he would have to gain from telling this shit to other people. Public opinion was already pretty low, and I wasn't planning on moving to politics anytime soon. But still. I perused the shelves I'd memorized over the years just to hide from my discomfort.

"I was thinking we should get dinner at some point," he continued.

My hand paused as I was turning the labels outward on a collection of jars.

"If you're game. I haven't had a chance to meet many people in the city yet and it seems like I'm guaranteed to get into some shenanigans if I'm with you." He laughed.

I resumed straightening the shelves. Okay, nothing to worry about. Dinner as friends, that's all.

"Yeah, I'd be up for that."

"Awesome. Looking forward to it."

"Looking forward to what?" asked Derfael. He had a large tome in his arms. I hadn't even heard him come down the stairs.

"I talked Evyn into taking pity on me and helping me meet people."

Derfael looked back and forth between us suspiciously but said nothing. My phone chirped and I saw a message from Percy.

"Huh. That's a new one."

"Is that Percy with the location?" asked Derfael.

"He wants to meet in a little whisky bar on the main floor of an event space on Hall. Not the usual dark alley."

"Public, well lit. A show of good faith."

I slipped my phone back in my pocket after firing off a response. "She also mentioned he doesn't trust me so it's probably for his own safety, not mine."

"Six of one." Derfael set down the book on the table with a thud and opened the yellowed pages. The handwritten text was cramped and spidery, some form of Middle English. I had to work to switch gears in my brain to be able to read it.

"The cycles," Derfael said, pointing to a certain section of script. "It rang a bell and I remembered this transcription."

"The Brotherhood of Levi." Derfael had almost a complete collection of the early grimoires of the brotherhood. Even though I hadn't needed to, I'd studied them growing up just because their form of magick was so unique.

"Levi?" asked Tristan.

"Leviathan," I explained. "Among other things he's associated with the knowledge of chaos. The brotherhood took a deep dive into that chaos"—I waggled my eyebrows—"and it started talking back." I ran my hand along the pages.

Tristan peered at the book. "It could just be my skills with Middle English are pretty rusty but this sounds like nonsense."

I smiled mischievously. "It always does at first. Once it starts making sense is when the real fun begins."

"I'll take your word for it."

"Good answer," said Derfael. "I regret ever letting her get her hands on these books."

"That bad?"

I shook my head. "I was only twelve. I didn't have that firm line formed between possible and impossible yet, so this all started making sense real fast."

Derfael grumbled. "Her aunt and I both had to construct a containment barrier around the daft idiot so she didn't destroy the city in a fit of pique. Try getting someone to see reason after she's had a peek under the skirts of the universe."

"You infuse dark matter into a teddy bear one time and people lose their minds. They never let me have any fun."

Tristan was at a loss for words.

"Still sure you want to hang out with me?"

"You were harnessing the raw power of the universe when you were twelve?"

"I was a precocious little scamp, what can I say?"

"I'm suddenly both terrified and turned on."

I barked a laugh. "I have that effect on people a lot."

"Can we get back to the matter at hand please?" asked Derfael, rapping his knuckles on the table. He shot me a glare.

Tristan and I quickly sobered. "This makes reference to the thousand-year cycles, great rites that need revitalization every thousand years or the magick dissipates or goes rogue. Those are the usual civilization sustainers guarding against drought, famine, disease, war."

"Been going a little lax on re-upping those ones, have they?" Tristan asked.

"Yes and no." I put my scholar hat on. "Keep in mind that the brotherhood is shrinking while the world is expanding. Not to mention the multitude of human inventions that interfere."

Tristan nodded thoughtfully.

Derfael spread his hand out on the page. "But these ten-thousand-year cycles aren't renewals. It's part of one big reavowal."

"Of what?" I peered closer at the pages.

Derfael shook his head. "Unless it's mentioned somewhere else in the text the brothers seemed to take it for granted that anyone reading this would know."

"Wonderful. Hopefully this nerd will know more. But if you're thinking the same thing I was about Göbekli Tepe, it was built twelve thousand years ago."

Tristan furnished the answer this time. "It was buried ten thousand years ago."

That brought the mood in the room down considerably. Tristan still didn't know about the connection with Solomon and the Ancients, but it bodes ill when an important unknown event coincides with the burial of an entire city.

"I'm guessing the informant was talking about those creepy cloaked fuckers. It'll be interesting to see how they're connected to all this. And if Moreno is involved."

"What's this now?" Derfael hefted the book closed with a riffling of pages.

Shit. I forgot I didn't tell anyone about them. "Weird cloaked figures, they look like monks. I saw them on a trip to the Strangefells, and then again when I was downtown. I actually ran into Adrian, and he couldn't see them. He thought I was crazy."

Derfael looked concerned. "If Moreno is in any way connected to this, you should bring someone with you."

"I'll go." Tristan volunteered immediately.

I shifted uneasily. "Are you sure? You were great backup when we dealt with Ro's human, but this is an entirely different ball of wax." I left unstated, but clearly implied, the previous debacle.

Derfael snapped the collar on his robes to straighten it. "I have given him a small... advantage. I am sure he is eager to try it out."

"Advantage?" I asked. "What kind of advantage?"

Tristan reached into his pocket and pulled out a thin brass bracelet which he hooked around his wrist. I could see a faint aura around him, so faint you'd miss it if you weren't looking for it.

"Seriously?" I hissed at Derfael, feeling suddenly like a kid that always got socks for Christmas while her friends showed off their new top-of-the-line toys. "You always refused to make one for me. Why does this guy get all the cool stuff?"

He tried to suppress a smile. "It would have made you overly confident and lazy. He actually needs it."

I reached down and drew a boot knife, swinging my arm in an upward arc and flinging the blade straight at Tristan's heart. It rang off the shield and bounced harmlessly away but not before he flinched, lamely slapping in the direction of the knife with a surprised "Fuck!"

Both of the men were scowling at me at this point, but I was too busy laughing, doubled over as I struggled to breathe through the giggling fit. Once I finally got myself under control, I stood up straight, clutching the stitch in my side. "I just had to see if it worked."

"And what if you were wrong?" asked Tristan.

"But I wasn't wrong, and you're fine." I retrieved my knife and stuck it back in my boot.

"That was still a dick move."

I shrugged and grabbed one more donut before I left. "I'll pick you up at seven. Maybe you can teach me some of that awesome slap fighting on the way there."

I smiled as I heard Derfael chuckling on my way out the door.

There was a fine mist hanging over the parking lot when we pulled in, the air crisp and a degree away from freezing. There were only a few other cars there.

I turned the Camero off and we sat in the dark car, observing the bar. I could see some patrons and several bar staff but it wasn't busy by any means. It seemed like a mostly human crowd, but I wouldn't really be able to tell until we were closer.

"Did you really summon dark matter when you were twelve?"

The abrupt question ricocheted around the silent cab. "I did."

Tristan whistled. "I don't even know what to make of that. It honestly breaks my brain to imagine a child harnessing that kind of power. The Ætherim barely go near it. Were your parents—"

"Let me stop you there. I only tapped dark matter once. It was a fluke that it didn't dissolve my bones into soup or leave a crater where Grand Rapids used to be. I'm sure it was because of my cluelessness that I got lucky. If I'd tried to exert any force of will on it there's a very good chance we wouldn't be talking right now."

"The fact that you even tried it." His voice held the awe of witnessing the impossible. "Forget controlling it. That it came to you at all, that it recognized you as someone with the ability to understand it, even if you didn't in the moment."

I held out my hands placatingly. "You're giving this way more thought than it needs. It was a fluke. Nothing more. I may be capable of a lot of things, but I couldn't and wouldn't go near dark matter again." I nudged him with my elbow. "Beginner's luck is a real phenomena."

"But—"

"That's all it was," I said firmly. End of conversation.

Tristan sighed. "Alright." He popped the door handle and stepped out. "We can talk about this again over dinner."

He shut the door before I could answer. I scrambled out after him. "Or we can not do that."

"Or not." He clapped his hand on my shoulder. "But probably. I'm very persistent."

"Great," I said, rolling my eyes and pushing past him to open the door. I walked into the bar with him trailing closely behind.

"You have many mysteries I'm eager to unravel." There was a note of something in his voice. Heat? Hunger? If so, what kind of hunger?

I stopped and swung around to look at him. I opened my mouth to speak but closed it again when I spotted a weaselly looking man at a high top by the window staring in our direction.

Tristan followed my gaze, and we walked over to the table.

"I didn't think the invitation extended to a second." His voice was high pitched and nasal. His short orange-red hair looked greasy and was plastered to his sweaty forehead. The body odor was rolling off him in waves and I tried not to gag as we stopped at the table.

Everything about this man was off-putting. He may not trust me, but he at least needed to trust a bar of soap.

"Nobody specifically said it didn't."

The man chuckled. "You've got me there."

I was about to grab a seat, but the man shook his head. "Not here. I don't want to risk being overheard."

"Where else did you have in mind?" The apprehension was plain in my voice.

"The third floor is empty. I know the owner, he gave me a key for the elevator." The man slipped off his seat and motioned for us to follow.

I looked at Tristan and pointedly raised my wrist to rub at it. He took the hint and slipped the bracelet on as we walked.

The elevator was just down the hall and we piled in, heading to the third floor in silence. The doors opened on another short hallway, painted bleak gray with the same stylish light fixtures as the first floor, the exception being these lights were almost all the way dimmed.

The man led us into a wide space with gleaming wooden floors, high raftered ceilings and industrial-style lighting. It still smelled of fresh varnish and wood glue.

When the hairs on the back of my neck stood up, I knew we weren't alone up here.

"She brought a second?" said a voice. I scanned the room again, but the light wasn't just dim, it was that yellowish light that makes it hard to see even when the lights are on full blast, especially when the majority of the room is dark varnished wood.

Small movement pinpointed the stranger's location, and in response to my spotting him he moved fully into a small pool of light from an overhead fixture.

The vampire was wearing a nicely tailored suit and while he was also of slight build, he carried himself like a predator. My mind immediately went to the adder and I regretted not checking to see if Tristan was fully loaded with his own weapons.

This man let his curtain of dark hair cover half his face and the unnatural glint in his too-blue eyes made me uneasy.

"Where's your other friend?" I asked the ginger. "I know there's someone else here."

From the opposite side of the room, I heard a chuckle that sent ice down my spine. "We had a feeling you wouldn't come alone, so neither did we."

"Although we had hoped that you would," said the first suit.

The second voice moved forward near the light, and I did that comical double take you see in movies. A twin. They even had their hair covering opposite sides of their faces.

The second twin spoke up. "We honestly didn't think you'd have any accomplices left that were willing to work with you."

They both smiled, wicked with malice and murderous intent.

Dicks.

"So to whom do I owe thanks for this set up?" I looked at Percy's contact and scowled at him as he attempted to soft-shoe back to the elevator. I leveled a finger at him. "Don't think I'm not coming for you."

He scurried off and a second later I heard the sliding doors close.

"Come now. I'm sure you know who sent us here," said the first twin. It wasn't a question.

"No, you're really going to have to narrow it down." I never found out for sure who sent the adder so it was possible this was round two.

"The patriarch that you struck down at the height of his power and left his family vulnerable," the second twin elaborated.

I pinched the bridge of my nose. I wasn't in the mood for twenty questions on this episode of "Who Wants Me Dead, Now?"

"I think she needs another hint, William," said the first twin.

"You killed the eldest son years later?" The leech named William looked at me with a comically confused expression.

"Closer, but there's still a few possibles," I said.

"Seriously?" asked Tristan.

"Don't sound so shocked."

At least William had unknowingly confirmed it wasn't the same family that sent the adder, but that only succeeded in making me feel worse about this situation.

Families that I had generational "interactions" with were high powered, more than likely tied to crime syndicates and had many branches. If they all got it in their minds to seek vengeance now there was no telling how many turns I'd have to take at this square dance before I reestablished my dominance or died trying.

"You seduced the new heir and stole the family's most treasured Book of Shadows?" William looked at his brother. "Richard, am I speaking clearly? Shouldn't she have figured it out by now?"

"There's two options left, guys," I said.

"Seriously?" asked Tristan, eyebrows in his hairline.

I threw an elbow and nailed him in the gut. "For fuck's sake, just tell me who wants me dead and let's get on with it!"

The twins both erased the bemused looks on their faces and got back to business. William placed his hand on his chest. "We're here on behalf of the Hensley family."

"Hensley? As in Anton Hensley? That was you?" asked Tristan. The glare I delivered him made him put up his hands and take a step back. Tristan stared resolutely forward and folded his hands in front of himself like he was guarding the door of a VIP lounge.

William nodded. "The remaining members of his family that have survived the attacks from outside factions in their time of weakness are still very eager to get revenge on the woman that caused them to fall so far out of favor."

"Well, then." I locked eyes with Tristan and nodded. His mouth was a thin, grim line as he nodded back. "Let's go."

# Chapter Fourteen

William disappeared from view and there was barely time to brace myself as I was hit from the side. I went airborne and sailed into the red brick wall a good thirty feet away. The brick buckled and I landed with the rubble, a huge gash on the back of my head bleeding down my neck and soaking into my shirt collar.

I got to my feet shakily, not happy with how this was beginning. William was on me, pinning me to the wall before I could react.

I tried to spit a hex to knock William back, but he squeezed down tight on my windpipe, and I winced, the word choked out of me. I scooped at his eye with my right thumb, and when he turned his head away, I rammed my left forearm into his face.

He broke his grip enough for me to force my palm up and jab his neck. William released me entirely and I attacked full throttle, launching into an assault with knees and fists, not allowing him to get far enough away from me to defend himself properly.

I noticed that Richard was stalking something among stacked chairs and folded banquet tables. Smart, preventing the vamp from getting too close and discovering the shield. And it would prevent them from tag-teaming against me.

My distraction cost me again as William clocked me in the face with the force of an anvil dropping off a cliff and I sailed backward, landing heavily on my right side.

I felt my shoulder jam and William flashed over to me and stomped, the snap as the bone broke ringing too loudly in that empty space along with my yelp of surprise and pain.

"Evyn!" Tristan broke cover and Richard was on him in an instant but was more than a little surprised when he couldn't get near enough to Tristan to strike. The cuff began to glow as it did its work.

"This one is quite well equipped," said Richard to his brother. "I wonder why you warrant such protection?"

I hoped the brothers would have no idea how those amulets worked, or how to get around them.

"We'll deal with Urquhart, and then we can keep beating on that one until the amulet wears down and breaks."

Fine, just dash my hopes.

"Then we'll ask him the serious questions." Richard was circling Tristan like a shark.

William leaned his weight on my shoulder and stared down at me with hunger. "Why bring a second that shields himself while you are open to attack?"

A shot rang out and William's neck spurted blood. He hissed and turned toward the source. I reached down and slipped a knife from my waist, stabbing him in the thigh.

"That's why."

It did little more than make him stumble and it pissed him off pretty good, but it gave me enough room to jump to my feet and grab my .45 from its holster. Here's to hoping I was faster than an angry vamp and still a good enough shot to kill him on the first try.

Richard was continuing his assault on Tristan's shield charm, flashing away as Tristan took a shot at him and attacking from another angle.

A nagging thought in the back of my mind was begging me to take care of stray bullets that Tristan may not realize he was firing in my direction.

As William moved toward me, I spoke an incantation that made time slow. Not for long, but it would turn two seconds into ten seconds and that was a huge advantage. I raised my .45 and aimed.

The main thing to know about killing vampires without staking or removing the heart is that your only other option is to destroy the pineal gland, a tiny spot in the center of the brain that functions as the seat of the third eye. Just a millimeter off in any direction and the vamp would recover quickly, if it even slowed them down at all.

I pulled the trigger. The bullet pierced William's forehead with a small spray of blood instantly followed by a blast of gore and skull fragments. Nailed it.

His body hadn't even hit the ground yet when Richard gave an anguished roar and charged me. I countered his attack and got the upper hand, tackling him to the ground.

Richard bucked me off and punched me in the gut so hard I felt something rupture. Blood came out of my mouth in a spurt of red. He swung at me again, but I caught his arm with my good arm, twisting it behind his back and punching him in the kidney.

I ran him into the wall and reached for a knife, but he grabbed a fistful of my hair, yanking me to the side and loosening my grip. He pulled away, hand still in my hair and flipped me to the floor. He tried to stomp on me, but I punched his foot away and kicked out, nailing him in the crotch.

As I got to my feet Tristan joined me, and together we assaulted him with blows to the face and body that left most of it a bloody mess. Tristan kicked Richard's chest and he stumbled back into a wall.

Richard became a wild, feral thing in a desperate attempt to save himself.

The ferocity of the attacks he unleashed was a combination of physical onslaught and flashing out of reach and popping back in for another attack with a speed that neither of us could keep up with. Tristan was managing just fine as far as not getting hit but he was having no luck with landing hits of his own either.

Richard nailed me in the face and left me seeing stars. I staggered backward trying to stay on my feet, blinking blood out of my face from a cut I didn't even remember getting.

Then several things happened at once. A cracking sound, a pained cry and a loud crash of metal and I looked up to see Tristan splayed out among toppled tables and chairs. The amulet's protection had been broken.

Richard didn't even seem to realize what he'd accomplished because he flashed back to me. Tristan lay motionless as Richard grabbed my shirt and yanked me close to him, the blood frenzy in his eyes so terrifying I couldn't breathe.

His jaws opened wide, and fangs glistened with saliva. He licked blood from my face and his eyes took on an edge of cunning only an apex predator possesses before it kills its prey. Richard slugged me in the gut again and I coughed up more blood, thick and warm as it ran down my chin.

Stirring and the sounds of objects shifting broke through the haze threatening the edges of my mind.

"Evyn!" Tristan called. I looked toward him as he raised his gun.

"No," I sputtered around a mouthful of blood as his finger squeezed down on the trigger. I watched as Richard's eyes slid focus as he realized what was about to happen. He turned and used me as a shield, anticipating Tristan's shot just before he fired.

The bullet landed in my back, close enough to my heart that it stuttered for a moment and I thought it wouldn't start again. A smile twisted Richard's face in a cruel facsimile of something human.

"This is a nice surprise. Your companion did my job for me." He growled. "But you will suffer first for what you did to my brother."

Tristan ran up on him with the knife in his hand but was easily batted away with Richard's fist and landed in a heap, unconscious. Blood leaked from a nasty gash in his head.

Richard threw me to the floor and pinned me by my neck with one hand, not a tight grip but enough to hold me steady in my weakened state. "I'll be a hero for killing you." He drew his arm back and made a claw with his hand, the nails extending into razor-sharp blades.

It happened so fast I didn't realize what he was doing until a scream of pain so loud it hurt my ears issued from my own mouth. I could feel his hand as he punched *into* my stomach, pushing my organs around and crushing whatever he fancied.

He was working his way upward, now elbow deep in my guts and moving toward my heart. My body spasmed in shock and my vision started to go black. I'd only been this close to death once before, but I didn't think I'd be getting out of it this time.

Suddenly, Richard went limp and fell away out of sight and then there was silence as I lay there in a broken mess, a growing pool of blood forming around me.

Tristan leaned over me, panicked, his image fading in and out focus. "Gods, Evyn, what should I do? Can you hear me?"

I sputtered around the blood in my mouth. "Go . . . Derfael."

"No, I'm not leaving you here." He was incredulous I would even suggest it.

"Can't help." I took a rattling breath around one collapsed lung. "Done."

"Not done," hissed a voice. Tristan's head snapped up but the most energy I could muster was a roll of the eyes toward the sound. A cloaked figure, taller than the others had been and somehow more tangible, coalesced from the shadows around it and moved forward with a smooth glide.

Tristan jumped to his feet and planted himself in front of me. "Who the hell are you?"

"That is not important. Do you want to save her life?" Every word came out in a labored breath from wheezing lungs and dry vocal cords.

"Of course."

The figure pointed at the limp body of Richard lying on the floor. "His blood is the only thing that can save her now."

"He's dead. How—"

"Not quite, but she will be if you don't listen carefully and do as I say."

I grasped weakly at his pant leg, and he looked at me. I shook my head. "Don't trust."

"You don't have to trust me. Only listen."

"What do I need to do?" asked Tristan.

"His blood will mix with hers as she drinks, a powerful elixir. It will heal her, but only if you do it now."

Tristan moved toward Richard's body and I could see there was a knife protruding from the vamp's back. As Tristan bent over him to grab his arms, the injured beast twitched but went still again.

He looked at me, but I could only blink at him. Anybody else would have been long dead, but my mage's heart kept beating rebelliously. Even so, I was almost positive this was a terrible idea.

"It's the only way." Tristan picked up Richard's body and dragged it closer to me. "Please. It can't end like this."

Tristan slit Richard's neck in a small cut, right over the artery and blood started to ooze out.

My eyes widened. "No." There were any number of bad things that could result, but to my knowledge that was mostly lore. I couldn't remember ever hearing of anybody actually attempting it.

"You must do it now. There's no time to waste," the figure hissed impatiently. "Do it now!"

Tristan moved behind me and propped me up against his chest. My whole body burned, and the pain was like nothing I'd ever experienced. Blood flooded out of the hole in my gut along with thicker viscera and I passed out.

I came to as a sweet, thick liquid filled my mouth. My eyes opened and I saw that Tristan had positioned Richard near my mouth and was transferring the blood as best he could with his hands.

I could feel death creeping up on me and I latched on to the wound, drawing a mouthful of blood and swallowing it, thick and syrupy. It tasted like spices and vanilla and deadly nightshade.

"It's working," Tristan said. I could feel my organs shifting and expanding, regrowing what was lost and moving back to their rightful sizes and places. I kept drinking and heard Richard moan. Fuck you, buddy, fuck you.

I felt stronger with each pull and marveled as the bullet in my chest worked itself out and fell on the floor with a small clatter. I felt around my stomach with one hand and followed the seam of my skin as it knit back together. I tossed Richard aside and licked my lips.

Tristan laughed. "It worked," he said again, running his own hand across my skin. I was suddenly very aware of his proximity as I lay against him. I placed my hand over his and he stilled as I twined our fingers together.

Stomach fluttering for reasons unrelated to the massive trauma, I paused... before lifting his hand away and pushing myself to my feet, letting my fingertips trail against his before I stood and stretched. I offered my hand to Tristan and pulled him up.

"I don't think I've ever felt this strong. I've heard vampire blood and mage blood are a nice cocktail when mixed but I didn't believe it." I looked for the entity that had saved my life, but he was gone.

Both of us looked around, bewildered.

"You saw him too, right?" asked Tristan.

I nodded. "I'm really getting tired of those creepy bastards."

Richard lay on the ground, not much blood left in him. I pulled my other .45 which had miraculously stayed put in the fight and walked up to the dying vampire. He opened his eyes a little, unable to move from the knife tickling his heart and I fired several bullets into his brain, more out of revenge than ensuring his death.

Tristan and I looked at each other a bit awkwardly, covered as we were in blood from multiple sources.

"Thank you."

"For what? Shooting you?" He rubbed the back of his head.

"What's a bullet between friends?"

He huffed a laugh.

"You're a really good shot."

A true laugh this time and he gave a teasing smile. "Good thing your heart is two sizes too small. Otherwise I wouldn't have missed."

Surprised laughter burst from me in a shower of spittle and Tristan got caught by the spray. He was still as he registered what had hit his face before dissolving into a fit of laughter.

Suddenly the laughter stopped and he wavered on his feet, hand going to his head. I grabbed his arm before he fell. "Let me check your wound."

"It's fine."

"You were unconscious, maybe twice. That's not 'fine.'" I started to examine him. Most of the injuries were surface only but that gash in his head was deep enough I could see bone. I took a small pouch from my belt that I kept at the small of my back and removed some poultice from the emergency medical kit.

As I daubed the wound, I caught his eye and smiled before turning back to the triage. "I guess we do make a good team. We had a few hiccups, but we rallied."

"Rallied? Is that what we're calling near-death experiences now?" He winced as the poultice started to do its work. "What is that stuff?"

"Don't ask." I finished dressing the wound and replaced the pouch on my belt. "That should do it. We'll head back to my loft so I can keep an eye on you. And you'll need those ribs wrapped up."

Tristan looked at me with a sly smile. "So this was all a ploy to get me back to your place? You play an intense long game."

"You should be so lucky," I said wryly. "I desperately need a bath and I don't feel like dropping you off across town first."

Tristan's eyebrows shot into his hairline, and he attempted to grin lasciviously. It was not a look that worked for him, especially when he was covered in blood.

I groaned and stifled a laugh. "Alone."

Tristan spent the night in the guest room, and we drove to Wolfe's the next afternoon. I'd briefly filled Derfael in about what went down but I didn't go into detail.

I'd made us a small brunch before we left. "You don't notice anything different about me, do you?"

Tristan looked at me, concerned. "No. Do you feel different?"

"I still feel like I stuck my finger in an electrical outlet but other than that I don't think so."

"Food still taste normal?" He pointed at my drink with his fork before taking the bite of hash skewered on it. "Did you make that Mary a little extra bloody?"

I smiled. "Gods, no. It's mostly vodka with a splash of Brewt's."

"Then you should be fine." He turned serious. "It would be a good idea to make sure you're not alone with a vamp until you're sure about their thrall gaze not having an effect."

My mind immediately went to my meeting with Grizz-Mo. She had been able to catch me with her gaze but was by no means the average vampire. She wasn't even an average Briste vampire.

But he was right, I couldn't take any chances.

When we got to Wolfe's, Jake hurried to the back room where he had a small stash of toys. Derfael met us at the door and gave us both the once over. "Thank the gods you're alright."

Tristan handed Derfael the two halves of the shield bracelet. "I think I might've voided the warranty."

Seeing the two halves of the broken charm made it sink in just how bad that situation could have been. Derfael's face was ashen.

"So what else happened last night?"

"Little of this, little of that," I said, skirting.

"Tell me everything."

His expression got more and more knitted until I got to the point about the "blood transfusion" and he went from intent listening to blustering fury real fucking quick. Jake backed out of the room, taking his rope toy with him.

"You did what!?" He turned on Tristan, rising so quickly from his seat he almost overturned the table. "And on the advice of some... some creature from the shadows!"

I kept my voice low and calm. "If he hadn't tried it, I wouldn't be here right now. Having your innards on the outside can be a bit hard to recover from."

"Do you like pushing your luck?" Derfael hissed, hands clenched into fists and starting to smoke. Tiny licks of flame appeared between his fingers.

I inclined my head. "It is something I've been known to do."

"You had no idea what would happen!" Derfael said, hitting the table with his fist and scorching the surface. Sparks flew at me, but I didn't move. "What could still happen!"

"It couldn't have been worse than dying, could it?" I asked.

"You could become a thrall." He began ticking things off on his fingers. "Your magick could be altered. Your body might start to mutate."

"Sounds like puberty," I joked. Tristan snorted behind me. "It wouldn't be the first time I've ingested vamp blood."

"Never in that quantity, and never on purpose."

"Look, you can say I told you so if it actually happens but we both know that mages are no more susceptible to thralldom than they are to fae glamoury." I pictured it for a moment before saying, "And if I sprout batwings or start shooting lasers out of my eyes it'll just add to my aesthetic."

Derfael was not amused. "You have not been in contact with another vampire yet. You cannot know this for certain." He snapped his robes around him again, but he let it go.

The bell over the door rang and Derfael sighed. "Tristan, if you could?"

Tristan nodded and went to attend the customer.

"You're more worried about this than you're letting on, Talulla. Why?"

I chewed my lip. "Something that happened with Moreno. Her gaze got to me."

"At the meeting?"

I nodded. Derfael schooled his expression, but I could tell he was furious I didn't mention it before.

"I broke it when I realized what she was doing so I still had a defense to it." Before he could come back with anything I cut him off. "What's done is done. I'll look into some fail-safes to guard against the potential but there's no taking it back." I looked behind me toward the main room of the shop and back to

Derfael, an edge of anger in my own voice this time. "And don't blame him for it, either. What else was he supposed to do? Let me die? I'm sure you would have understood."

Derfael's mustache fluttered as he grumbled under his breath.

"They're right back here." Footsteps approached as Tristan escorted the customer in this direction. The curtain pulled back and I was surprised to see Lorraine.

"Hi, what brings you here?" My mind created answers for me. Dire news, ill omens, impending doom?

Lorraine looked around with interest at our inner sanctum.

"I saw something interesting this morning and I noticed your car outside, figured I'd stop in."

"This is the Seer?" asked Derfael.

"Lorraine Rollins," she said, offering her hand to Derfael.

He grasped it with both of his. "Very good to meet you."

"I appreciate that you're still pursuing this, but isn't it too dangerous? I don't want Vivianne on my ass if something happens to you."

Lorraine pursed her lips. "They know this is my choice. I can't stand the thought that someone is able to hide something from me." She pulled out a chair and sat down.

"Would you like some tea?" asked Derfael.

Lorraine nodded. "Please." She gave Jake a scratch under the chin, and he rested his head in her lap. "Most of the time I avoid delving too deep into anything. It takes the zest out of life when you know what's coming. But this one." She shook her head. "The fact that they are actively trying to keep me out, I'm taking it personal."

"Dare I ask what you saw?" Again, my mind answered. Dire news, ill omens, impending doom?

"Griselda has one of the artifacts here, in her safe house. It's one of the keystones that makes the others function properly."

"So why would she bring it here?" asked Tristan. "Why not keep it with the others?"

"You haven't met her," I said. "She may be a mastermind, but her ego usually takes precedence."

Lorraine nodded. "She wants it as a showpiece in her personal museum. A display of her power and proof of concept for the other syndicates."

Derfael turned to the table with the fresh pot of tea. "The safe house is heavily protected by enchantments of the highest order. And there's no telling what alterations she may have made since acquiring these latest prizes."

I looked at him. "How do you know?"

At this question he looked slightly guilty. "I'm the one that advised on its creation."

I popped my hand into the shape of a T. "Wait, time out. When was this?" I asked. He'd never been a fan of hers, and he wasn't prone to consulting for people he didn't respect for the money alone.

"Shortly after you were presumed dead. I was approached by one of her lieutenants and asked to consult. I figured she was trying to find out if you were still alive and in hiding." He paused. "She is a lot of things, but stupid is not one of them."

"And it's easier to control the narrative if you deal with them directly." I couldn't hold that against him, I'd have done the same.

"So is she confident that nobody will be able to get to it? Or is it a setup?" That seemed to be a question I couldn't escape and it was wearing my nerves thin. Did Moreno think too highly of herself or was—fill in the blank—just part of the plan?

Lorraine nodded apologetically. "Yes?" She sipped her tea, her brows furrowed. "I can't tell you much else. There was something brief about a river of spirit, but I couldn't tell if it was the undercurrent of the magick in that place or something more physical. And there was a point where someone disappeared completely out of my consciousness but then reappeared. I think it was you, Evyn."

"Disappeared?" That sounded ominous. "But you're not sure in relation to what?"

She shook her head. "Only that it happens while you're in that house."

Derfael chimed in. "Could you tell if it was voluntary? As in some kind of defense she utilizes?"

That made her pause. She searched around thoughtfully before she gave an answer. "You go willingly, but there's fear. You've been to that place before." Her eyes focused on me with new interest. "Where have you been before that's outside of consciousness?"

I shot a look at Derfael and he shook his head ever so slightly. "I was playing around with parallel and pocket dimensions for a while. I managed to make a pocket big enough for a person to fit so I tried it out." I grimaced. "I don't recommend it."

Lorraine chuckled. "That could explain it."

"And there are some traps, or at least there were, that functioned somewhat like that," offered Derfael.

"So what I'm hearing is"—I rubbed my hands together gleefully—"we're planning a heist!" I waved my hand at Derfael. "And we've got an inside man. This'll be cake!"

"They're bound to have added extra security since I last saw the place," Derfael cautioned.

"At least the Ancients won't be popping up just yet." Lorraine said it offhand, and I thought Tristan wouldn't catch it for a minute.

But he did. "I'm sorry, I think I misheard you."

"I said at least the Ancients won't be popping up just yet." Lorraine missed the note of worry in Tristan's voice and moved on like we were all on the same page. She was looking into the space around me, nodding her head occasionally.

Her eyebrows shot up and she looked at me. "You almost died last night? And drained a vampire to heal yourself?"

She stood abruptly, almost knocking her chair over. "That sorcerer. He's one of the people keeping me blind to all this."

She gathered her coat in a rush and headed for the door. "I have to go."

The three of us were standing there staring after her, the door opening and closing behind her before we could even say "thanks for stopping by."

After a moment, Tristan piped up. "So I have questions."

# Chapter Fifteen

It doesn't take very long to explain the potential catastrophic resurrection of eldritch horrors. What does take a while is the processing of such information.

Tristan retrieved the bottle of scotch from the cupboard and poured a triple, much like Derfael and I had when we first discussed this.

He mulled things over while Derfael and I planned the heist.

"If you can get me a layout of this place and all the potential security as you remember it, we can plan from there. I'm sure whatever else she's added since should be defeatable if we take it slow."

"Who is 'we'?"

I looked at Derfael like he was going senile. "Me and Tristan?"

"After what happened last night, I'm not trusting the two of you again so soon." He put up a hand to silence me. "You were faced with an impossible choice, yes, but mistakes were made in plenty leading up to it. He needs more training before he's ready to go with you into the field again."

"Fine. I can do this alone no problem."

Derfael scoffed. "You think I would allow you to go alone?" He layered on a thick helping of disbelief. "Into Briste territory. After everything that's happened? After the new information you finally remembered to mention?"

"You just said Tristan wasn't with me on this."

"He is not." Derfael looked at me poignantly.

"Oh, no. No, no, no, no, no. I'm not working with him, not now, probably not ever again."

"Call him."

"No."

"Talulla, call him," Derfael growled.

"No."

"If you do not call him, I will."

I crossed my arms. "Go ahead. He won't come anyway."

Derfael's eyes shifted out of focus, and I could feel a pissed-off Adrian respond. I could only imagine how that conversation was going.

Adrian was putting up a fight, but I felt a wrenching pull as Derfael forced him through the lines and the angry demon appeared next to me, spitting and spluttering in his rage.

"What the fuck, Derfael? What the hell do you want?" His head snapped over to me and he took a big step away.

"There's a job that needs doing and Evyn will not be going alone."

"Like hell. I'm not going anywhere with that bitch."

I felt a sting of air whip by as Derfael lashed out and punched Adrian without so much as lifting a hand. Adrian staggered back a few paces and rubbed at a red spot on his jaw.

Fire flared in his eyes and he took a step toward Derfael. A whole flurry of strikes hit Adrian from all angles and he stumbled under the onslaught. When Derfael let him up Adrian still looked pissed but far less lethal.

"You make a compelling argument," he conceded.

"I think so as well," Derfael said, smiling the way he always did when he won a confrontation before it even really began. "I am not at all pleased with the way you two have been behaving. I have let it go, thinking that you would work it out on your own, but I no longer have that kind of time."

"And you trust me to have her back?" Adrian asked.

I narrowed my eyes at him.

"Should I not?" Derfael had the same expression. He rose from his seat and approached Adrian, standing inches away and leaning his huge frame down to get into the angry demon's face. "I should not have to warn you, should not have to threaten." Derfael's voice was low and dangerous, and a chill ran up my spine. "But since it has been a few years since we have dealt with each other I will remind you."

A dark shadow began to crawl into the room and Adrian began to shift nervously. "If you let anything happen to her that you could have prevented, let your anger cloud your judgment for a second," said Derfael, so coldly I could hear the ice cracking and breaking off every word, "it will be the last thing that you ever do." He backed away. "The time for hurt feelings and child's play is over."

Adrian's olive skin was pasty, and his eyes had a glassy quality like he had been ill for a long time but was on the up-and-up. I guess if I couldn't expect an actual partnership anymore, a healthy fear of Derfael and any revenge the old druid could conjure up would be a good consolation prize.

"This is your familiar?" Tristan had snapped out of his reverie.

"Who's this d-bag?" Adrian looked Tristan over with extreme dislike and crashed down into a chair, propping his feet on the table.

"Adrian," I sighed.

"Oh, his name is Adrian, too?" An obnoxious smile. When nobody gave him any reaction to his "joke" he moved on. "So what am I here for?"

"A heist."

Adrian blinked a couple of times. "Of what?"

"Moreno has one of the artifacts in a safe house. Lorraine just told us about it. It's a key piece of whatever she's planning on doing."

I shot a look at Tristan, silently pleading with him not to say anything about the Ancients.

He smiled. "That's wonderfully vague, isn't it?"

"If you'll stop being a dick for two seconds, we'll explain."

"'If you'll stop being a dick for two seconds,'" Adrian mocked in a high pitch.

"That is enough!" barked Derfael.

Adrian and I both flinched. "You are three hundred years old, not three. I suggest you start acting like it."

Adrian grumbled something unintelligible, and it was better for his safety if it remained that way.

"So are you in?" I asked.

"Do I have a choice?" he asked, casting a side-long look at Derfael who narrowed his eyes for what must have been the hundredth time that evening.

"No, but if I know you're going to be invested in this job it would be a weight off my shoulders."

"How invested do you want me to be?"

"For fuck's sake!" My fingers twitched, itching to wrap around his throat.

"Okay, okay. I'm in."

The bell over the main door jangled loudly like someone had shoved it open with force. Heavy boots thundered toward us and Adrian and I both stood to face the newcomer. The curtain tore back and Percy appeared carrying a bowling bag.

Without a word she opened it, pulled out a head and thunked it on the table. The clouded, sightless eyes of the man that orchestrated the set up last night stared back at me.

I blinked and looked at Percy. "I take it you heard about what happened?"

"Yes, I heard," Percy growled. "Why the fuck didn't you tell me yourself?"

She didn't give me a chance to answer. "I had to hear about it from the ghoul management guy! I hate that guy, Evyn! Especially when he knows things I don't!" She took a breath. "Are you okay?"

"It got a bit hairy for a minute, but we're both fine." I motioned to Tristan.

"Who are you?" Percy looked at him suspiciously.

Tristan offered his hand. "I'm Tristan. Derfael's new apprentice and occasional backup for Evyn."

I noted the stink eye Adrian shot at Tristan but ignored it for now.

"Hm." That was all that Percy said, but she shook his hand despite her reservations. "Anyway, I saved you the trouble of hunting him down. You know I had nothing to do with that treacherous bullshit, right?"

The question was aggressive, not apprehensive. She was implying the answer was obvious and she'd be real mad if I thought anything different for even a second.

"The thought never even crossed my mind," I answered truthfully. "Underhanded backstab-ery isn't your style."

"Damn right it's not." She sneered at the head. "You're lucky I managed to bring you this much. There's not much else left that's even identifiable after I tore into him." Her fists clenched and there was a faint ripple under her skin as the fury threatened to force the change into wolf form.

"Traitorous scum." She bared her teeth at the head once more and turned away from it. She finally notice that Adrian was there. "Oh. Are you two talking again?"

\*\*\*

Adrian and I were driving in relative silence, only the radio playing a dull tune in the background. Even if we did have a somewhat amicable agreement on working together for this one mission, I didn't want to risk a song of all things pissing him off and putting everything we were going after in danger.

Not that he would've noticed. He was tuned out, like he was lost in thought. Anything to keep him quiet I suppose.

Derfael had never looked more nervous or earnest as he gave me my instructions on our way out the door. "Talulla, you are only going to have one chance to get this right. I don't need to tell you that if you fail to get the artifact it will disappear for good."

So with no pressure at all, I was going to have to Houdini my way into that room and past all the defenses, with the added caveat of Adrian and his begrudging "help."

Navigation Robot politely informed me I had reached my destination and I started, realizing I had been on autopilot. I looked around at the quaint little neighborhood and the quaint little house with a quaint little garden that I was parked in front of.

"Griselda keeps a safe house here?" asked Adrian, stirring from his thoughtful silence. "It's not that far from her headquarters."

"The way Derfael tells it, she uses it less for a safe house than a museum. She wants her treasures within easy reach."

"And we're relatively confident Derfael got the layout right?"

"Relatively. If you notice anything at all that wasn't on the schematics do not hesitate to say something, please."

I got out of the car and he followed, slamming the door behind him.

"Why don't you alert the entire neighborhood that two people in black spandex are outside a nice house at three in the morning?" I hissed at him.

He actually had the decency to look sheepish. "Sorry." He followed me silently up the walkway to the front door. "You're not actually going in that way, are you?"

"Give me a little more credit than that, would you?" I put my hand lightly on the door frame and felt around it, checking for any sigils and spells worked into the wood. I only found a couple and wasn't worried about them.

I nodded my head for Adrian to follow and we moved around the house, looking at windows and doors to see if they were bespelled as well. Much like her main house, I only found one window that wasn't marked so there was no chance I was going in that way.

"Not fooling me twice," I mumbled under my breath.

"What?"

"Nothing."

"So where's the point of entry?"

I stood back and stared at the house, hands on my hips. I blew a stray slip of hair out of my face. "The front door."

"What?"

"It's the best option." I shrugged. "It's hexed but not like the other entrances. It's the obvious entry point so it's the least heavily protected against burglars. As for anyone that actually knows what they're dealing with here, there are much worse things inside that house to worry about."

Adrian nodded. "Fair enough. It's been a while since I've been on a good old-fashioned heist."

I appraised the door. "Breaking the hexes would alert her that we were here so we're just going to have to deal with them."

"What are they?" Adrian asked, wary. He probably thought I would just shove him through the front door like a sacrifice and let him take the brunt of the magic.

Out of the question, I could never do something so underhanded... but if he pissed me off at any point, I'd be sure to keep that in mind on the way back out.

I cataloged the various afflictions for him. "Temporary paralysis, blindness, and speechlessness."

"Sounds fun. You still using those shitty little talismans to counter hexes, or have you upgraded?"

I rolled my eyes. "Seems like beggars with sad, chaotic demon magic that's not good for much other than sloppy destruction shouldn't be choosers, but since you asked so nicely." I chanted a much more robust curse breaker than those talismans would have ever provided back in the day. "There you go."

Adrian scowled. "It was just an observation, you didn't have to add the insult." We stood for a minute in awkward silence. "So, are we good?"

"Yeah, should be fine," I said with a smirk.

"Should be?"

"No, no, don't worry, it's fine." I flapped my hands in dismissal. "You go first."

"Evyn—" Adrian started with a warning tone.

"It's fine," I said firmly. I pushed him out of the way and manually picked the lock. It clicked and the door swung inward on silent, well-greased hinges. I stepped through and said pointedly over my shoulder, "Ladies first."

As I crossed the threshold, I could feel the hexes reaching for me, trying to latch on to something they could sense was there but failing to find purchase. I was glad I upgraded my defenses from those "shitty talismans."

Derfael may have been the one to design this place, but the marks of other mages and sorcerers were everywhere. Nothing against Derfael, but he's always been the type to work magick that does the most effective job in the quickest time frame. Not the best for robust, long-lasting defense without constant renewal.

I could feel the High Order magick here. The living, breathing thing that permeated the air itself, constantly shifting and changing as the situation called for, finessed and honed to such a point that a simple hex almost had sentience. I was kind of jealous and more than a little tempted to go back to studying the Brotherhood of Levi's grimoires.

Adrian followed and noticed nothing, although he swatted at something like he'd walked through spiderwebs. This place was spotless, so he wasn't completely oblivious.

I felt a pang of sadness at our loss of connection. In the past he would have been just as attuned to the magick around him as I was. We shared our strengths and mitigated each other's weaknesses; that was the whole point of being familiars. But all of that was so faded we could really only feel each other when we were called or when emotions were riding high.

Once the door closed behind us with a heaviness that made this place feel like a tomb we stood still and reached out with every sense, searching for any threats that might be hiding. We found nothing.

I lit a ball of witch fire and let it hover above us. The place was full to bursting with all sorts of priceless artifacts that had been lost to history.

I moved through the house, picking my gaze over everything and recognizing cuneiform tablets from Sumer, a ritual cartouche belonging to a long-lost Egyptian queen, an Iron Age golden torque with boar's heads and what looked suspiciously like King Arthur's seal, a scimitar engraved with the goddess Kali's epithet, even...

"Is that a freakin' crystal skull?" asked Adrian, seeing the object at the same time I did.

"Looks like. There's another one." I pointed to a shelf on the left, the gleaming quartz flanked by two other skulls that very clearly had been part of a living creature at some point. One had the characteristic sharp cheekbones and subtly elongated cranium of some fae creature that had been bound over with iron bands and covered in runes and goetic seals. The other was blackened from fire and had two stumps of broken horns as jagged as the multiple rows of pointed teeth. I'll let you make your own guesses as to where that one came from. I was awestruck. "Quite the collection. I'm almost sorry we're here for a job, I'd like to take the time to look around."

"Once she's dead we'll know the first place we need to visit," said Adrian, giving me a sideways smile, which I returned.

We kept searching, keeping an eye out the entire time for some internal defenses, mundane security systems, even trip wires, but there was nothing.

Derfael marked the wards and traps he'd put in place on the blueprints but even with the upgrades from the new magicians I couldn't find any sign of security other than on the exterior of the building.

"Am I the only one that's starting to get really uncomfortable with how easy this has been so far?" asked Adrian.

"No," I murmured. "Something can't be right here."

The farther into the house we moved I could feel a growing presence, something just at the edge of my mind that was purposefully staying there, taunting and elusive. To bury my nerves, I tried to keep the conversation going. "I am glad that you're with me on this."

Adrian eyed me with suspicion.

"I'm serious. We always made a good team, we always made it back alive." I nudged him. "And you were more than gracious in the after-actions with the Council in giving me more credit than I deserved. Our ops were far less dominated by me than people were led to believe."

"I seem to remember there being certain sexual favors on offer before those after-actions, so I was more than happy to oblige." Adrian's smile turned more wolf-like, and a hungry glint lit his eyes as he remembered.

"Oh, yeah," I reminisced, getting a little hot under the collar just from the thought. "We weren't the first ones to use the torture room as a sex dungeon, but we made damn sure we were the ones that everyone talked about."

I turned and found him standing directly behind me. He closed the distance until he was inches away, looking down at me with the full power of that infamous smile. My knees got weak.

He put his hands on my hips and jerked me forward, our bodies touching. I became aware of the bulge in his pants as he pressed against me and heat pooled between my legs as I remembered all the delicious things he could do with it.

Adrian leaned in and brushed his lips against mine. "I don't recall you complaining when my 'sad, chaotic demon magick' made you writhe with pleasure and scream my name."

He ran his fingertips up and down my side in silence, but it was heated with memories of moans, heavy breathing, and sweat.

"You certainly weren't complaining when I drew up my incubus magick and ravished you over every inch"—he ground his hips into me—"of your body."

His magick licked across my skin, igniting desire within me. With nothing more than fingertips skimming my body I was ratcheting quickly toward climax. Then everything halted and I opened my eyes to his smug face staring back at me. "What the hell?" I spluttered breathlessly.

"Just admit that it was a petty insult and I'll finish you off any way you want."

I shoved him away. "Forget it."

So we mounted the stairs instead of each other and made our way slowly upward after clearing the first floor. Adrian seemed a little disappointed but just shrugged it off and I had to resist punching him in the dick.

The second floor was completely open, organized as an exhibition hall with a long promenade down the center. And at the end of that promenade was what we were here for.

"This is a joke, right? How obvious of a trap could that be?" Adrian asked.

"I think it's a safe assumption only completely idiots would try to steal from her, so she probably doesn't feel any need to hide it."

I was visibly on edge at this point. The lack of opposition, magical or otherwise, combined with a heaviness in the air that was getting worse by the second was torturous. A smell started to permeate the space, the rank, acrid scent that belied magic of the darkest caliber.

Adrian voiced the words I'd just been thinking. "Where's it coming from?"

"I don't know."

"Do you think she already knows we're here?"

I shook my head. "If she had goons on the way they'd be here by now."

"This has to be a trap. Has to be. So where—" He stopped. "Evyn, stop walking."

I stopped dead, not even turning to look at him. "What is it?"

"Look down."

Unsure of what he could have seen, I studied the floor beneath me. It took me a second to make them out, but when I did a shock spiked through me. Among the intricate patterned wooden tiles on the promenade floated ancient runes that I barely recognized from my studies centuries ago.

They were visibly moving with a sense of purpose, entwining with other runes and reforming into a new shape before detaching and going on their separate ways. More of the living, sentient spells. And beneath them was the ebb and flow of the eternal, ephemeral waters, the otherworldly sheen on the soft waves undeniable.

"S-styx." The word came out of my mouth in a barely audible croak.

I could feel Adrian's fear notch up in my own gut as he whispered, "What do we do?"

"Say hello to Hades?" I said grimly. "It's been a while since I've seen him."

"That's not funny."

"Did it sound like I was joking?" My stomach twisted in knots. "I'm not sure what I'm looking at here, but I'm in it either way." As if to further drive home the point that I was contending with sorcerers far more devious than I, a face swam up from the current and appraised me.

"So we figure it out, we always do."

"Adrian," I said, watching the face as it stared back at me with white, pupil-less eyes. He didn't hear me.

"Good thing you've got my outside-the-box brain, right?" Adrian tried to force some humor into his voice.

"Adrian," I said, looking over my shoulder as best I could without moving my feet. I met his eyes, tight with anxiety. "We've got company." I looked back around at the face. I heard him curse behind me.

"Do we make a run for it? Regroup?"

I shook my head. "You heard Derfael. If we don't get it now, it'll disappear."

"If we keep going, *we* might disappear," Adrian hissed.

Lorraine's words made plenty of sense now.

"We're not good to anybody if we're dead, pretty sure Derfael would agree. At least in your case," he blanched.

I heard him and agreed with him, but running and regrouping when we were this close to the artifact wasn't something I was ready to consider yet. Even with the creepy floating face staring at me from a bespelled mirage of the Dark's most infamous body of water.

"What if we freeze it?" I asked Adrian.

"Freeze the noncorporeal smoke river?" he asked, monotone and unimpressed.

"Not exactly. What if I create a sheet of ice on top of it?"

"Where are you gonna go then? The only way to that artifact is by stepping on this damn pathway."

"If I can at least get free of the immediate danger we can figure that out with a bit more breathing room," I snapped.

Adrian started to say something but bit off his response and huffed out a breath. "Okay, fine. I don't have anything better."

I looked back at him for—I still don't know what. Reassurance or encouragement, maybe? Whatever it was I was looking for, I didn't get it. Instead, just a distant, worried glance before he went back to studying the floor.

I crouched down carefully, not moving my feet an inch. I hovered my hand over the floor and started to speak the words that would put a sheet of ice between me and whatever doom lay under my feet. Ice started to spread from my fingertips and crystalline shards arced in fractals across the floor. The face was still staring at me, and I could have sworn—

"It winked at me."

"What?"

"The face. It winked at me." I was trying to figure out what that meant but got my answer quickly.

A rattling growl like a million hungry ghosts rumbled through the house, a sound deep enough to set my heart palpitating. My feet slid out from under me on the ice sheet and I collapsed to the ground.

Everything was shaking now, priceless artifacts falling from the walls and sliding off shelves to shatter into pieces. I struggled to get up, succeeding only in dragging myself toward the edge of the ice.

I could sense Adrian was shouting at me but couldn't actually hear any of his words. My vision was blurry, and my head buzzed with what felt like an electric shock. I looked up, every inch of movement an entire battle waged until I finally caught sight of him.

He was on his knees, reaching for me, frantic. I could see him looking at something over my shoulder and just then the noise cut out and the room settled, returning to normal, not a thing out of place. All my faculties came rushing back and I whipped my head back to see what had Adrian so panicked.

There was nothing there.

We both collapsed back, sitting heavily on the floor, and trying to catch our breaths.

"What just happened?"

Adrian was just as puzzled as I was. "No idea. Was that some kind of hallucination?"

"With the level of spellwork we're seeing in this house, I wouldn't doubt someone found a way to mess with our heads that badly."

"So do you think it's safe? Maybe they were counting on people getting the fuck out of dodge after that experience."

"Doubtful. That's too kind for Griselda." I looked below my feet and found the ethereal Styx had disappeared. It was just your everyday plain tile.

I took a baby step toward the edge. Nothing happened, nothing moved, even that pungent smell was gone. I took a larger step and still everything remained quiet.

The way the room was designed the artifact was set into an alcove that was about eight-feet square embedded into the surrounding wall, the entire width of the pathway. Even if I walked alongside the now tile promenade, I'd still have to step back onto it to reach the artifact. Sigils set into the corners of the alcove made it apparent that going through the wall from the outside wasn't an option.

"Evyn, I know you aren't thinking about walking down that floor. That's a kill zone no matter how you look at it. If you won't leave without it, at least let me call Derfael and get his input."

"Why, so you can be absolved of his wrath for not completing the mission?" I asked, a bit harshly.

Adrian scowled. "Maybe he has some ideas that we're not thinking of. Maybe we're a bit more out of practice than we thought," he spat back.

"He'll have to come down here himself to get a look at it and that'll take too long." I only half believed my own bullshit.

Truth was, I would risk whatever this was if it meant not having to call Derfael in for help. It wouldn't have been the end of the world, but he would certainly think less of me, and that was just as bad in my estimation.

"Evyn, don't."

I ignored him. Throwing up the strongest all-purpose shield around myself as possible I turned on my heel before he could stop me and sprinted down the tile walkway. I was inside the alcove, the magick of the place beating down on my shield from all sides, my fingertips grazing the artifact when I was thrown backward a good twenty feet.

I landed hard on my side and my shield broke as the pungent smell returned. If I had any color left in my face, I'm sure it all left in the next moment.

A giant wave of vaporous water and ghostly faces rose from the alcove, gaining momentum and changing shape, first into a giant version of the face that had watched me, then into a wave of serpents, finally settling into the grizzled and smirking visage of Charon, the ferryman.

I leaped to my feet and started to run toward Adrian but the ether was already lapping at my heels. The only way out of this one was going to be through, and of the two of us, I had the best chance at making it back alive, Lorraine's prediction not withstanding.

Adrian couldn't follow me where I was going. His outstretched hand was inches away, but I lurched forward, shoving him in the chest and sending him stumbling backward and off balance, landing several feet away.

He was pissed, but I'd only have to ask forgiveness if I had the gall to survive.

I stopped running. Adrian twisted around and crouched, ready to leap toward me. "Evyn, no!"

But the wave was already closing around me, and I felt myself start to fall through the ether. If anyone had been there to witness it, they would have seen Adrian jump after me, trying to follow, not willing to let me fight this alone despite the hate for me he still held so close to the surface.

The part of the story he doesn't like to constantly remind me of however is where everything disappears and he hits the floor facefirst and skids on the last remnants of the ice sheet. But I'm sure it was a very heroic skid.

My fall didn't come to an abrupt end, rather a slowing before I found myself suspended, upside down in midair. I couldn't see anything past the gray haze and hear the now very corporeal waters of Styx writhing beneath me, sensing a new sacrifice had arrived.

"Shit." My voice bounced and reverberated in different pitches and tones all around me and then cut off into abrupt silence. I hung there for what might have been years for all I knew. Waiting.

Finally I heard noise besides the blood rushing in my ears. A soft splashing, as of an oar dipping in the water at a slow rhythmic pace. An eerie whistling started up, a tune that sounded vaguely like a sea shanty but if a humorless, two-star, half-dead, all-asshole ride-share driver was the one singing it.

Charon.

# IRON-FORGE CROSSROADS
## REMEANT - COMING MAY 21ST, 2024

Remeant (adjective): coming back, returning

When the whistling sounded like it was just a few feet away the gray dissipated suddenly, and I gasped when I found myself face to face with the ferryman himself.

"I thought you'd be back much sooner," said Charon in his monotone voice.

I frowned, still hanging in the air. "Do you mind?"

A smile spread across his lipless mouth, his ashen gray face cracking and flaking off in places. One of his eyes twitched and I fell with a thump into the bow of the boat.

I settled in, making myself as comfortable as possible among the bare wood skeleton of the ferry and watched as Charon dipped the oars soundlessly into the water. "So what have you been up to since last time we met?"

No reply. I watched the shores of Styx slip by as we moved deeper into the Dark. This place was another "layer" of the Strangefells, a version of the underworld like you may have heard in myths and legends.

It's where the dead reside, where the chthonic Ætherim and those entities strongly tied to the earth called home. Most Strangers that found themselves here were in a holding pattern. They rested, recuperated, prepared for another turn at life.

It was possible for the living to visit and leave again but the pull of this place, the magick of the shadows and the in-between, tended to sink all the way down to the bone. It kept calling, even after you left. Even now, some part of me was grateful to be home.

If you didn't find something to anchor you to the world of the living, chances were good you'd wind up back here one way or another.

The bare flat plains gave way to tall grasses and the occasional rise of a sand dune and eventually into fields of golden wheat and then vast green swaths of lush grass.

I watched the mountain range in the background, gleaming in the cold gray light and pointed. "Are those new?"

Charon's eyes slid to me with heavy disdain and away again.

"I'm just gonna keep talking. I can make up your side of the conversation if you'd like."

"Whatever stories you can come up with will be greatly entertaining, I'm sure, and you'll have plenty of time to share them with people who might care. Which isn't me."

"Come on. What else do you have for entertainment besides mindless small talk or attempted bribes to turn the boat around?"

"I count the blissful hours of silence between these insipid interactions."

I sat with that for a minute. "You must be really fun at parties."

Charon offered me nothing, just kept rowing and stared ahead like I wasn't even there. "So do you know anything about the kind of magick that brought me here?"

Nothing.

"Somehow somebody figured out how to bring Styx into the mortal realm."

That got his attention. It was just a tiny flicker of his eyes in my direction, but I knew he was listening.

"Yeah, I thought that was interesting." He frowned at the knowing smirk in my voice. "It felt ancient, that kind of magick. Not a whole lot of people have that kind of knowledge anymore. It was quite beautiful to witness, even if it sent me here."

Charon was silent for a time, but I could see his wheels turning. Finally, he spoke. "Sorcery."

I shifted my weight and tried to get the pins and needles out of my legs and feet and ended up sitting like a child during story time. I even propped my face in my hands and leaned forward.

"I'd say you fell prey to a trap laid by a Mesopotamian sorcerer. Always an unpredictable bunch, more mercenary than magician."

"No offense taken, don't worry about it." I plastered a wide smile on my face.

"What were you doing to fall into this trap, I wonder? Robbing tombs? Drawing a mustache on some poor soul's statue? Pissing on graves of the dearly departed?"

I scowled. "As fun as those things sound." I tried to rein in my impulse to strangle him. "I was attempting to steal an artifact from a sociopath that's intent on releasing the Ancients. Not a huge deal, but it'd be nice to have."

Charon stopped rowing and froze, the boat continuing to move forward despite the placidness of the waters. His Adam's apple bobbed a couple times before he said, "Don't be absurd. Are you honestly suggesting—"

"I wish I wasn't, but that's exactly what I'm suggesting. Griselda Moreno found a whole cache of artifacts underneath Göbekli Tepe. And there have been plenty of informants helping us piece together this puzzle. Solomon's name has come up more than once and I'm not entirely sure I haven't met the guy already." The cloaked figure that advised on the unorthodox blood transfusion came to mind.

"It all adds up to a giant shit sandwich with the Strangefells and the mundane caught between a genocidal maniac and eldritch horrors."

Charon shook his head, still refusing to believe it was possible. "For anyone to release them would be suicide. No one can control them. They'd unmake the world and all of us with it." The first notes of panic started to appear in his voice, and he spat into the Styx to avert the evil of his words.

"If it makes you feel better Griselda is mostly intent on wiping out humans." Yes, I was being sarcastic. "She seems to have a plan for controlling them and there are clearly very capable sorcerers involved, even if they're less than scrupulous."

"So they'd only allow Them to destroy three-quarters of the world then?" he asked bitterly. Then his gaze shifted, and Charon's mind went somewhere else, finding some buried memory.

He refocused on me with growing fear. "We no longer have the kind of power it took to lock them away, even together. We were almost destroyed in that war, at the height of our strength, with Stranger and human fighting side by side. If someone set loose the Ancients now, we'd have no hope. None. And all for a foolish power grab."

"So let me go. Let me secure that artifact. That will strike a huge blow to their plan."

Charon shook his head. "I can't do that. Someone else will have to finish the job. You're not the only mercenary in the Council's employ."

"In the time it takes to get somebody else caught up on the situation with everything that I know so far Moreno could have moved the artifact and we'll never have another chance to find it before she uses it."

He had gone back to ignoring me again, paddling silently along.

"Or would you rather take your chances that you'll be saying hello to the eldritch horrors before the year is out? Would you like to explain that to Hades right before we're all wiped out of existence?" I looked around. "Real estate is going to be at a premium around here."

That got his attention.

I leaned in. "If he knows what's happening and what's at stake, I think he'll be okay with delaying our meeting for a little longer."

"You are very confident, aren't you?" asked Charon.

I sat back, the hard lip of the boat digging into my back, but I refused to readjust. "That's why I'm so good at my job. And we're all going to need plenty of confidence for what's to come."

Charon stared at me for a long moment, having a long debate with himself. Then his eye twitched.

And I found myself back at Moreno's safe house.

"Evyn!" shouted Adrian, running and sliding toward me like he was stealing second base.

I was still trying to get my bearings, but I smiled up at him from my landing place on the floor. "I made it."

"Are you okay?"

I suddenly felt like I was moving through sludge. I turned my head slowly, feeling myself being as creepy as it must have been to him. I vaguely registered the look on his face, a mixture of worry and fear.

"You're not alright. What happened? Where did you go?"

I was going to answer but his gasp made me go quiet.

"Your eyes... they just turned black. Completely black."

I sensed myself reach up to my face but I couldn't feel my fingers near my eyes where I knew they should have been. Suddenly it felt like a vacuum had closed around us.

"What's happening now?" He got to his feet and hauled me after him, palming my face roughly and staring into my eyes like they held the answers.

My gut twisted as everything in me told me to get the fuck out of there. The sluggishness released me at the same time the vacuum dissipated.

"Fuck." I hissed, pelting toward the statue and grabbing it while simultaneously shouting "Run!"

We both sprinted toward the nearest window, Adrian on my heels. I threw my hand forward and blew out the window with a directed blast of air, allowing the added force to carry us both faster and fling us out the window as far away from the house as possible.

We hit the ground outside just as the air ignited and the house was engulfed in flames, every window shattering outward and shaking what must have been the entire block.

Adrian used his own brand of magick—sad and chaotic—to put a shield up around us and protect us from the debris just as a splintered piece of the house shattered against it like a spear. That would have hurt.

Adrian helped me sit up and gave me a moment to catch my breath, the two of us preparing to run before the authorities showed up. The house was just a fireball on top of a shattered foundation.

But no lights went on. Nobody screamed. There were no sirens in the distance as we watched the house burn. And then the flames reversed back into themselves with a rushing noise, the house pieced itself back together and it was like nothing had ever happened.

Adrian and I looked at each other and he sniffed. "That's new."

What else can you say?

I started, remembering that I'd grabbed the artifact on the way out and opened my hand. There it was. A small artifact, shaped like a scorpion with a skull on its back, its tail piercing that skull. A tiny stone carving that could end the world. I wish that was just me being hyperbolic.

"What if we just destroyed it? Smashed it on the ground right now? I can make a power sink with my knife, we put up a barrier to keep any magick from leaking out, shatter the thing and let all that old, crusty magick get sucked back into the earth where it belongs." Adrian laid out a surprisingly effective plan and I considered it.

The world would certainly be safer without this thing in it. But anything containing magick this old that's been dormant for so long is like a pressure cooker that's been building up steam for thousands of years.

Popping the cork could result in a catastrophic blast of energy that would not only kill the two of us, but possibly flatten the entire city. Or, it could just sink into the ground like Adrian hoped. Given the odds were pretty fair in favor of either of those things being the result, I wasn't willing to take that chance.

"Better to let the Council take possession of it. Even if they don't destroy it, it'll just end up in a private collection and nobody but us and a few people outside of Moreno's team will ever remember it existed." I paused. "And Moreno isn't going to be alive much longer anyway."

"What, my method isn't good enough for you?"

I stood, brushing myself off best I could given I was covered with ash and my clothes were singed. "Actually I thought it was a rather good idea."

Adrian was ready with a retort but then he realized what I said and snapped his mouth shut.

"I just don't want to risk leveling the neighborhood. Do you?"

He grumbled. "That's fair." He appraised the tiny statue. "So what now?"

"I'll keep it with me until I can get it to the Council. I haven't spoken to the Matron since I *disappeared* myself. Not sure how that's going to go down."

Adrian grimaced. "You have fun. Let me know if you need help again." That smoldering smile. "Or just hit me up when you're ready to finish what we started earlier."

I pushed past the little thrill that went through me and proceeded to ignore him altogether. He chuckled knowingly as I headed back to the car.

Once we were back on the road Adrian asked, "So what happened after you got swallowed by the ghost wave?"

"A short trip to the Dark and the longest conversation I hope to ever have with Charon." I fell silent and could feel his eyes boring into the side of my head. I turned to look at him with a shocked smile. "Oh, did you want to hear more?"

# Acknowledgements

I don't think I would've had the guts to forge ahead with this project had it not been for a couple of people.

Ma, you were a cheerleader and a voice of reason when I started to feel the pressure of the overwhelming task of bringing this book to fruition. Love you lots.

Samantha H., my intrepid friend. Instead of insisting I was crazy when I revealed my thoughts about starting over with a new career, you went full-tilt with that ride-or-die support. Thank you, Samantha the Brave.

And a special thanks to my editor, Kat Betts, who dealt with my new-author jitters in stride and helped get this project on its feet.

Coming Soon

May 21st, 2024
Iron-Forge Crossroads: Remeant
Death's Left Hand Book 2

And MORE coming soon in the *Death's Left-Hand* Series!
Book 3 – October 8th, 2024
Book 4 – November 12th, 2024

And Coming in June 2024
An exciting new Romantasy novella series from Gwydion Royce!

Visit gwydionroyce.com for the latest information!